BITTEN BY DEATH

VEGAS IMMORTALS: DEATH AND THE LAST
VAMPIRE

HOLLY ROBERDS

Cover Design: Holly Roberds

Editors: Jolene Perry & Christie Hartman

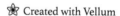 Created with Vellum

BOOKS BY HOLLY ROBERDS

VEGAS IMMORTALS

Death and the Last Vampire

Book 1 - Bitten by Death

Book 2 - Kissed by Death

Book 3 - Seduced by Death

The Beast & the Badass

Book 1 - Breaking the Beast

Book 2 - Claiming the Beast

DEMON KNIGHTS

Book 1 - One Savage Knight

Book 2 - One Bad Knight

LOST GIRLS SERIES

Book 1 - Tasting Red

Book 2 - Chasing Goldie

THE FIVE ORDERS

Book 0.5 – The Knight Watcher

Book 1 - Prophecy Girl

Book 2 - Soulless Son

Book 3 - Tear in the World

Book 4 – Into Darkness

Book 4.5 - Touch of Hell

Book 5 - End Game

* For recommended reading order, visit www.hollyroberds.com

To my Hellions in the reader fan group, Holly's Hellions.

You inspired me to write this series. I feel this book was a co-creation harnessing the hilarious yet often dark hive mind of the group.

Thank you for raising hell with me.

Let's never stop.

1

I woke up with a gasp.

Am I dying?

Cold wrapped around me and cut into my bones like a thousand daggers.

Despite being in total darkness, I could easily discern my surroundings. I was in a metal box, the size of a coffin. There was a strange red tint to my vision. I tried to scream but nothing came out. When I closed my mouth, I bit my own lip with a precise slice. Reaching up to touch my canines, I found sharp elongated incisors. Fangs?

What the unholy hell?

The taste of metallic blood slid against my tongue and something savage tore through me. Before I knew it, I had beaten the steel door off the coffin-sized enclosure with only my feet.

The need to cover up my naked breasts and pubic region was a fleeting wink of a thought as I gaped at the steel prison I'd just been in. The sharp sting of antiseptic over-whelmed my senses along with the reek of cold, decaying flesh. I wasn't dying. I was already dead, a cold slab of meat in a morgue drawer up until a few minutes ago. The freezing cold penetrated to the marrow of my bones.

Emotion and panic swelled inside me only to be drowned out by hunger...for blood.

Oh god, I needed to drink, feed, gorge myself, or I was going to die.

Never mind that; I had clearly already died.

I streaked through the swinging doors, passing by a half-full mug of coffee. I could smell it, instantly discerning the coffee was cheap and that it had gone cold hours ago. I followed my sharpened senses, homing in on the target of my blinding thirst.

My heart didn't beat, but something deep and primal drummed inside me, controlling me, driving me to a room where I ripped off the door to a refrigerator with little effort. I threw the rectangular slab of steel behind me, not caring about the tremendous crashing sound it made as it smashed into the cabinets along the wall. I had found my prize—clear bags full of red, life-giving liquid.

The need doubled down, gripping me so hard it almost brought me to my knees. Instead, I grabbed a bag and bit into it, sucking it dry like a dehydrated child with a juice pouch.

The blood was cold. I wanted it hot, fresh, full of flavor and slick texture, but I couldn't wait. I drained the bag in seconds, then reached for another. I tore into a fifth and then a sixth bag of blood, then by the time I'd sucked two thirds of the hospital fridge dry, the drumming inside me abated. Despite the cool liquid, warmth spread out to my limbs. The crisis vibrating in my cells subsided. I didn't feel like I was going to die anymore.

Looking down at my naked, blood-smeared body, the

reality of the situation crystalized around me. My legs turned boneless and I slid to the floor. The drawers of the open fridge bit into my back, but I didn't care.

What the hell was I?

Vampire, my subconscious whispered.

Who was I?

My mind drew a blank.

I was a woman, scratch that...a vampire who'd just gorged herself on blood, naked, in a hospital in the middle of the night. Despite there being no window, I instinctively knew it had been dark out for five hours. How did I know that?

My thoughts raced as I reached for more information—a name, a life, the faces of people I knew, anything. I came up empty.

A snout pushed the door open, interrupting my existential crisis. I was startled to meet the unerring gaze of a dog. It was sleek and black, but its narrow face and bushy tail reminded me of a fox. Its fur was an inky black and its eyes were golden, near luminescent. Across the room, it stretched its neck out toward me, sniffing the air. There was no collar or leash attached to the pooch.

Sure, a dog roaming free in a hospital. Why not?

Instinctively I lifted a hand, wanting to touch the soft fur and enjoy the vivid dream I was obviously caught up in. "Hello," I said softly, finding my voice though my words came out hoarse.

When it tilted its head, regarding me, its face shifted for the briefest of moments. Instead of a furred face, I saw its canine skull. The dog's lip peeled back, baring its teeth at me with a low growl.

I snatched my hand back, pressing it against my chest. Doggie-poo did *not* like me.

The growl deepened. The dog was going to attack.

Despite the danger, I couldn't force myself to my feet. Maybe I should let it tear me apart, I mused, oddly disconnected from my body and the situation.

Then the dog was gone, turning the corner from which it came.

Okay, then.

I woke up in a hospital morgue, a vampire with no memories, I destroy a fridge full of blood like a girl's rampant ice cream binge after a bad breakup, and then a weird dog shows up, threatens me, then disappears.

Sure.

Something bubbled up inside of me. It pushed its way up past my throat until it spilled out of my mouth.

I laughed.

At first it started out as a giggle, then turned into a full-out howl of laughter and soon I had tears streaming down my face.

The second thing I learned about myself, after realizing I was a vampire, was I had a dark, jacked-up sense of humor.

That or I was crazy as a loon.

"Pl—please," he stuttered. "Mercy."

"Mercy?" I stood, towering over the shaking man who pleaded on his knees. My words came out crisp and concise. "Do you really think you can ask death itself for mercy and expect to get it?"

Clenching his hands together in prayer, he shook his head. Our voices echoed in the shadowy, stone antechamber. The orange firelight from the torches flickered over his face and mostly bald pate.

"You wish me to think you humble, good, and special." My shoulders tensed and flexed under my suit. "You believe death itself should spare you because *I* care." I nearly spat the last words. Then grabbing the man by the lapels, I lifted him up onto his feet and leaned in, practically nose-to-nose with him.

"You are not special. No one is spared. Everyone must meet their end as such, and you've already placed your bets. Now it's time for you to cash out."

Then I showed him the true face of death.

His piercing scream reverberated all around me as his pure terror permeated the air.

After I finished with him, I straightened my jacket and returned up the few stairs to the lone, red velvet chair in the room. Picking up the demitasse of espresso, I sipped the dark, bitter elixir. It had been a long day. The exhaustion I felt had nothing to do with a lack of rest. It was the same thing day after day, and while I valued my duty, the work was punishing, never-ending, and it was my burden alone. There was no use thinking of how things could be different, nothing would ever change.

The rhythmic and efficient click of expensive polished shoes alerted me to the presence of my aide. When I turned to Timothy, his normally carefully tousled hair seemed in more of a disarray and worry pinched his eyes.

"Sire, we have a problem."

Setting the cup down with a clink, I gave him my full attention. "What is it?"

It wasn't like Timothy to hesitate. One of his best qualities was being forthcoming with news, no matter good or bad.

"There has been a sighting of a..."

"Spit it out, man."

"A vampire, sire."

"You must have made a mistake," I said, slowly.

Shaking his head, his lips pursed with displeasure.

I was wrong, something had changed. And not for the better.

My life had sucked the last two weeks. Living in the sewers, feeding off rats, I tried to piece my former life together. I only scored one lead to my past.

And wouldn't you know, the potential keeper to my life's secrets just had to be named Chad.

"What do you want, bitch?" Chad spat at me, a loogie landing squarely on my face. Chad was a six-foot dirty blond in his mid-thirties, with heavy acne scars and bad breath. No, never mind that I was hardly the picture of good hygiene. With all I'd been through the past two weeks, this was the closest thing I'd had to a shower.

Wiping away the spittle that was rapidly cooling against my cheek, I didn't bother to hide my expression of disgust. My other hand tightened around his throat. A dainty squeak popped out of Chad. His bulging eyeballs flicked south to confirm he was indeed a foot off the ground, his feet dangling like a rag doll's.

Okay, so my newfound undead existence came with a few cool perks.

We stood out back of the bar he frequented, The Hairy Harbinger. Chad had stepped out for a smoke, and that's when I cornered him. No one was likely to hear his yells over the pounding classic rock and raucous slot machines coming from inside.

"Come on, Chad," I purred. "Don't be like that. You were there the night that girl was murdered."

"What are you talking about?" he rasped, still trying to pry my fingers off his throat with no success.

The guy seemed more defensive than confused by my presence. There had been no spark of recognition in his eye when I showed up, which made him an even less likely suspect for my murder.

"I'm talking about the girl who was found with her throat ripped out. You were spotted on the scene." I jerked my head in the direction of the alley, two blocks over.

"I told the cops what happened. They let me go," he protested. Resentment simmered in Chad's eyes. Chad wasn't the brightest bulb in the vanity.

I lowered Chad so his feet touched the ground, but I kept my grip tight. At the prospect he might get loose and run, a thrill went through me, tightening my nipples as the predator inside me awoke. I blamed the fast thrum of his veins under my palm. His blood was distracting, tantalizing, and despite his ugly mug, arousal curled in my belly.

I recoiled at the thought. Not for him, *eww*.

Still, the prospect of a hot, human meal...his blood sang to me. It would be so sweet to sink my teeth into his neck and drain him dry. I suppressed a shiver. It was risky to be this close to a human when I barely got enough vermin blood to stay sane. But I had to track down the truth. Find out what happened to me.

I pushed away thoughts of ripping his throat out and

said, "Yeah, well, I ain't the cops, so tell *me* what happened." I gave him a shake, hard enough to leave his teeth rattling.

Before leaving the morgue, I'd managed to locate and read my file before I stole a lab coat and hightailed it out of there. In the manila envelope were pictures of my body. My limbs were splayed out at awkward angles, my lips bluish gray, eyes wide and empty. Head tilted to the side, the mangled meat of my ripped-up neck was on perfect display for the camera. I was wearing a little black dress and heeled boots, but there was no trace of a purse, phone, or any form of ID. There was a note attached that it was a possible mugging, but the wounds looked like they were inflicted by an animal. I was tempted to grab a pen and write in "vampire attack," next to the original note.

The coroner had also tried to run my fingerprints, but the scanner errored out. I'd examined the pads of my fingers, finding they were unusually smooth. Too smooth. As far as the coroner was concerned, I was still a Jane Doe.

Ugh. What a lame name. I was tempted to grab the pen a second time to write in a better one.

But the most important thing I'd gleaned was the location where my body had been found. I resorted to hanging around that very alleyway, looking for clues, when I picked up bits of conversation from a couple guys smoking outside a bar around the corner, The Hairy Harbinger. The place was a dark hole in the wall that stank of weak beer and vomit. *Can I serve you a knife wound along with that cheap whiskey?*

The two men casually chatted about how Chad stumbled on "that dead chick with the nice set of legs." They mused on whether he'd done it, since it wouldn't be the first time he'd gotten rough with the ladies.

After two weeks of hanging around to see if Chad would

show up, I finally approached one of the smokers. For the low price of 250 dollars, he would coax Chad back out. I'd managed to get the dough, and now that I had the sole lead to my past in my hands, it was worth it.

"Like I told the cops"—Chad over-enunciated each word with palpable hate—"I was smoking outside, waiting on a friend when I heard someone scream. Coupla tourists straight off the Strip stumbled onto the body. I didn't see shit."

His heart pounded erratically, and his eyes darted here and there, confirming what I suspected of Chad the Charming.

"You're a liar," I said, giving him my best psychotic smile. His eyes widened, and he went still as his gaze fixed onto my mouth. Right. Vampire fangs. Forgot those would come in handy for scare tactics.

Suddenly words were spilling out of him in a waterfall. "I was smoking, like I said, but while I was waiting, I saw someone in the alleyway. It took me a minute to realize they were dumping a body."

Anticipation gripped me. Finally, a freaking clue what happened that night. I'd been killed somewhere else. I'd need to figure out where I'd been and why the vampire moved my body. Weren't bloodsucking fiends uncaring of the bodies left in their wake? "What did they look like?"

When Chad emitted another squeak, I realized I needed to loosen my grip a bit. "Sorry, you got me a bit excited. Now tell me what they looked like." A part of me still insisted no one would miss this lowlife scumbag. I could drink him dry and leave the world a little brighter.

No. I clamped down on my instincts and fought the thirst with everything in me. My thirst would not control me, and I would not become a murderer.

Chad's gaze moved passed me and something changed. His face drained of color and if I weren't holding him up, his legs would have failed him. The tiny hairs along the nape of my neck stuck up at attention. As if I knew with certainty lightning was about to strike me right on the two inches of exposed flesh between my coat and hairline.

Releasing my grip on the man in front of me, I twisted around, already wishing I hadn't.

What I saw was scary enough to kill me...again.

The figure stalking toward us was no regular being. Despite having the visage of a man, power flowed out from him in a majestic dark mantle. Though I didn't need to breathe, panic sliced through my chest as the air was sucked out of the space around me. My stomach plunged and my already cold body dropped to arctic temperatures.

It was like setting eyes on a solar eclipse; not impossible, but it burned. His square jaw clenched with visible tension. Vengeful eyes burned with golden fire, and his muscular build filled out the suit he wore. His movements were liquid, unnatural. The only sign he was human was the dark scruff perfectly framing his full lips.

"It's the devil." Chad's whisper came out hoarse. I hadn't realized I'd let him go, but he remained frozen in place, staring at the approaching creature with abject horror and dread. "He's finally come for my soul."

The man oozed power. In his presence, I was a mere ant. He would smush me without any regard.

He's just a man, I told myself, swallowing hard.

As if hearing my thoughts, the man's face flickered. I got glimpses of what I guessed to be his true form—a skull with eye holes of black, sucking darkness that threatened to drag me in and swallow me whole. Looking at him was like meeting with the end of everything.

Based on Chad's reaction, you didn't have to be super-natural to see this guy had major mojo. More importantly, the dude looked seriously pissed.

Chad stumbled away from me, and I didn't try to stop him.

Maybe because I knew I was in the last two seconds of my undead life.

The powerful being paid no attention to my hard-won mark, making a beeline for me.

Shit shit shit. What do I do

A hand reached for me. My instincts kicked in as I dodged his grasp, then grabbed his arm and did the only thing I could do.

I bit his hand.

He stopped cold.

"What the hell are you doing?" he growled, and a shiver rippled down my body before sweeping back up through my stomach. Fear and...lust?

Great, whoever I really was, I was also dumb.

My lips still wrapped around the side of his palm, I said with a full mouth, "Biting you?"

His look of incredulous disgust would have reduced any other human being into a puddle of regret at having ever been born.

It was then that I realized my fangs had retracted, and I was gnawing on him like a toddler. Releasing him, backing up a few steps, I put my hands up in the air. "I was just trying to defend myself. It was clear you were coming at me with a lot of heat."

Examining the dull teeth imprints on his hand, then me, the god said, "And you thought you could..."

"Bite you?" I winced at my lack of conviction. I didn't know what tall, dark, and scary's deal was, but I was pretty sure being a vampire who couldn't bite was a pretty epic failing. Was I this big of a loser in my last life? Vampires only did the one thing, right? Bite people and drink blood?

Who was I supposed to see about revoking my V-card?

Oh right, V did not stand for vampire in that instance.

The god wiped the back of his hand against his very expensive-looking pants. He gave me a strange look.

The squeal of tires filled the air. Chad had made off like a bat out of hell. I dropped my hands, slapping one knee in frustration. "Seriously? Now I have to track his ass all over again. I barely had the money to bribe his buddy to lure him out the first time." I held out a hand expectantly to the god. "You owe me two hundred and fifty bucks."

After all, I'd stolen that money in a crumbling, smoke-filled casino fair and square. I'd been trying to pick a mark to steal from when I heard a man, rooted to a poker table, make a lewd suggestion as he slapped a cocktail waitress on her ass. She bit her lip instead of responding, probably not wanting to ruin her chances of a tip. He'd had a lucky day, judging by his chips. As he leered at her retreating form, I'd activated my super speed mode to nab his neat, colorful stack. I made sure to drop half of them on the waitress's tray when she was looking the other way. I was like the Robin Hood of vampires. But I wasn't so good that I'd let this beastly hot man get away without paying me back what I'd rightfully stolen.

Clearly taken aback, the god looked at my outstretched hand as if it were the hand of a leper's.

This time when he reached for me, he succeeded in wrapping his fingers around my throat. My feet lifted off the ground several feet, like I'd done to Chad only minutes ago.

Seriously, what kind of karma had I racked up in my previous life?

Despite not needing to breathe, I felt the instinctual danger that he wanted to rip my head off. In the list of methods I had tried on myself to see if the vampire myths held true or not, I was fairly certain that he would take me out.

I clawed at his hand, but he didn't release his grip.

"What are you doing here, sekhor?" he snarled.

I'm definitely going to die.

Despite the pressure around my throat, I could squeak out. "Fuck you."

What? Do you want to die faster? my logical brain cried.

His nostrils flared and the golden light gleamed from his eyes. Okay, he was some supernatural being. Maybe he was a vampire? Maybe the one who turned me?

Still, he had barged in, scared off my mark, called me what sounded like a dirty word, and assaulted me. I wasn't cowing down to this son of a bitch, no matter how bone-melting gorgeous he was. Or how pee-my-pants terrifying.

"What was that?" he said, cupping a hand around his ear. "You want me to rip your head off right now, bloodsucker?" A faint, cultured accent curled around his words seductively despite his threat. The low timbre of his voice reverberated through my skin, striking my bones with a devastating blow.

Bloodsucker? Okay, maybe he wasn't a vampire, but I wasn't entirely ruling it out. Despite being a nearly starved vampire, I didn't hear his blood the way I could most people's. I was salivating for different reasons. The things I wanted to do to his jawline had nothing to do with drinking blood.

I settled for a glare this time, imagining every bone-breaking maneuver I could use on him.

Understanding dawned in his eyes, as if he heard my

thoughts loud and clear. My gut clenched at the possibility this supernatural dude could read my mind. But no, I was just doing a stellar job of broadcasting my "Fuck you" this time.

He released me. I half-expected to crumple to the ground. Instead, I miraculously landed on my feet. Score one for vampire abilities. One side of his mouth curled up in a smile as his eyes flattened like a shark's. He was now ten times scarier.

"Tell me how you came to be, and I'll make it quick," he promised. Where there had been raw fury a moment ago, he slid into a smooth professional demeanor. His voice was silken. There was a soothing, well-practiced quality to his tone. I instantly believed he could convince terrorists to hand over their guns simply because he asked.

"Make what quick?" I rubbed my neck, wondering if I could bruise.

The smooth mask slipped as he bared his teeth at me. "Your death."

"Yeah, well, the last time didn't exactly take, so what makes you think you'd be successful?"

Taking two steps toward me, he seemed to suck all the air out from the space between us again. "Trust me."

If I still had a beating heart, it would have been hammering out of my chest. As it was, my nipples hardened at the rough tone of his voice. To both our credits, our eyes remained locked despite the stiff peaks now pushing through my tank top.

"That's what I'm working to find out," I said, waving an arm in the direction Chad had taken off. "You chased off my only lead to finding out who bit me."

Something hardened in the god's face. "Someone bit you?" I was tempted to ask what type of accent that curled seductively around his word. It was cultured yet comprehensive, as if he were from everywhere and nowhere.

Maybe I'm a linguist; how else would I know about accents?

"Isn't that generally how vampires are made?" I pulled the collar of my leather jacket and tank top aside to show the scar tissue where my neck met my shoulder, where someone had taken a chunk out of me. Nothing like those beautiful, pristine twin bite marks you saw in the movies. The sucker had gnawed on me as if I were a chew toy.

The gold drained from his irises, leaving warm mahogany as they regarded my scar. "You don't remember?"

A few strands of my hair tickled my nose, but I was afraid to make any movement to push it back. "Nope, sure don't. Don't remember my name, my family, my home, my life. Pretty sure I would like all of those back."

"So, what?" His tone was derisive and incredulous. "You think you can go back to living a normal life though you must live off the blood of others to survive?"

I jutted my chin out, glaring at him. Okay yeah, it was a pretty stupid plan when he said it out loud, but damned if I was going to tell him that. Judging by the amused glint in his eye, he knew anyway.

This time he grabbed me by the arm, dragging me along. "What the hell, dude?"

"Dude?" He raised a perfect dark eyebrow at me. There it was again, that spark of amusement. When it drained a second time, he said, "You will answer my every question to help me find the one who made you."

Sounded like a brilliant plan when I was on my own. Coming from him, it sounded like a suicide plan. "And once I do?"

He stopped, jerking me to an abrupt stop, bringing me face-to-face with him.

Damn, he smelled insanely good. Whatever cologne mixed with the scent of his skin was enough to make my brain go fuzzy. Warmth spread through my stomach, then pooled between my legs. I wanted him. Maybe even more than blood.

His gaze lingered on my lips. Holy hell. He was going to kiss me. Every fiber of my undead being begged for it, wanting to be set on fire by those perfect, full lips. I was dying to feel the dark scruff rake across my face as I discovered what he tasted like.

Instead, his words washed me in cold fear. "I will end you."

3

"You're— you're Death?" she asked. "Like actual death? The grim reaper Blue Oyster Cult sings about?"

I grinned. It made things easier when I was recognized. "Exactly, and *you* are an abomination." I gripped the back of her neck, still debating whether I should kill her right away.

"Let's not be hasty, sire," Timothy said from behind me. "We must question the subject first."

Timothy came up with his tablet in hand. The man was glued to that iPad, yet his eyes kept sliding up to regard the vampire.

I couldn't blame him. She wasn't beautiful by the plastic sparkle of Vegas standards, yet neither of us would deny the glow emanating from her. The vampire shone, soft, alluring yellow light that made her as brilliant as a beacon. Any human who passed by would be blind to her gleaming aura, yet I was loath to tear my eyes away from it.

Something at my center pulled me toward her. Though it had been centuries since I'd last been near such a being, I didn't remember the draw to be so powerful.

Underneath the grime, I could just make out the woman underneath. She had a heart-shaped face and a short, even nose, but what struck me was her eyes.

I'd place the woman to be early or mid-twenties. She wore ill-fitting pants, a beat-up jacket, and a baggy tank top. They looked like they belonged to a man. The dark, stringy hair that had slipped out of her ponytail showed a desperate need for a proper washing. There was an allure to the curve of her lips and hooded eyes.

Staring into the vampire's emerald green irises, my core shifted, warming and responding to the haughty set of her chin. The reaction was overwhelming, and my immediate instinct was to rip her head off to stop this feeling.

Instead, I released her arm. She blinked, then narrowed her eyes at me.

"Move one muscle, and I'll kill you in an instant," I said, my voice a low warning growl.

She looked at me in wide-eyed astonishment.

"There," Timothy said. He finished typing and looked up, pushing his glasses up his nose. "Who turned you?"

"What?" she stuttered, looking back and forth from Timothy to me.

"This is an exit interview," Timothy enunciated as if speaking to a child. "Please tell me who turned you into a vampire." Her eyes fell back on me and I saw uncertainty there. "I don't know."

Timothy's fingers remained poised over the screen.

I asked this time. "The question is, who is your master and how many more of you are there? How did you come to be a bloodsucker?"

She blinked. "I don't know."

I exchanged a look with Timothy.

"Memory loss after a turning is not unusual. Perhaps she's the only one," he said with a small shrug.

"Then this problem will be solved before it has barely begun," I said. We'd dispose of her and the problem would be contained with very little effort. Why couldn't all jobs be this easy?

Still, a part of me bucked at the idea of extinguishing such an inviting power.

When I looked back into the vampire's face, there was something curious about her expression. Like she was caught between being resigned to her fate and wanting to fight or run. I'd seen every reaction to death, yet this vampire gave me pause.

Probably because I hadn't seen one in so long.

Something crashed behind us.

"Oh dear," Timothy said. "Perhaps not."

I turned to see three figures surrounded by an ethereal glow. More vampires. There were two men and a woman— blood smeared their lips as they hissed at us. Their eyes were crimson. They had been feeding. Unacceptable.

The idea of "easy" all but evaporated.

Though they shared the same aura as the vampire next to me, theirs were dullened, as if I were looking at them through murky water. Neither did they possess the same magnetic pull.

I stepped away from the green-eyed vampire, who seemed more dazed than a threat. Addressing the newcomers, I asked, "Whom do you serve?"

"Death," said the woman with a shaved head and muscular build.

"Oh, do you?" I asked, taking a few steps closer. "Is that what your master told you?" I could hear the amusement and disgust in my voice. "Did you hear that, Timothy?"

Timothy tucked his tablet in his jacket. "I did, sire."

"I was not aware these three were under my employ. Did you hire them?" I asked, sending them a grin that should have made them turn and run like hell. Instead, they crouched in a ready fighting position and their hisses intensified.

"Not as such, sire," Timothy said in a calm, almost bored voice, then politely to the vampires, "Do you have references?"

One of them lunged at me. I smacked him to the ground so hard the pavement broke under his impact, spider webbing out under his body.

Seeing more vampires should have left me giddy with delight. *Hey guys, I'm part of your bloodsucking club, let's go for drinks and talk about how our lives have taken such a crazy turn.*

But it was clear the three vampires weren't down for the "gosh, why did this happen to us" commiseration I had in mind.

My bet was on the big scary guy who claimed to be Death. Which was exactly why I ran like hell as soon as the fighting started up. I couldn't say I hated my newfound super speed as I hightailed it out of there.

Unfortunately, I hadn't gone too far before someone stepped in my way. I skidded to a stop. He looked like a swole gym-bro who spent most of his life pumping iron. Seeing as he was also over six feet tall, his stature was impressive. Even his bald head looked like it had been pumping iron. His nose was wide and flat, making me think of a boxer who had taken a pounding in the face one too many times.

Despite his mega-creepy smile, I paused. He took a few steps toward me.

"Don't even think about it, buddy," I warned.

He grabbed my arm, but I shook him off.

"This will be easier if you don't fight me." His tone suggested the same open sexual invitation I saw in the dull glint of his beady eyes. *Ugh, no thank you.*

If he was taking me to the vampire who made us, I might find out what the hell was going on. Except there was the part where there was no freaking way I was trusting this guy.

"You're going to want to let go of the girl and back away," a woman's voice interrupted.

We turned our heads to see a black woman with an afro and an expression that said she meant business. She set down the canvas bag of groceries at her side and pulled out a taser from the leather purse that hung around her shoulder. It sparked blue twice, a warning.

Bruiser's face lit up as he looked her up and down.

Blood bags, I inwardly cursed.

Turning to face her, he said, "I suppose we have time for a snack." I wasn't sure if he was talking to me or just himself, but the idea of bonding over a drink did not appeal.

"Get out of here," I warned the woman.

Cool, calculating brown eyes slid to me, then back to Bruiser. "No, ma'am."

This wasn't an average citizen. Her posture suggested she'd had training, maybe armed forces.

How did I know that? Was I in the army in my past life?

Bruiser smiled at her, showing off his fangs. Her eyes widened in realization that this was no ordinary meat head. He streaked toward her. She was in the last two seconds of her life.

I crashed into him before he could reach her, sending him hurtling into a brick wall. I yelled at her this time. "Go."

The way her eyes flitted down to my teeth, I knew my fangs had elongated. Thankfully, the woman wasn't a dummy. She turned to run, leaving the groceries behind.

She got one step before Bruiser was on her, fast as lightning. She hit the ground and Bruiser easily rolled her over and pushed her head to the side, revealing the length of her neck.

Before fang could scratch skin, I threw a roundhouse kick at his head and it snapped to the side. I shot out a second kick that sent him rolling off her body. The woman wasted no time crab-crawling backward.

Blood rushed through her veins hotly, and her heartbeat was impossibly loud. The whites of her eyes nearly swallowed her irises. Hunger pounded in me as instinct demanded I jump on her next. I gritted my teeth as the thirst took hold of me. I should have found more rats to feed on before going topside. I wanted to tear into her. Bad.

Do not feed on the woman you are trying to save.

The woman got to her feet and ran. She sprinted with an athletic gait.

Digging my fingernails into my palms, the urge to hunt her hit me like a Mack truck. Oh god. I wanted to chase her. Play with her, then corner her and rip out her jugular. I took one step in the direction she'd fled.

Oh, fuck no. I squeezed my eyes shut and tried to think of anything else. Mud. That weird dog in the hospital. The sexy line of Death's jaw.

Something hard hit me from the side, and I was on the ground under Bruiser this time. He leered down at me with a slightly unhinged look in his eye. "So the girly wants to play."

My instincts warned me this guy brushed up against, if not crossed over, the line of psychotic. Was that a vampire thing? I wasn't demented...or so I liked to think.

The memory of laughing until I was crying after binging on blood flashed in my mind.

Bruiser flew off me, landing an impressive twenty feet away. When I looked over, I saw Death standing there, his suit slightly rumpled now. The dark hair that had been slicked back now hung over his forehead with a slight curl. His eyes had turned completely golden again, and he looked seriously pissed. His energy shimmered in the air around him, a dangerous, dark power. His hand was still raised, and I realized Death had tossed big boy like a rag doll.

The vampire was on his feet in the blink of an eye. Hunching over, he was ready to charge back at Death like an incensed rhino. But then his face emptied of expression and he stood in a neutral pose. It almost looked like he had a sudden attack of amnesia, then streaked off in the opposite direction.

Death looked at me, then in the direction Bruiser had gone, as if weighing his options. Lucky me, he decided not to give Bruiser chase. He yanked me to my feet, his face too close to mine.

"Did you call for them to come save you?"

"Are you kidding me? I don't know who the hell they are, and I don't know what they want with me."

"It is clear they were trying to get a hold of her, sire," said the slimmer man with the tablet.

He was Asian with square features, and what might have been a thousand-dollar haircut. He wore a blue pinstripe suit that screamed uptight, organized, and always packing an extra pen or five. Even the pink pocket square matched his socks and tie.

Where the pinstripe-suit guy reminded me of someone who enjoyed train schedules that ran on time, Death was more the sexy, dark playboy type. I imagined he could pick out any girl and take her to an exclusive backroom of a club to fuck her until her body gave out, then walk away without a second glance. Or maybe when he took her behind the curtain, he'd cleave her like a cow for the butcher.

Shaking off my disturbing, if not vivid fantasies, I ground out the words. "I don't know them, or you. I only came to talk to the schmuck who hightailed it out of here when you showed up."

The gold in Death's eyes softened, revealing hazel eyes that searched mine as if trying to ferret out any lies. I set my jaw in a hard, defiant line.

"Then they'll be back for her," Death said. My gaze flitted down to his mouth. I couldn't help but notice how full his bottom lip was. This close up, his sex appeal was magnetic. Like I knew sleeping with him would *actually* kill me, but it was probably worth it. Of course, Death resembled sin itself.

"You're coming with me," he growled.

I opened my mouth as my brain calculated the odds of fighting Death and getting away.

"I wouldn't if I were you," the other man cautioned, as if reading my thoughts. "Come along with us or he can kill you right now."

Death had already laid waste to the three other vampires in ten or so minutes. My odds weren't good at all.

My hands shook, so I balled them into fists to hide the tremor. Fighting Bruiser had spent almost all of my energy. Then there was that woman tempting me with her blood. The thirst had struck up in me again, like a match that threatened to burn me from the inside out. Strangely enough I wasn't drawn to either of the men in my presence. It was as if my senses were blind to their blood. I knew Death was, well, Death. But what was the other guy? If I had to guess from his formal, business-like demeanor, my first guess was robot. My second guess was cyborg. Or maybe he was just British.

I considered my limited options. Even if I were to make it back to my makeshift camp, people would be in danger. I couldn't risk it.

Dammit to all. If I was going to be backed into a corner, they sure as hell didn't need to know that.

I shook off Death's grip and brushed off my tee-shirt and straightened my jacket. "Yeah, well, I guess I shouldn't leave until you give me my money, anyway. Take this down, Jeeves: two hundred and fifty dollars in cash...no, scratch that, three hundred for my trouble."

The two men exchanged a look.

Death growled.

His sidekick interjected. "Remember, sire, she is more useful now than she is dead."

I shot Death a smug smile, crossing my arms. "Ya hear that? Jeeves thinks I'm useful."

I set my hands on my hips and tapped my foot. "Well? Are we taking a car, or a hellish carriage drawn by your demonic hell horses?"

4

The vampire was duly impressed by the limo, bouncing around and finding every secret compartment and button she could press. She seemed less like a bloodsucking monster and more like a hyper juvenile on her first joyride. I sat in the back with my legs crossed, one arm stretched along the seat. I never took my eyes off her. She resembled a scrappy urchin child, but I knew better than to be taken in by emotion or appearances. And I absolutely refused to succumb to her siren-like draw, no matter how it called to me.

People were all the same; vampires were worse. Full of hubris, drunk with power, and an unending hunger for death. That was my territory, and I wouldn't stand for these creatures to interfere with the natural process of life or endanger souls.

Yet the sekhor seemed to have no designs to escape as she popped from seat to seat, landing on the side bench.

As the vampire pulled out a crystal glass by a decanter of scotch older than this city, she said matter-of-factly, "I'm hungry. If you turn around and drive east ten minutes, I know a sewer brimming with rats."

In the seat across from her, Timothy dragged his attention away from his tablet. "Is that how you've been surviving?"

"Yeah." She rolled the glass in her hand. "They do the trick in a pinch," she mumbled with a grimace. Then she looked up at me from under her lashes and an electric current zinged through me. "What did you think? That I ate people?"

Timothy responded, while I continued to hold her gaze. "That is usually the case with sekhors."

"I don't know what the blood bag a sekhor is, but I'm not a monster." There was defensiveness in her voice. We'd offended her.

Intriguing.

"Yes—well," Timothy said, losing his composure for a moment. "No need. I will make the appropriate arrangements."

She looked back down at the glass in her hands before returning it to the drink compartment. "So what do I call you?" she asked. "Death?"

"Yes," I said without pause.

She snorted and pushed her long, stringy hair away from her face. "Yeah, no. How about I call you D? Short for Death?"

I forced breath out through my nose. "If you insist, you may call me Grim."

"No need to get huffy, G," she declared before turning to Timothy, who was doing his damnedest not to laugh. If he weren't so valuable and we hadn't known each other for almost as long as time itself, I would have let him know his humor displeased me.

"And you are?" she asked him.

My number two straightened. "You may call me Timothy."

"So you're what, like his secretary?" She hooked a thumb at me.

Timothy's nose wrinkled. "I consider myself to be his aide."

"Right, sorry," she said, her finger finding the button to the window. "We don't say secretary anymore, do we?" Her eyes met mine with the expression of a guilty child, and I knew she was considering pressing it.

If she thought she could escape through the open window of this limo, I'd be forced to change tactics to make sure she stayed where I wanted her. She wouldn't like my methods. I was known to be punishing. Still, instead of saying anything, I waited to see what she would do.

Her finger slid away from the button, and she moved to the seat all the way at the other end of the limo as if finding something interesting over there.

"And what should we call you?" Timothy rolled a hand.

"I..." she faltered.

"Fang caught your tongue?" I asked, tilting my head.

Her eyebrows shot up. "Oh, so he's funny?" she said to Timothy.

My aide sent me a strange look. "Not typically, no."

"Well, since I don't have a trace of an idea who I was or my name, I guess you can call me, Vivien."

I dropped an arm from the car seat. "Vivien?" I didn't bother hiding the skepticism in my voice.

She frowned. "Yes, Vivien. I totally feel like I would have been a Vivien in my past life."

Not knowing what possessed me, I said, "You strike me as a Martha."

She made a face of disgust, sticking out her tongue at me. "What? Martha? That's so boring. I was probably a Persephone, or Anastasia, or maybe if I had a simple name, Hope."

She'd put thought into this. "Hope? You really believe your name was Hope?" The sekhor was likely mad from spending all her time in sewers hunting rats. Still, she arrested me with her crazy.

I caught Timothy staring at me, and realized his attention was affixed to the smile at the corner of my mouth. I emptied my face of expression and leaned back in my seat to look out the window.

Remembering what happened when I followed madness down its rabbit hole of merry amusements, I shut off the curiosity I had for this vampire. It was as simple as turning off a spigot.

The sekhor shrugged. "Okay, maybe not Hope. But I'm naming myself Vivien. Call me Vivien." She shot out a hand to Timothy. He was closer. His eyes flitted down to her hand in surprise before taking it and giving it a shake.

The limo stopped, and we exited. I kept a tight grip on "Vivien's" arm, pulling her along. The night air smelled of cigarette smoke, car exhaust, and the earthy palm trees surrounding the entrance. Though people partied all night on the Vegas Strip, there were very few milling about with the sun to rise soon.

Vivien looked up at the massive hotel, colored lights shining bright in the night to highlight its impressive construction, a siren call for all who wanted to experience sin and luxury at its finest.

"You're staying at the big pyramid hotel?" Vivien asked, her brows furrowing.

"I *own* the big pyramid hotel," I said, mimicking her phrasing.

"I told him he should try to have more fun," Timothy said, now standing next to us outside the limo, still absorbed in his tablet. "So he went to Vegas like anyone else would do...and bought a hotel, turned it into the most exclusive luxury location on the strip, and works harder now than he ever did before."

The sleek black lines of the hotel appealed to my aesthetic. It was now the favored hub to the powerful and rich, not only in the country, but worldwide. But to me, it wasn't a home; it was a place I occasionally slept and where I did my work.

My aide's tone was chastising and tiresome. "Not now," I said in warning. He could bother me later about my deplorable work habits.

Timothy looked up as if realizing where we were and who was at my side. "Yes, well, ahem, welcome to the Sinopolis."

"Let's go." I started toward the front doors.

Vivien tripped over her feet.

"I thought vampires were imbued with great strength and grace?" Irritation lined my tone.

"Graceful as a ninja ballerina now," she confirmed. "I just don't feel like we need to be in a rush."

Dragging her closer to me, I was ready to spout off another menacing threat, but I stopped before pushing her out to arm's length.

"What?" she asked.

"You reek of garbage and a man's body odor." I held my breath.

She glowered. "Well, excuse your highness, but living in

the sewers hasn't given me a lot of time to clean up or launder my stolen threads."

Instead of answering, I resumed my quick pace with Vivien in tow, keeping my nose a safe distance from her.

We walked through the lobby, and Vivien's face tilted up to take in the dazzling heights. The rooms all had balconies that overlooked the restaurants and shops below. A massive oasis sat at the center with lush trees and foliage that filled the air with the scent of fresh flowers and freshly turned dirt. There was the soothing rush of water from the falls all around the clear pool. Massive gold and obsidian chandeliers were suspended above.

Vivien slowed down, except this time her mouth gaped as she drank in the surroundings. I didn't push her any faster, allowing her to absorb an environment I took great pride in creating. She looked out of place in her smelly, ill-fitting clothes, yet I appreciated the open awe on her face. The wealthy guests who entered the doors rarely paused to observe the surroundings with wonder. Instead, they barely glanced at the luxurious, cultivated environment as if they expected it to look like this everywhere they went.

The hotel was a masterpiece in ink-black glass and marble, embellished with aged-gold accents. Tropical plants and red velvet furniture served as pops of color. Unlike other casinos, there were few slot machines here. The primary draw was the private backrooms for the gambling elite. If people wanted slots, there were plenty of places on the Strip where they could find their cheap thrills. But at the Sinopolis, patrons could enter with their fortunes and leave with a kingdom in their pocket if they knew how to play the game.

Instead of heading toward the elevators at the center of the lobby, we cut to the right to one of my private lifts.

Timothy excused himself to his duties, leaving the two of us to enter the car. When the doors closed, the ambient echo of the hotel cut off. The padding on the walls made it so quiet you could hear a person's heartbeat in here. Except Vivien didn't have a heartbeat. I still released her arm as we were in an enclosed space for at least a few moments.

She turned her head to the side, not quite looking at me, her voice low in the quiet elevator. "You're not taking me to some kind of dungeon, are you?"

There were only three buttons. The middle, a white button for the lobby, and there was a gold one above it and a black one below. I reached past her to press the top gold button. The buttons had fingerprint recognition so they would only work for the designated few. "No."

"Good," she said with sudden confidence. "Because I came for my three hundred dollars and then I'm splitting."

"And then what will you do?" I asked, genuinely curious.

"I've got a list."

"Pray tell."

"A, find out who murdered me. B, kick their ass. C, remember what my life was."

"And D?" I goaded.

She faced forward again. "I'm still working on that one." Her shoulders fell. "Don't suppose I could go back to the life I had."

I didn't answer. None of that would be happening. I could not permit her existence. Though the soft longing in her tone tugged at something in my chest.

I hardened inside as I did whenever I had to take care of business. When the lift opened with a soft ding, I took hold of her arm again and dragged her into my penthouse.

"Hey, watch it, bucko," she protested. I released her. She rubbed her bicep while shooting me an angry glare.

"You will stay here until I come for you. You are only alive because I allow it. Because you are useful for drawing out the master vampire. But the second you inconvenience, or otherwise vex me, I will not hesitate to dispose of you."

Vivien stomped up to me, mania gleaming in those green eyes. "Whoa, I'm here for my money and then I'm out of here."

Strange creature. She was still trying to act like she was in control here.

Looking past her, to the windows that slanted upward, 180 degrees around the pyramid top of the hotel, I said, "It will be dawn soon."

As it was, her eyes drooped, fatigue and weakness evident on her face. It would be so easy to end her right now. Wipe her from existence. I was tempted to be done with her. But I needed to return order to this world, and I intended to use her to root out the cancer that threatened to upturn everything.

"Do you really wish for me to throw you out?" I said, gesturing to the sky that was fast turning from night to dawn.

The vampire looked out at the lightening sky, opening her mouth and then shutting it.

Not waiting for a response, I turned to the lift, pressing a button on the wall. Wood paneling and shades lowered over every window.

"And might I suggest," I said, stepping back into the elevator, "taking the opportunity to shower before rubbing your unclean body on the furniture." My nose wrinkled at the thought of the havoc she could wreak on the upholstery.

Just as the doors shut, there was a giant crash against them—something ceramic by the sound of it. Hmm, perhaps I should have thrown her in a dungeon somewhere.

5

I hoped the statue I hurled against the elevator was expensive, though I suspected Death didn't truly care about material things or money. Still, the explosion of ceramic was satisfying.

I considered pressing the elevator button to make the doors open, but then I'd potentially bring big, dour, and scary back up. I planned to give it a few minutes. Then I would attempt to find my way out of here.

And into broad daylight...

I rubbed my hand, still remembering my first test to see if sunlight really was lethal. The pain had been excruciating. My charred skin had healed after I emptied an entire blood bag I'd taken with me down into the sewer. I'd only been able to carry out three bags before I had to resort to sucking vermin dry.

While I wasn't in a hurry to burn to a crisp, I had to get out of here. Or Death would come for me. Literally.

Who would have guessed Death himself would b impossibly sexy? Peering into Grim's eyes was like drownin in a vat of warm, liquid chocolate. Convincing myself I w just hungry, which was true, but chocolate wouldn't do it for me anymore.

The penthouse was massive. The roof sloped up over the living room, making up the top of the pyramid. The gothic chandelier in the kitchen resembled the ones in the lobby. It lit up as the wood panels and shades finished sliding into place. Impressive feat having total window coverage on a slanted angle. Was Death worried about snipers? Not that he himself could die. Could he? Ugh, a girl's head could explode trying to figure out all this crazy supernatural stuff.

What was next? Werewolves and the tooth fairy? I still hoped I would wake up from this nightmare, but after two weeks in the sewers, and trying to find my murderer, my new reality had set in.

The least I could do was find out all about how my life— or unlife?—came to this.

Even as I resolved to break my way out of here to resume my personal investigation, heaviness closed around me, threatening to pull me under. The sun had that effect, and I knew as soon as it set, my strength would return. My stomach gurgled, then settled for gnawing on itself. Maybe that bastard intended for me to starve. The shaking in my hands had intensified.

I walked over to the kitchen, which exuded masculine elegance. A sleek, onyx waterfall island matched the coun-ters and black cabinets. The steel appliances gleamed as if never touched. A metal wine cooler sat next to the fridge. A quick glance inside and I gathered many of the bottles in there were older than me, times fifty.

The thought of being trapped up here, slowly eating from the inside out, made me queasy. Then again, who knew what I would do if I was out on the streets below with all those blood bags walking around.

Humans. Ya know? Human, like you used to be?

The elevator softly chimed. I snatched my hand off my stomach and righted myself.

Grim's aide stepped out of the elevator. He grimaced at the porcelain mess on the floor and gingerly stepped between the pieces.

"Do you have my money?" I demanded, though my head was foggy, and my stomach was likely to cave in any second.

Timothy lifted a small red and white cooler.

Relief swept through me, though I tried not to let it show on my face. "Did his majesty bleed off one of his many kills for me?"

Timothy crossed the room to set the cooler on the black island. His tone was delicate and clipped. "That's really not how it works. He doesn't kill people."

Splaying my hands on the cold marble to suppress my need to rip the cooler open and drink whatever blood was inside, I asked, "So big, dark and scary has never killed anyone?"

The aide paused, taking the lid off the cooler.

Yeah, that's what I thought. Death has gotten his hands dirty.

"So if he doesn't kill people, what does he do?" I asked as I grabbed a blood bag from the cooler. There was a label on it. Oh sweet Jesus, it was human. A shudder of anticipatory pleasure ran through me.

Human tasted one thousand percent better than rat. But my conscience niggled at me, when I thought of trying to steal more blood from the hospital. Which led me to conclude that Bruiser was a real dick in his previous life if he had no qualms about snacking on that woman who tried to save me.

Instead of handing me the medical bag, Timothy rounded the island to grab a large goblet and turned away from me. When he handed the cup to me, I had to use both hands so as not to spill it. The shaking had intensified.

"Is that a pineapple and hibiscus garnish?" I asked, incredulous.

Timothy smoothed a hand down his suit. "Yes, well, just because you are a blood-sucking fiend doesn't mean I have to skimp on presentation."

If I hadn't been so damn hungry, I would have continued to stare at him like he was the crazy one. As soon as the blood hit my lips, I let out a low moan of pleasure. It would have been better warmed, but I wouldn't look a gift human in the mouth.

Timothy averted his eyes and went about unpacking the rest of the blood into the fridge.

"The master guides souls into the afterlife, preserving the sacred cycle of life."

I lifted my mouth from the glass for a moment. "There's an afterlife? For real? No shit. What's it like?"

Timothy's expression grew increasingly pinched. I wouldn't squeeze any more out of him on that front.

"You seem to have this whole suck whore thing figured out."

Timothy blinked, unable to hide his shock. With a few more blinks, realization seemed to spread across his face. "Did you mean sekhor?"

"Yeah, that," I held up a hand to him. "My fingerprints are gone. Is that a sekhor thing?"

He regained his composure. "Yes, your skin and body underwent a significant transformation when you turned. There is a certain elasticity in your DNA now that allows you to heal quickly from otherwise traumatic or even fatal injuries."

So I had super healing abilities, but I wasn't invincible.

The empty goblet clinked against the marble when I set it down. I asked in a low tone, "He's not going to let me go, is he?" Despite my new fullness, fear churned in my gut. At least I wasn't frozen anymore. Warmth ran through me, and I was a new girl. Err, vampire.

Timothy closed the fridge and turned to face me. His eyes were solemn behind wire-rimmed glasses. "He's charged with preserving the sacred cycle of life," he repeated.

I didn't understand.

He continued to stare at me. Somewhere in the penthouse a clock ticked with precise, measured clicks, time expanding between us.

I'd tested the sun theory. I had gotten my hands on some silver, a cross, a bulb of garlic and even some holy water, but not a one of them hurt me like lore suggested. But there were some things I didn't dare test.

"I'm immortal, aren't I?"

Timothy slowly nodded his head.

I licked my lips. Did vampires even get dry lips? "And he can't allow that, can he?"

Timothy's voice came out quiet and measured. "No, he cannot."

"I didn't ask for this," I said, hating that my voice cracked.

Timothy grabbed the cooler and walked back to the elevator. As it opened with a ding, his eyes remained averted. "I suggest you get some rest. I'll be up later to clean this. If you need anything, pick up any of the phones and dial three. That's my direct line."

When the elevator closed, I had the overwhelming need to throw something again, but it wouldn't help.

No matter that I could live forever, I'd have to face the same hard truth everyone else did. Death was inevitable.

I SAT in the lone chair of the antechamber, thinking on how a vampire could appear after all these years. Not one, but five. This was a catastrophe. That sekhor upstairs in my penthouse right now clearly had no concept of the chaos she presented. If I did not contain the situation, sekhors would run rampant; murdering, power-hungry creatures.

A door opened, and Timothy entered. I looked up from where I'd rested my chin on my fist. Two of my reapers trotted in on either side of him, Yelhsa and Nerual. I could tell by the golden glow of their eyes, they'd returned with yet more souls requiring my judgement. They went over to wait against the wall along with Aicila, Eener, and the fifteen others. Tension coiled into my neck and back like a compressed spring. Work could be demanding, but my duty was sacred, and I never forgot that.

Timothy stopped a couple feet from the stairs of my platform. He didn't say anything, and neither did I for a few moments. The weight of the situation was more than pressing, and we didn't need to comment on the fact of the catastrophe. The dire situation was self-evident.

Timothy finally broke the silence. "Why after all this time?"

"I don't know, but whoever is orchestrating this is moving quickly. We've encountered five sekhors, but Vivien..." I paused, thinking on how hard the vampire had deliberated on picking a name for herself, "has been on her own for two weeks, if we are to believe her. Whoever wields the ability to turn people, they aren't wasting any time on growing their numbers."

"Only a vampire can turn others into one of their own, and you have long made their kind extinct. How could they simply appear after all this time?" Timothy asked, echoing the question that now tortured me.

I pressed two fingers in my temple, feeling a headache develop. "I don't know." Then I got up from my seat and walked down the stairs, gesturing for Timothy to follow me. "At the moment, how they came about is inconsequential. Foremost, we need to find the master. When the sun sets, we will take the vampire back out and use her as bait. The others came for her; I presume they will do so again. If there is one thing I recall about vampires, it's that they are fiercely territorial of their own kind. They will attempt to get her under their control as soon as possible."

There was hesitance in Timothy's voice. "You believe she doesn't remember her turning?"

I paused. The vampire who spent all her time pressing buttons in a limo like a child and insisting she drank animal blood because she wasn't a monster was...unusual. Not like the creatures I remember, nor like those in the alleyway. She would have me think her guileless, but I was not new. I was as old as dirt, as Timothy sometimes liked to joke.

"Trusting her would be a grave mistake," I said. "One I don't intend on indulging."

Timothy held his tablet in front of his body. "I don't think we should either, sire, but those other vampires came for her. Someone thinks she is special."

"Which will make her the perfect bait."

We had much to plan. But first, there were souls needing judgment before I could deal with the sekhor issue. It was going to be a long day.

_____

6

Predictably, the elevators did not come up, no matter how many times I smashed the button.

Agitated that I was trapped, I had to resist the urge to take a chair and try to beat out a window. Even if I waited until night and succeeded, it wasn't like I could surf down the side of the glass building as if it was one big slide.

Or could I?

Then again, I was pretty sure I was only immortal if I didn't do anything too extraordinarily dumb to get myself killed.

Instead of hurling myself off the building, I wandered the expansive penthouse. There was a mix of slate gray walls, dark wood paneling, and exposed brick from room to room.

Deciding to take advantage of the digs while I had them, I found my way to a bedroom and the adjoining bathroom. Though tempted to touch the pristine white comforter on the way, I kept my grimy digits to myself. Then thought better of it, rounded back and pressed my filthy hands on the duvet, making perfect imprints. Then I drummed on the duvet as if I were performing a show until it looked like a little mud-covered piggy had a ball.

I slightly regretted soiling the covers for Timothy's sake, who seemed as uptight as a bleached starfish on a stick. But worth it, if I irritated his majesty even the tiniest bit.

Peeling my clothes off and throwing them in the bedroom haphazardly, I made my way toward the shower. Not because his highness wanted me to, but because I felt like it. Though being dirty wasn't the worst thing in the world—maybe I was a wilderness explorer in my old life?— a steamy shower appealed.

The shower could have fit a party of five. It had pulsating heads positioned all the way around. As soon as the jets hit my skin, I moaned. The stream turned black as I scrubbed away sewer grit, not skimping on the blackberry sage body wash. I didn't stop until the water ran clear.

Despite being cold as a corpse, I enjoyed the spray of near-scalding water, like a lizard. I spent the next five minutes wondering if vampires were descendants of lizards. I considered how I nearly froze when I didn't get to drink blood. So if vampires could withstand the sun, would they splay out on hot rocks all day long?

Apparently, exhaustion had caught up to my brain. I wasn't sure if it was from the bizarre turn of events or because dawn was breaking. The daylight seemed to always sap my energy.

With an impossibly fluffy white towel wrapped around my body, and one around my hair, I padded back into the bedroom. The closet was packed with clothes. Women's clothes, to be exact. Were they here to accommodate all the women who passed through? Or did women come here, do the deed with Grim, and then pass...on?

My skin crawled at the idea of wearing his majesty's

dead concubines' clothes, but they smelled and fit better than what I'd stolen from a laundromat.

Most of the options were short, glitter party dresses, so I dug deep for more. I shucked on some supple leather pants, a silver tank top, and donned a denim jacket over it. Though I had to go without panties or a bra, I didn't mind the feel so much. After rooting through the closet some more, I even found some heeled boots in my size. At the last minute, I grabbed a long leather lace from a corset and wrapped it around my neck and tied it off. The makeshift choker mostly covered the gnarly bite scars.

Next, I moseyed around the penthouse despite being dead tired.

Haa. At least, I knew I was a funny person.

I wouldn't be able to relax unless I scouted out the layout. To my surprise, not a single door was locked. I discovered a two-story library room, complete with fireplace, fancy old dude's bar, and big tufted leather chairs. The thick volumes didn't appeal, and I searched for a magazine with some celebrity face on the cover but came up empty.

Wasn't that the damnedest thing? I had to reacquaint myself with my face in the mirror—while ruling out the no-reflection myth—but I never forgot a Kardashian. Hell of a joke.

There were two other bedrooms, and there was no doubt which was the master. Walking in his majesty's bedroom was like strolling into a gothic theater. Heavy, black curtains with gold fringe and tassels lined the walls. The scent of smoke and sex lingered, along with *his* musk. The combination made for a heady aphrodisiac that warmed and curled in my belly. A shiver went through me. Similar to the rest of the penthouse, this place was masculine sophistication, but there was something underlying this room. Lust, sin, but above all, danger.

I half-expected to see shackles, whips, or some kind of fancy BDSM equipment laid neatly out somewhere. Aside from the precisely arranged watches and clothes, there was nothing personal.

The true centerpiece was the extravagant bed. More expansive than any king-size, the backboard was a tufted forest-green velvet surrounded by large gold filigree vines. Someone had folded the dusky plum bedspread back to frame black satin sheets.

The only reason to have a mattress that massive is if you are going to fill it with people. Images of tangled limbs from Grim's orgies flickered in my mind.

Then I wondered how many women or men—I didn't know Grim's preference if he even had one—had been up here. When he finished with them, did he kill them? Or if one of them begged him to take them before reaping their soul? Would he take a chosen few on those sheets and fuck them until they died? No, I didn't want to think of that.

Despite myself, a warmth blossomed in my stomach as I imagined what he looked like stripped of his expensive suit. A girl could wrap her legs around that tapered waist, grab hold of those muscled arms and go to town.

No no no, bad vampire, I scolded myself.

After weeks of isolation, loneliness and the need for touch nearly swallowed me whole. I spent an inordinate amount of time fantasizing that someone was waiting for me to get back to them. A boyfriend, a husband, someone who loved me so much they were going out of their mind thinking I was dead. Then when I returned, they'd be so grateful and happy we would make it work, even though I was a vampire. I'd promise never to bite him in bed, and he'd warm my blood for me every morning in a mug that said, "Bloodsucker in the streets, vamp in the sheets."

But Grim would never do anything so domestic or mundane. Death took what he wanted, when he wanted. I could imagine those dangerous amber eyes watching a human writhe under him while he remained in complete control.

I backed out of the bedroom. My imagination had gotten away from me, and it was leading to a dark place that made me deeply uneasy.

After sufficient snooping, I lay down on one of the long leather couches. I'd only rest for a minute, then I'd come up with a plan to get out of here. The muscles in my body had turned leaden. Even my eyelids drooped. When I finally woke up again, most of the day had passed while I went into a mini coma.

The need to roll over and sleep for several more hours was strong. The sun was still up. But then panic crawled up my throat. *He* would come back, and who knew how long I would have then?

I needed to find a way out of here. Groggily getting to my feet, I was weak as a kitten, but at least I was clean and safe, for now.

Warming up another blood bag in a mug— black, of course—I tossed it back, barely allowing myself to enjoy the texture and flavor.

My innate appreciation for my meal made me wonder if maybe I'd been a chef or a food critic in my former life. I stole apples and bread in the first week of my vampirism to see if I could still eat like a normal person. My senses were heightened. The flavors of an apple transported me to the taste of the very farm where it had grown. Unfortunately, when my need for blood arose, food did nothing to abate the thirst.

The blood helped wake me up some, so I drank two more bags' worth until I was practically bursting. My body sang, buzzing with energy. Maybe I would try to surf down the pyramid after all.

One way or another, it was definitely time to go. But not before I got paid. Rounding back to the library, a heavy executive's desk sat off to one side. I rummaged through several drawers before I found a stack of cash under some paperclips and a stapler. Counting off three crisp one-hundred-dollar bills, I pocketed them with satisfaction. I thought of leaving a note thanking them for the hospitality, but seeing as they put me up only to use me as bait and kill me later, I figured I could forego the pleasantries.

I stared at the elevator with a critical eye. What if it magically opened now? I pressed the button to call it up and open the doors.

Nothing. *Blood bags.*

I spotted the pinhole at the top right of the door where a magnetic elevator key fit. Bingo.

It took an hour, but I discovered it in a utility drawer off the kitchen. Sticking it in the hole and turning it, the doors released, and I could push them open. Looking down into the dark shaft, I wondered if I shouldn't come up with a less dangerous plan than sliding down thirty stories. I gulped.

If I stayed, I died. If I fell, my vampire abilities would kick in and heal me, right? I sucked another cold blood bag clean, though my stomach had distended from so much. I'd need all the healing powers I could get.

Reaching out, I grabbed the thick cable, then wrapped my body around the twisted steel. Pausing there until I was sure I could easily hold my weight, I then inched my way down the cord.

As I slid down a little at a time into the engulfing blackness, my vision turned red. I could see in the dark. Gaining confidence in my ability to hold my weight, I realized it was going to take forever to hit the bottom at this rate. Feeling bolder, I relaxed my grip and slid down ten feet. Not too bad.

I eased my grip again, sliding down. Stopping once more, a smile spread across my face. The feeling of power, ability, and knowing I couldn't die emboldened me.

I decided to have a little fun. Releasing my legs from the pole, I dropped, speeding down the steel, air whooshing by as my hair flew up. Unable to help myself, I let out a yeehaw as I rode the line all the way down. As soon as I caught sight of the top of the elevator car, I tightened my grip ever so slightly, gradually slowing myself until I soundlessly landed on the roof of the car.

Looking at my hands, some skin had scraped off, but it knitted back together before my eyes. The feeling was incredible. I truly could do so much more than I'd given myself credit for.

I found the latch on the top door and slowly opened it to make sure no one was inside. Seeing it was empty, I jumped down and into the car, as silent as a cat. The elevator doors were open, but it wasn't at the lobby level. Peeking out, there were ancient-looking sandstone walls lit by torches.

Holy crap, did Death have a medieval castle built underneath the hotel or something?

Voices echoed, and I stepped out to hear better. There were massive pillars everywhere, so I took care to remain hidden as I crept forward.

A woman was sobbing. "You don't understand." She was middle-aged and wore a sweatshirt and jeans.

Grim sat back in a stone-cut throne, with a bored, contemptuous expression on his handsome face. "No, I never do, do I?"

"I'll do anything, just please don't do this."

Gold sparked in his eyes as he leaned forward, fingers grasping on the arms of his chair. "You'll do anything?"

Holding out her hands in prayer, she cried out, "Yes, yes, anything."

My stomach clenched as I waited to see what would happen. The desperation in her plea tore at my undead heart.

Something wet touched my hand, and I jumped. Looking down, I found the same black, dog-like creature that had been in the hospital. A low growl rumbled in its throat. Before I could think of what I was doing, I reached down and scratched its head. The growling stopped. Then, after a minute of heavy petting, the canine leaned into my touch.

Great, my crazy dog fantasies followed me here. Thankfully, I didn't draw any attention as I continued to scratch poochie behind the ears. There was no way a dog could have been roaming around the hospital on its own, and it was less likely I'd see the same mutt down here. I must have lost a chunk of my mind when I'd been turned...if I had it to begin with.

In a moment Grim was inches from the woman, cradling her chin with his knuckles. The tension stretched out as he let her continue to sob. I wanted to jump out and tell him to leave her alone, but I forced myself to stay hidden.

Grim then leaned forward to whisper something in her

ear. I drew back as he stared past her, afraid he would catch sight of me behind the pillar.

Then Grim stood, and a heavy stone door to his right opened with a loud creak. He waved his hand and her body jerked through the air, flying into the darkness with a terrified shriek that rang in my ears. Another sound emanated from the blackness, a growl. So deep, loud, and guttural; it wasn't like any animal I had ever heard before. I held fast to the pillar to keep from shaking. The woman's screams echoed as if she were being torn apart. Her cries cut off when the door shut again.

A soft whine from the dog reminded me my hand had gone still. I resumed petting poochie, perhaps harder than necessary but he leaned in.

Timothy suddenly appeared with the tablet, offering it to Grim to sign. Neither showed any hint of emotion or remorse.

And here I thought Timothy was a good guy, but he lied. Grim killed, and he enjoyed it. I knew it from the gleam in his eye, and the lift of his lips when he toyed with her.

I had to get the blood clot outta here. Silently backing up, I retreated into the open elevator. I needed to escape. The dog trotted after me but didn't follow me inside.

Whatever lay behind that massive stone door was a fate worse than death, and I was all full up on weird, terrifying shit for the day. Yep, all full up. No más.

Pressing the button, the elevator dinged loudly. The voices hushed, and the dog whined.

7

F ucking perfect. I might as well have stripped down
to my underwear, run around, and quacked like a
duck. Might have been less subtle. I hid in the
corner, drawn into myself as the doors shut, waiting for
Grim to appear in a fury and then throw me to whatever he
had behind door number one. Unable to help myself, I
pressed the white button repeatedly. But I didn't have the
key to the elevator like Grim did. I was totally screwed.

Footsteps were approaching. My heart lodged itself in
my throat. Backed into the corner, a helpless mouse, I
waited for the predator to come and rip me to shreds.

Maybe I could escape out the top hatch. Then again, if I
hopped on top of the elevator and they sent it back to the
penthouse, I'd be smashed into a pancake. *A vamp-cake?* I
shook my head.

You're a vampire now. You'd survive that...probably...maybe.

I was super strong and immortal, but I still had no desire
to be maimed.

Magically, the doors slid close and my shoulders

dropped in relief. Guess you didn't need a key if the destination was the lobby.

As soon as the elevator opened on the main level, I wasted no time hauling ass across the black marble floor. I was almost to the front doors when they opened. A couple strode in, followed by orange rays of sun. I reared back with a reactive hiss.

Shit, it was still daylight. I'd have to hide for a little while longer. A ding reached my ears. They were calling the elevator back down. *Blood bags.*

Instead of running out onto the Strip, I booked it farther into the hotel.

I slowed down to a fast walk when I got pointed stares. The hotel staff eyed me, while a security guard lazily made his way toward me. Death owned this place and everyone inside. There were security cameras littered everywhere, so no matter where I went, I'd be easy to find.

If memory served, there were windowless corridors that connected some of the hotels.

And yet, you don't remember where you lived before all this. Tragic.

I shook off the pathetic thought and made my way past restaurants and shops. Hotel guests milled about, but there was no blending in here. I stuck out like a janky, half-crumbling donut amid five-tiered wedding cakes. From their cutting gazes, it was clear they also knew I did not belong. I should have donned the short slinky rhinestone-bomb dress and a fur coat if I wanted to fit in here. Ah, to be a high-class hooker.

After making a few wrong turns, I eventually found the corridor that led to the neighboring hotel. I had to get away from Sinopolis's cameras.

The décor morphed from sleek chic to a colorful,

childish castle theme. The metal ping of the slots competed with the pop music playing in the background. The crowd thickened as people were all out seeking dinner. Cigarette smoke choked the air. The masses here were less posh than those at the Sinopolis. Less Louboutins, way more fanny packs. It was a cinch for me to blend in now. While I was pretty sure Death didn't have access to cameras in here, I ducked when I spotted one. I disappeared in the crowd, wondering if I could keep this up until the sun set?

I pretended to be interested in some of the shops, sticking close to other groups of people. I hadn't been around this many people since I turned vampire. Countless heartbeats pounded around me in excitement, and I heard the blood rush through their veins. The prospect of a delicious, hot meal straight from the source left me with a heady faint feeling.

No. You had plenty to drink. Do not do it. You are not a monster.

Thank god I drank until I almost exploded before leaving the penthouse prison. I'd never sunk my fangs in anyone's neck. Part of me desperately wanted to know what it was like. I feared it would be too good. If I drank straight from the source, would I lose control? A knot formed in my stomach.

I needed to stay focused. Only about a half hour before I could blow this joint.

The crowded cafeteria was the best place to get lost. I waited by a fountain near a group of girls who were taking selfies. Their giggles reached shrill decibels only a dog could detect. They reminded me of a rabid pack of hyenas.

My attention caught on a kid who was off at a table by himself. He looked ten years old, wore an Iron Man shirt, and his thick, curly hair was cropped close to his head. He was alone, hands folded in his lap as if patiently waiting for someone.

Two men and a woman argued at the table next to him. Their slurred voices rose as the fight escalated. One man jumped up, flipping the table before diving at the other dude across from him. The girl let loose a shrill scream. They started throwing punches. To me, it all happened in slow motion. They were about to fall into the lone kid, and he wouldn't get out of the way in time.

Everything slowed down as I used my super speed to dart over to the kid. I grabbed the boy, yanking him back, as the two men crashed into his chair. I set him down and crouched down to eye level. "You okay, kid?" We stood at the far wall by the McDonald's now.

There was more shouting as someone intervened in the fight.

The boy's eyes were wide, bright white against his dark brown skin. His heartbeat thundered as he bordered on hyperventilating. I didn't know if he was amped up from the almost miss, or because within a blink of an eye, I had him across the room. With a quick glance, I tried to determine if anyone else had seen, but all eyes were on the hot-headed drunkards.

"Jamal, are you okay?" a woman called nearby.

I stood up. "I think he's alright, just a bit shaken up from watching a couple of douche nozzles."

Turning to the woman, I stopped cold. She blinked in twin surprise. It was the woman who tried to save me from Bruiser last night.

Next thing I knew, I was looking down the barrel of her gun. With a quick scan of her outfit, I realized she was in hotel security garb and it had been her voice I'd heard breaking up the fight.

Slowly raising my hands, I considered the possibility of me surviving a gunshot to the face. I should have asked old Timmy more questions about my kind. Even if I survived her shot, I imagined it would not be a good time.

We were off to the side enough that no one noticed, and she kept her gun trained on me, but aimed so that her body hid the gun, avoiding a public panic.

"You're a..." She faltered.

She'd seen the fangs. She saw how Bruiser and I had moved. Even if she couldn't say it out loud, she knew what I was.

"Mom?" Jamal's worried voice broke through the glazed terror in her eye. Her jaw hardened, and she narrowed her eyes at me.

"It's okay, baby, come over and stand behind Mommy."

Jamal seemed reluctant but obeyed his mother's command.

"I didn't hurt the boy. Have no intention of it," I said, trying not to spook her. Did I have a calming voice? I should have asked his highness.

She snorted in disbelief.

Jamal tugged on the back of her shirt. "We flew like Superman, Mom."

This was not good. Time to bolt. I turned and ran. I got two feet before colliding smack dab into the hard chest of someone who smelled like lilies, fresh-turned soil, and a musky cologne.

When I tilted my head up, the rugged, handsome face of his majesty greeted me. Gold arced from the center of his irises. Fury tightened his impossibly handsome face.

"Going somewhere?"

Blood clots.

8

The vampire had not only escaped the penthouse somehow, she had snuck into my private work chambers and then tried to run for it. I had underestimated her, a mistake I would not make a second time. I squeezed her arm with bruising force. Only the corners of her eyes gave away her wince.

If we hadn't been in public, I might have throttled her.

The hotel security guard looked back and forth between Vivien and me, uncertainty in her eye, gun still drawn.

"Thank you for your help, Miss—?"

"West. Miranda West." Her posture and tone remained rigid. Apparently, my charm was a bit rusty. Used to be I could have a woman fawning over me with a mere look.

The way she regarded Vivien with wary, wide eyes tipped me off she was cognizant of the *strange* in her midst.

"Ms. West." I bowed my head. Turning, never losing my grip on Vivien, I said, "Timothy, if you could properly thank Ms. West for her help, I'd greatly appreciate it."

"What has she done?" Miranda asked, skepticism as thick as the waft of greasy fries in here.

"My aide will explain everything." I attempted to smile but based on how the kid both jerked and grasped at his mother's hips, it came off menacing. A side effect of spending too much time judging souls in the antechamber.

As I dragged Vivien off, Timothy stepped forward.

"What's he going to tell her?" Vivien asked in a sulky tone. "That I've been a bad vampire, and you need to put me back in my kennel?"

"He has a talent for making questions and problems disappear, whether by explanation or money." Though I doubted from Ms. West's demeanor she'd be amenable to bribery, but that was yet another quality that made Timothy invaluable. He'd find some way to explain why I dragged a young woman off.

I pushed us through the throng of vacationing tourists. "And here I thought you'd appreciate being allowed to stay in such a nice kennel."

"Mad I chewed through the bars?"

I turned on her so fast, she almost ran into me again. "Do you think it wise to test me so, when your existence is only permitted based on your usefulness?" Despite my efforts to stay cool and in control, she was skating on my last nerve.

Her gaze flew to where I held her arm between us, then up into my eyes. Judging by her gasp, I'd let my death mask flicker through.

While her aura was bright before, Vivien shone as bright as a star now. She was nearly unrecognizable since she'd cleaned up. Her long hair was not a dark, muddy brown, but a glossy auburn. Transformed from straight and limp, it was now a voluminous, textured mass that begged for fingers to wrap in it. No longer streaked with dirt and grime, her face was the shade of cream with a sprinkling of freckles across the bridge of her nose.

Before, she was attractive. Now, she was a wild kind of beautiful that made me think of jungle cats and the lush, inviting jungles where they played. The shade of her hair reminded me of a sunset I wished would never end. Her eyes still crackled with the same energy as when we first met, warning me not to rub the soft skin of her forearm, though my thumb itched to do so. If she was aware of her power over me, she didn't show it.

Instead of cowing down, her expression hardened as she leaned in until we were almost nose to nose. "Oh, I'm sorry. Am I not being useful enough? Should I have been cleaning the toilets in your penthouse? Making lunch for you, or perhaps sitting still and quiet until you come to retrieve me like a pair of house slippers?"

"You are infuriating."

"You want everyone to be afraid of you, but guess what, buttercup? I'm not."

Despite her irksome behavior that inspired me to lock her up in an actual dungeon, I couldn't help the twitch at the corner of my mouth. "Did you call me buttercup, bloodsucker?"

She responded in a haughty tone. "I prefer the term sekhor. Seems more formal, *your majesty*. No, you're right. You're so easily shook, buttercup is a much better nickname for you."

Blood rushed in my ears. Her green eyes crackled with electricity and she pressed the tip of her tongue behind her front teeth as if goading me to start a fight with her. She very well might have seen what I was capable of in the antechamber. She knew I was death itself, yet she was baiting me.

A select number believed they could defy death, many out of arrogance. Some offered money, others challenged me, thinking they were above the *end*. But when I revealed death's true face, they all cowered. Vivien wasn't defiant because she wanted to stop me from doing my duty. From what I could tell, she provoked me for the sheer joy of it.

A hand slapped me on the back as the stench of cheap beer and sweat assaulted my senses.

"Haha, get a room, you two," slurred a twenty-something boy with a popped collar and cap turned to the side. When he stumbled back to his buddies, they all laughed and punched each other on the arm.

"Uck, dude-bros are the worst," Vivien muttered.

For once, I didn't disagree.

I led her back to Sinopolis, not liking how easily she provoked me. I told myself I was on edge after such a long day of work; that, coupled with the stress of this vampire problem, and I'd lost my temper with this insignificant sekhor. But it was no excuse for me to lose my cool. I couldn't afford distractions, but she was a flashing neon sign with screaming bells and whistles. Hard to ignore, and harder not to toss out a window.

A trio of men were about to pass by, when one of them halted. His face drained of color as he regarded us.

"Fan of yours?" Vivien asked, her tone dry as the martini I planned on having later.

The man was average height with brown hair and blunt features. He wore cargo shorts and a Hawaiian shirt. But he wasn't looking at me. Vivien received the full force of his startled, wide-eyed gape. He stared like a rabbit confronted by a hunter.

He took off sprinting, knocking into people as he made

his way across the hotel, in the opposite direction we were headed.

Vivien followed him, but I yanked her back.

"Did you see that? He recognized me. We need to follow him."

"He wasn't a vampire," I said, not giving her an inch.

Vivien still strained against my grip, trying to keep him in sight, though he was fast making a getaway. "He knows who I am. We can ask him how he knows me."

"I would guess a past lover based on his speed," I muttered.

She whirled on me, vibrating with anger. "We have to talk to him." Her shout drew attention. I sent a reassuring smile to the guests around us. Thankfully, Vegas was not unusual grounds for rambunctious, shouting people. I dropped my voice low, encouraging her to follow suit.

"Who you were is of no consequence. If he can't lead us to a master vampire who turned you, he is also inconsequential."

"Maybe he doesn't know anything about vampires, but maybe he knows something about the night I died that could lead us to the master."

Her case was weak, thready at best. To assume that man had been there the night she was turned was a stretch. I also had no interest in involving mortals in the sekhor matter.

"Please." Her voice became hoarse. "He's the only lead I have to figure out who I was. You can't imagine how it feels to not know who you are." Her sea-green orbs searched mine, also begging me to let her follow him.

Pleas, nothing but pleas, all day and night for centuries had long hardened me to their effects. Yet Vivien somehow plucked on a cord of guilt deep inside me with her earnest entreaty.

I turned away, dragging her back toward Sinopolis. The vampire tried to pull in the opposite direction. She was strong, but I was stronger.

We earned some concerned looks from guests, as I hauled her through the lobby of my hotel. Vivien turned despondent, now dragging her feet. I half-expected her to launch into a full-on tantrum.

I relaxed my grip, so it wouldn't appear as though I was her pimp or abusive boyfriend. At least the staff knew to pay no mind to me or my companion.

"Of all the clothes available, you chose to dress like a delinquent punk," I muttered under my breath, pressing the button to call down the private elevator. Timothy assured me it was still in working order despite Vivien's tampering, but running a little slower than usual.

Vivien's tight-fitting clothes revealed a figure that was both lean and toned with muscle. I was careful to keep my eyes averted when I realized she'd forgone a bra with the sparkly, low-cut top. She looked like she'd walked offstage after a rock performance. Rest assured, no groupies would be bowing before those impossibly long legs any time soon. I'd make sure of that.

Vivien raised her head at my comment on her clothing, noticing the attention we were getting.

"Oh, I'm so sorry to embarrass you. What was I thinking? I should have dressed up like a slutty piece of glitter, so I fit in with your clientele." Her eyes slid back to the onlookers before she exploded. "Ricky, I'm sorry I didn't get the money. I promise I'll get it up front next time. The John said he had it, but I'll make sure next time. Please, just give me my cut. Little Billy needs his insulin, and I can't afford it if you take all of my green again." She pretended to struggle in my grip without any real fight.

Chatter started up around us along with a startled gasp or two.

I stared at her, wide-eyed, in shock. A devilish smile flashed across her face just as the steel doors slid open with a ding. She walked of her own accord into the elevator car, no longer bothering to hide her evil grin.

As soon as the doors shut, I slammed both hands on either side of her head. She jerked, and her smirk evaporated. Anger burned through me as I bore down on her. My fingers spread across the tufted, black leather wall behind her, so Vivien didn't see them shift and elongate into sharp, black claws.

"Did the insanity set in after you turned, or has it always been your affliction?" I shouted, fighting the change, my hands returning to normal.

"If we followed that guy, we could have asked," she shouted back. She blinked with defiance in the face of my fury, but she still drew back against the wall. "And what do you care? You are death itself. What does it matter what those Richie Riches out there think?"

"I do not require their approval. But I do take pride in creating a haven of luxurious sophistication. While you"—I pointed a finger in her face—"are like a rabid mongoose berserk on crystal meth and worse yet, I have to be the one to muzzle you."

Her eyes narrowed. "You just try it, bucko."

Fire swept through me. My composure didn't melt away, it exploded in an inferno. My hand clamped over her mouth as I pressed my body against hers, bringing my mouth to her ear. "I need you as bait, but perhaps you are of better use without your tongue. I wonder if it would grow back? How fast? Rest assured, if it was too soon, I'd be happy to rip it out for you again."

Suddenly, I was all too aware of the way I was pressed against her. My chest flattened her breasts, and my thigh thrust up between her legs, trapping her hips. Images of fucking her into submission in this elevator flashed through my mind.

Leather, my personal soap, and something divinely sensual invaded my senses. Her scent threatened to drag me in and under. The feel of her silky lips against my palm heated my blood before sending it south. My breath turned shallow as I pulled back so I could look into Vivien's face, amazed at the reactions running rampant through me. For a moment, I thought I saw a twin flame of arousal in her eyes. Maybe she too considered me taking her right here.

A wet cold smushed against my hand.

She licked me.

I wiped my palm against my pants and pressed the gold button with my other hand. Her childish behavior was an instant cure for my temporary insanity.

My work-driven celibacy was clearly driving me to madness. It had been a long time since I'd invited anyone into my bed. It seemed crucial I do so at the first opportunity.

VIVIEN SAT at the kitchen counter, sulking at me, while I stood in front of the elevator doors with my arms crossed. At least there were twenty feet between us now, allowing my senses to cool down from the lust-filled rage she'd somehow worked me into.

"What are we waiting for?" she asked. Arms also crossed, mirroring me, she sat on a stool on the other side of the island.

"My aide will arrive soon, hopefully with a report on the whereabouts of any recent vampire activity." I couldn't help the disdain in my voice. I hated biding time, but I had no way of tracking the bloodsuckers.

"And then what?"

"Then you get to serve your purpose."

"Bait." Her tone was flat.

I didn't bother answering.

She dropped her arms as her frown deepened. "Are you going to put me on a hook and ask me to wriggle out on the line?"

A similar image sprung to mind, but in my version, she was wearing no clothes as she writhed about with a wanton expression.

"Oh good, glad you think that is a such stellar idea," Vivien scoffed. I wasn't sure what facial expression I made, but I cleared it away.

"What's the big deal, anyway?" she asked. "Is it because vampires are soulless demons? Evil monsters of the night? Because I don't feel particularly evil or murdery." She uncrossed her arms before scrunching her shoulders up and then rolling them back. Was she restless?

I certainly had a few ideas how to work off that extra energy.

Don't be absurd. You will not touch the sekhor...again.

"Your existence is not permitted," I said.

"Yeah, but whhhhy," she whined, stretching her arms along the counter and resting her chin on them. She resembled a petulant, bored, yet adorable child.

Ridiculous. Sekhors were not adorable. They threatened all of humanity and more.

"Immortality is dangerous. Humans seek longevity, but

they do not understand the repercussions of living for centuries."

She sat up, her brow furrowing. "What does that mean?"

I debated not telling her, but I calculated my odds of her leaving the subject alone and came up quite one-sided with the figures.

"Immortality, for a human, corrupts absolutely. Once they get power and near-invulnerability, they eventually turn into violent, power-hungry tyrants."

"You don't know that," she said, though uncertainty lingered in her eye.

"Do you know when last vampires roamed the earth?" I asked, knowing she of course did not.

"My guess would be around the time that old dude wrote Dracula. What, did he run into one?" She gave an unladylike snort.

"Thousands of years ago."

She stilled. Though she tried to hide her surprise, I saw it register a moment before she buried it.

I dropped my arms, focusing on the cabinet over her head. "I faced the oldest vampire in a great war. She was convinced sekhors were the superior race. She set out to enslave all humanity and turned vast numbers into her own kind. The battle to kill her and the hoard she had created was bloody and continued on for years before we finally destroyed them."

My eyes landed back on Vivien. She didn't interrupt, only bit the inside of her cheek. She might actually be listening.

I went on. "The vampire started out as a regular human woman, like yourself, but eventually she felt the call of power and pursued it to the extreme. So you see, the longer you live, the more invulnerable you feel. You'll strive for more, no longer satisfied with a mundane existence. Like her, you'll become bored and hedge behaviors you once claimed you would never cross. You'll come to see mortal humans as less-than—food, pawns, disposable. Then over time you'll play bigger and bigger until you end up like her. Sekhor hubris erases any trace of humanity, leaving only destruction in their wake. It was decided, that to preserve the natural, sacred cycle of life, they could not be allowed to exist."

"Who decides?"

I'd said too much. I cursed my indiscretion. Instead of answering, I let the question hang between us in stony silence.

"That would never be me." Her words were barely above a whisper. Her eyes had rounded and turned serious.

"Do you know what it means to be a vampire?" I asked, taking two steps forward. I let the sneer of disgust manifest on my lips. "In the way a grave robber would dig up a body, an unnatural, twisted force has raised your corpse. Now you are a walking plague, able to infect and damn countless souls to your same base existence."

Her eyes glazed as she gave an almost imperceptible shake of her head, as if trying to deny some truth she'd known all along. Suddenly, she seemed alone, standing in front of a tidal wave that was about to crash into her and send her into oblivion.

For the second time, she'd somehow plucked a cord of guilt inside me I was not aware even existed. It rang out, vibrating through my body, urging me to take back my biting words, or wrap her in my arms until I could quiet whatever thoughts now tormented her.

I had been harsh. Too harsh. Was I telling her all this for her sake? Or was I trying to convince myself that she was nothing?

She could never mean anything to me. It did not matter how different she was from the vampires I'd once faced, or the billions of souls I'd encountered. I could not allow myself to believe she was special.

Yet, I already do.

The glow around her called to me, invited me to step into her space and claim her in a way I'd never permitted myself to in all my existence. More than her ethereal aura that dazzled, Vivien's vivacious spirit was positively arresting. I wanted to kiss that smart mouth; swallow whatever inflammatory witticism she was spouting off.

Instead, I clenched my fists at my side to keep from reaching out to her.

The vampire is bait, and nothing more. Her existence shall not be permitted. You know the others would never allow her to roam the earth.

My duty to protect this world was more important than eyes that sparked green fire, a sharp wit, and a mouth I couldn't stop thinking about. There was no choice in the matter. As soon as I contained the vampire situation, I would eliminate her.

Only when my phone rang did Vivien emerge from her inward, haunted expression.

I took the call. It was brief.

"Time to go," I said, hanging up. "Your master has struck again."

For once, she didn't fight me. She walked to the elevator, and this time we stood at opposite ends as we hastened to what I expected was a trap set for Vivien. Perhaps this would all be over before the night was out, and my sekhor problem would be solved.

Eyeing Vivien out of the corner of my eye, my chest tightened.

—————

9

While Grim cast his hard stare out the window, Timothy kept occupied on the far end of the limo with his tablet per usual.

Is the limo smaller than the last time?

Nope, same size, but traveling in silence, trapped in a vehicle with his majesty, was making it hard to avoid certain thoughts.

The memory of Grim pressed against me in the elevator warmed me a good twenty degrees. I'd felt his hard sculpted abs even through our clothes. His hot breath fanned against my ear as his delicious scent surrounded me, a cloud of sexually charged opium.

And those rich, amber eyes were dangerous and seductive. His stare was so intent, I worried his scrutiny would melt my panties right off my body...had I been wearing any.

Pinned against the wall, a needy ache had pounded hard through my center, developing a mind of its own. It'd urged to me to slide and buck against his hard thigh. Knowing there was nothing but his pant leg and my skirt trapped against my sex sent electric zings of anticipation to my already tight nipples before pinballing back downward with a flood of hot, wet want.

It wasn't only his physical prowess that had turned me on and inside-out. There was something in Grim's eyes, an almost desperate hunger. It was the look of a prisoner straining for freedom, as something inside him yearned to come out. Everything about Grim was heavy and serious, but there was a light inside him. I wanted to coax it out of him. My gut told me it wanted to come out and play with me.

I had been frozen in place, scared I would succumb to all my urges at once. And they were all screaming at me as if through a loudspeaker.

Wriggle. Grind. Kiss. Lick. Suck.

Was Grim aware that he was sex on a stick? Because my body had been ready as hell to jump on that rod and take a long, hard ride.

The desire had hit me so intensely, it reminded me of my thirst for blood. And while I desperately wanted to give in, I refused to let my cha-cha lead the way. I was crazy, not stupid. If Grim didn't smack me down in refusal within seconds, he'd likely laugh at how pitiful I was—a loathsome bloodsucker trying to nail a being as old as time and as powerful as a god.

So, I gave into only one of my urges. *Lick.*

When I tongued his palm, tasting salty skin, his dark, lust-filled gaze drained of all hunger, leaving disgust in its wake. I'd done an expert job defusing the situation. I deserved a ribbon.

And right now, I could use some ice; sitting mere feet from the scowling being inspired too many distracting, lust-filled thoughts. As soon as the limo stopped, I nearly jumped to get out of the car.

It took me all of two seconds to realize where we were. We'd parked by the alley where my body had been dumped. A chill swept through me that had nothing to do with temperature or my thirst. Darkness blanketed the alley, but I could see into the gloom where a man lay dead. The flesh where his shoulder and neck met was torn up and chewed on, in an all-too-familiar fashion. It was Chad. He stared up into the night with empty, sightless eyes. I wanted to look away, but I couldn't.

Before I'd left the hospital, I'd found copies of the police photos of my corpse in the morgue. The murderer had arranged Chad in a copycat position. He lay on his back, one leg bent at an unnatural angle and staring up at the sky. Like someone broke him, then tossed him aside like a piece of useless garbage, a discarded banana peel.

Seeing pictures of my own body had been disturbing, but this blatant reproduction of my death evoked a heap of nervous butterflies in my stomach and left an acrid taste in my mouth.

Worse yet, there was a pile of bodies farther in the shadows beyond Chad's corpse. Three more dead. Two women and a man, all drained of their blood.

Grim's prediction echoed in my ears. Was I doomed to evolve into a monster? How long had this master vampire been running around, killing people? Did the master start out like me and slowly morph into a lawless savage? Was I weeks away from turning into the same soulless creature? Would immortality and power corrupt me?

My brain clogged with too many questions; I needed a plunger to clear the way.

"Will they turn?" I asked. My words came out quieter than I meant them to. I wondered where the cops were. Then again, if it weren't for my dark vision, I would have likely walked right by the alleyway without a second glance until morning shed light on the gruesome scene.

"No," Timothy said with a sniff, peering at the bodies. "If they were going to turn, then our reapers wouldn't have found them. Their souls required collection and sorting, which is what led us here. And it appears as though most of the blood went toward leaving you a message." His gaze rose with a pointed focus.

"Me," I repeated, still in a daze. Of course, I saw it. The presence of the sweet coppery scent of blood sang to me no matter where it was. But this scene stank with soiled, wasted blood. Smeared on the dirty brick alley wall, someone had used written in large, jagged letters, "You thrill me."

Grim moved behind me. His mouth drew even with my ear, causing goosebumps to rise along the nape of my neck. "Is that the man you were questioning?"

I tried to respond, but my throat had gone dry. I swallowed. "That's him."

"Do you now see what chaos and destruction your kind wreaks?" The hard edge in Grim's voice told me he was on the verge of adding to the body count.

Despite his bitter tone, and the disturbing scene, mere steps away, I wanted to lean back into his warmth. I wanted to turn and bury my face into Grim's chest and inhale his scent until I forgot everything else. Then again, if I tried, he'd probably kill me.

"Do you smell their blood? Do you crave the violence?" His voice had gone raw with emotion. Somewhere inside, I registered how strange it was for Death himself to be outraged. He saw this kind of thing all the time. Why did he care? That would be tantamount to sending an overly empathic nurse to work in hospice. That environment would tear them to shreds from the inside out.

Was it the violence that offended him so? The vampires? Or me?

"No," I answered honestly. "I don't want this. I would never..." Would it be a different story if I hadn't binged on blood earlier? Would I fawn and feast on the bodies here?

Grabbing my shoulders, Death whisked me around, flickers of gold whipping in his eyes. This was it. I was dead. Would he send me to hell? Chuck me in the room with the mysterious beastie that made me want to hide under a bed and pee myself?

My one regret was I never regained my memories of my past self. I still ached to know. I'd been carrying that ache around with me since I woke up in a freezer drawer. It wrenched and nagged at me so much, sometimes I worried it would turn me inside out. Who had I been? Did anyone care I was missing? Was I supposed to be doing something important? Curing cancer? Taking care of a baby? At dinner with my family and my husband?

"You would, and you inevitably will resort to this," he said, with no small amount of menace. "You will continue to feed and then one day, you'll desire to make yourself a play-mate, and force one of your victims to drink your blood while they are on the brink of death. And with that act, you will continue the spread of your kind, like a disease."

The realization that the master vampire had likely forced me to drink his blood to change me, sent a shiver of revulsion through me.

Grim's earlier words in the penthouse had penetrated, striking fear in me, suggesting I was helpless against my nature. I'd done everything I could to fight what I was, and so far I'd managed to control the inner-animalistic hunter of my vampire side. But was I in a losing game against myself?

My defiance sparked, chasing away the ache. How dare

he judge me. He didn't know me. *I* didn't know me. I pushed him off and he let go, though he could have overpowered me.

"I'd die first," I said, craning my neck to look up at him.

"That can be arranged." His amber orbs slid down to my lips and his expression turned inscrutable, as if he were engaged in some internal conflict.

Anger boiled inside me. No part of me was onboard with this kind of carnage. Grim said I would eventually believe I was better than the rest of humanity. Pfft. What a load of crap. I wasn't better than anyone else. I was worse. The thirst controlled me the way booze controlled an alcoholic. And I absolutely fucking hated it.

Grim believed I was a slave to my nature, and his poor opinion of me bothered me more than it should have. Why did it matter what Death thought of me? He planned on killing me any which way, yet part of me craved his approval. I wanted him to see me as more than some bug to be squashed. Not because I wanted to feel important in the face of death, but because I wanted him, *Grim*, to think well of me.

Still, Grim set me up for failure and had zero faith in me, which was infuriating and made me want to prove him wrong even more.

"Stop trying to mansplain my own nature. You think because you've been around since the beginning of time you know everything. You think you know me." I poked his chest. He didn't rip my finger off right away. I poked him again. "You may be old as hell, but that doesn't make you an authority on who I am."

I wasn't interested in power. The idea of feeding my blood to a human after nearly killing them made me sick to my stomach. Right now, I only cared about hunting down whoever had done this to make them pay. Let them know I didn't care for their creepy-ass love note left in blood while I wailed on them.

"Sire," Timothy interrupted with a delicate cough. Grim turned and stalked off so fast, the air where he'd stood remained warm for a moment before cooling.

They stepped off to the side, lowering their voices, but my sensitive vamp hearing picked up their words anyway.

"Was bringing her here wise? This is likely a trap," Timothy said.

I'd moved on to examining the alley for clues, but felt Death's laser-beam gaze tracking me. I did my best to act as though I didn't notice.

As I neared Chad, I spotted a glimmer of something. Edging closer, their voices faded to the background as I realized it was a necklace. My heart leapt with recognition. I lifted the chain off Chad's mangled neck. His wound sucked at the necklace, but I pulled it free. The chain was cheap, not even genuine silver, but the charm captured my attention. It was a cupcake with pink frosting and a cherry on top.

My stomach somersaulted as familiar feelings and images returned to me in a rush. The smell of fresh baked cakes, bowls of colored icing, laughter and warmth. My eyes stung with unshed tears as the deep ache returned with a ferocious pain that rivaled the thirst for blood. I wanted to get back to that. I needed to get back there, wherever *there* was.

Chad's lids flew up. Crimson filled his eyes, making him appear downright demonic. He hissed, fangs elongating, then lunged at me. I stumbled away with a surprised yelp, yanking on the thin silver chain, breaking it off his neck.

Looks like the reapers missed one soul. I bet Grim was going to dock their pay or suspend them for the slip-up.

Vampire Chad leap-frogged over me and at the two supernatural men. They all fell in a flurry of fists. Without hesitating, I saw my chance and bolted.

I barely had time to recognize the irony that while they'd been worried about this being a setup, the "trap" helped me escape. Pocketing the bloody cupcake necklace, I knew with certainty it was mine from before. Someone had wanted me to find it. A gift from the master? With this new artifact, I was more determined than ever to find out who I was. And I couldn't do that from Grim's penthouse prison, nice as it was.

We were far from the Strip, so there was no crowd to disappear in. Suburban houses whipped by in a blur as I ran like hell, like Death was on my heels, which he most likely was.

I was debating ducking down into the sewers, hiding in someone's backyard, or running straight into the desert when a powerful force hit me. I smashed into a Suburban, leaving a me-sized dent in the side of it.

Ouchie.

A quick internal scan told me I had broken no bones, but yeah, ow. After brushing myself off, I looked for what hit me. A man with one milky eye, stringy black hair, and a face made for a mugshot leered at me. Milky-eye was a hunk of tall, lean, veiny muscle. His cheekbones were a sharp contrast to the hollowness of his cheeks, as if he spent so much time sucking on cigarettes that his face stuck that way. Meanness radiated out of his one good eye.

He smiled, showing me his pretty fangs. "You're coming with me."

"No thanks, I have a prior engagement. I've got tea with

the queen, and then I've got therapy with Bert and Ernie, then…" I said, holding my hands up. "Check back tomorrow. In fact, don't bother. I'll have my people call your people."

In the time I blinked, he'd crossed the distance between us and sunk a fist into my gut. I doubled over, wondering if he'd punched straight through to a kidney. I head-butted him.

"Argh." He wobbled on unsteady legs, pressing his palm into his bum eye. Damn, should have aimed for the good one.

He came at me again, fists swinging like giant hams. I avoided a few, but the ones that connected had me ready to cry uncle. While I didn't need to breathe, the urge to curl up in a ball to protect myself from the onslaught overwhelmed me. I punched, clawed, and gave my all trying to poke his dumb eyeballs out. Still, he laid into me like I was a sandbag at a gym.

I stumbled, unable to continue fending off his blows. Just when he laid off, I heard the *snick* of a switchblade opening. He grinned with malice as I groaned. "On second thought, I'm going to cut you up, little vampire, and see what's inside."

Steadying myself on the car behind me, I said, "Let me spoil it for you." I spit in his face. The blood-tinged gob landed in his milky eye. "Sugar, spice and everything nice."

Before I could move out of the way, his blade cut into my belly. The searing pain turned to unbearable agony when he jerked it up, then twisted. I thought I heard myself cry out. My hands flew to my wound with the fear my viscera would fall out.

Violence flared in his good eye. Then something strange happened. Just like Bruiser, when I'd last saw him, Milky-eye's face emptied of all expression as if someone had lobotomized him. The knife clattered on the asphalt and he backed away. His vacant stare and slack jaw reminded me of a zombie. Whatever was happening to him, it was not in his control.

Then, with a violent jerk, his head twisted off before bouncing once, then twice on the street. The body remained standing, and for a split second, it looked like he'd gotten a new head. Grim stood behind the decapitated form, seething in anger. The rest of Milky-eye hit the ground with a tremendous thump.

"Going somewhere?" Grim asked, his voice an unholy layer of echoes. Power seethed off the shoulders and back of his suit in dark clouds.

His eyes dared me to give him a reason to rip my head off next. There was no running when all my focus went to keeping my guts inside my body.

Milky-eye's body cracked and grayed, pieces of ash flaking off him before he disintegrated into a heap of dust.

Huh. How about that?

I faced Grim again and gave him my best innocent smile. "I was looking for a bathroom?"

10

I demanded the driver make haste, driving us back to the hotel. Vivien needed blood to heal...before I killed her.

I drummed my fingers on my knee, seeking to release my agitation in some small measure. "We could have taken that sekhor for questioning, forced him to lead us to the master, but thanks to you, I had to kill him before he finished you off."

That was the cause for my panic. She'd forced me to slay our only link to the master. It had nothing to do with my fear that the sekhor had gained the upper hand on Vivien.

Nothing at all.

She squirmed in her seat, still pressing into her stomach with both hands. Blood mushroomed out from under her palms, soaking her shirt. "If you are so mad about Milky-eye, why didn't you just keep ol' Chad for questioning?" Vivien asked with a pout. Her face had paled, and she seemed wilted, her strength waning before my eyes. We needed to get her blood, now. I fought back the unexpected wave of panic.

"Because," I said, "a freshly turned vampire is unlikely to have as much information as the sekhor who was sent to retrieve you."

She slouched. "Fair point. Well, Milky-eye did a terrible job escorting me to the master. He went all psycho and wanted to cut me open. But right before you popped his top off, I saw something switch in his head, forcing him to stop."

"Can you stop bleeding everywhere?"

"You're not even listening to me."

"You are not here to think. You are not here to speak. I only need you to draw out the master. And you managed to find a way to screw even that up."

A flush returned to her cheeks and the knot in my chest loosened. If I could still rile her, she would make it the short distance left to Sinopolis.

"Again," she said, "you are the one who ripped the dude's head off. While you definitely qualify as a grim dude, you should have everyone call you cranky pants. Do you even hear how macho and overbearing you sound?"

"Oh for heaven's sake," I said, unable to sit back one second longer. I pulled my jacket off, and slid over to the seat next to her. Nudging her hands away, I pressed my jacket against her wound.

Vivien stared up into my eyes, mouth slightly parted. Caught in her gaze, I wanted to lean down and capture her lips in a kiss, carry her into my bedroom, and keep her in there until danger forgot about her existence. A deep protectiveness had been stirred inside me. I desired to keep her safe and all to myself. When she infuriated me, I could chain her up, gag her, and do creative, pleasurable things to her body until she was worn out.

What was it about her that drew me in so? Was it because she was a sekhor, and it had been centuries since

I'd encountered such a being? Perhaps. But more likely, she made me feel as though I weren't alone. She'd been dropped in a world of supernatural danger and took it all in stride. Her tenacity to do things her way, while foolish, and bull-headed, was refreshing. The saucy retorts this spitfire threw my way sometimes made me want to break out laughing. Everything about her stimulated me for better or worse.

"Your jacket is ruined." Vivien's voice was low and husky.

I was tempted to say my life was ruined when I met her, but I wasn't one for dramatics. Instead, I studied the gold flecks near her irises. "You can buy me a new one with that three hundred dollars you stole."

She frowned as her eyes sparked. "I did not steal. You cost me that cash when you chased Chad off, so you owed me. I simply took what was mine when you *conveniently* forgot to repay me."

"Well, now you owe me," I said, silencing her. "Bleeding all over my car, my jacket, and..." I slid a finger under the cupcake charm that dipped between the swell of her breasts. "What is this?" She hadn't been wearing it earlier.

"It's a clue, Scooby Doo." Despite her sarcasm, her words came out breathy as I continued to finger the necklace with interest. "It was on Chad's body. I think it used to be mine because when I saw it, disjointed memories and impressions came back to me. I think I might have been a baker."

I raised an eyebrow. "Cupcakes, cookies, sweets?" My tongue curled around the words, while my eyes drifted down past the charm to what I suspected was far sweeter than any baked good. She audibly gulped and squirmed as my gaze touched her, traveling down her breasts and then to her thighs.

After seeing her nearly gutted, I wanted to reassure myself of her liveliness. While I would never seduce a woman in an injured or compromised state, it didn't mean I couldn't imagine what it would be like tasting her. Or wonder what sounds she made in the throes of passion while I filled her again and again until she lost her mind. Would she ball her hands in the sheets or rake her nails down my back?

I gently removed my jacket and then pushed away her hands to get a better view of the wound. With an audible rip, I tore off the bottom half of her shirt, careful not to brush up against her laceration, revealing her torso.

"Looks like it's already healing," I said, unable to keep my eyes from drifting to her navel. Indeed the skin was knitting itself together over the exposed muscle more rapidly than I expected. Still, she would need blood to recover.

Heat filled what little space remained separating us as my thoughts continued to fuel my arousal. Dragging my tongue across my teeth, I fought the deep hunger I felt for her. Though she didn't need oxygen, her chest rose and fell as if her breathing was labored. Her verdant orbs glazed over, reminding me of sea glass.

There was something here more than lust. Something far more dangerous and sinister. I couldn't afford to fall into whatever was yawning between us.

Licking my lips, I slid back and a mewl of disappointment escaped her. I clenched my jaw and turned away.

Get a hold of yourself, man. She is far more dangerous than even she knows.

As soon as we returned to the penthouse, I wasted no time retrieving a bag of blood from the refrigerator, which Timothy made sure to stock, and poured the contents into a mug. I did my best to ignore Vivien, as her lips formed a dumbfounded gape, while I heated up the cold liquid in the microwave. She blinked when I handed the cup to her.

"The words you are searching for are *thank you*," I said.

She blinked a second time before peering into the mug. "You made me dinner."

"What? No, I—"

In a sing-song voice, she said, "Grim likes me. He made me dinner." Then with an evil grin, she said in a normal tone, "What's next? Flowers, chocolates?"

"No."

Vivien bit her lip thoughtfully. "Or is your love language gifting me souls of the dead? Maybe a skeleton? I mean, I wouldn't say no to a spiffed-up skull. Or can you get me one of those shrunken heads?"

I rolled my eyes. "You are impossible."

She rocked on her heels, that impish twinkle in her eye. "The words you are searching for are *impossibly cute*."

When Vivien started toward the living room, I pointed in the opposite direction. "You can either drink over the sink, or in the bathroom; you are covered in blood."

"I wanted to change anyway," she said, sticking her tongue out before disappearing into the bathroom, shutting the door behind her.

With a sigh, I rubbed my face before pulling out my phone. The hotel was a well-oiled machine, but some decisions required my approval. I sifted through my inbox of requests from DJs and esteemed chefs asking for the honor of working at Sinopolis. Vivien emerged only fifteen minutes later in a black sweatshirt and boxers. *My* sweatshirt and boxers.

Irritation warred with another intense wave of arousal. She was impossibly sexy in my clothes, with her lose, wet hair. Her clean scent was almost too enticing to resist. My thumbs itched to hook into the boxers to drag them down her hips and...

"Is the fact your entire wardrobe is black because it's a 'death thing,'" she said, making air quotes, "or because it's slimming?"

My regular bouts of lust for her were more than irksome, especially since she had the mannerisms of a willful child. I was about to lay into her when my phone vibrated.

With a glance at the screen, I pointed at Vivien. "I am stepping into the next room to take this call, but if you so much as make a wrong move, I will drop everything to make your life a living hell."

Vivien bounced on the balls of her feet with nervous energy. There was a flush to her face I hadn't noticed before. The blood must have invigorated her. She looked positively hyper now. *Fantastic.*

Reluctant to leave a keyed-up Vivien to her own devices, I still had a call to take. It was a short walk down the hall to my office, and I closed the door behind me and slid behind my executive's desk. As I answered the call, I turned on my computer, lighting up multiple screens.

"Hello." I spoke with monotone disinterest, as though the caller had interrupted me while I was dealing with tedious paperwork.

"Is it true?" a female voice asked.

"Is what true?" I asked, though my stomach dropped.

"Oh gods, it is, isn't it?"

I pulled up the security cameras focused on my penthouse. Vivien was tearing through the kitchen, pulling out metal bowls, spatulas, and flour.

What is she up to?

"I have the situation under control, Bianca," I said.

My reapers were out sweeping the city. While my reapers couldn't track the undead, vampires left a trail of death in their wake. It wouldn't be long before their destruction hit my radar and then I would move in with swift, violent action of my own.

A firm tone entered Bianca's voice. "We must meet. Tonight. And bring the sekhor with you. I have to see her."

It was useless pretending I didn't know who she was talking about. Checking my watch, I saw that it was 12:30 a.m.

I pinched the bridge of my nose. "Fine." We set up a time and place, though I was already dreading it. The last thing I wanted was more people involved in this matter. The plan had been to contain things quickly and quietly, but if Bianca was calling, there was likely more I needed to know.

Stalking back into the kitchen, I found Vivien covered in flour, furiously stirring something that resembled Play-Doh in a metal bowl.

"I was gone for two minutes. How did you make such an absolute mess in that short of time?" I stared at my kitchen in horror. Flour and goop were splattered across my black countertops. White handprints covered my cabinets, making it look as though a handsy ghost had been in here.

Vivien glared at me, still attempting to stir the heavy glop in the bowl. "I'm baking cookies."

My mouth opened and then snapped shut. When I finally found my composure, I asked, "Why are you making cookies?"

Vivien dropped the gigantic dough-like blob onto a baking sheet. "Like I said, I think I was a baker in my former life, elbow deep in muffins and cakes all day. So I figured, hey! Muscle-memory. Maybe if I started baking, whip up something fabulous like I used to, I might jog my brain into remembering more about my previous life."

Then the vampire opened the oven and to place the

mound of dough on a rack. Before she could close the door, I was at her side, my hand on her arm. "You are not putting that in my oven."

Attempting to push me away with her body, she rolled her eyes. "Listen, I know what I'm doing. You are going to thank me when you are chowing down on this super-delicious, cake-sized cookie." Then she gave me a skeptical onceover. "You do eat, right? I mean, I found food in the kitchen, but why would Death eat? That's kind of dumb."

"Yes, I eat. I also drink, which you are inspiring to do more of lately."

Vivien huffed with impatience, as she had the audacity to look short with me. "Well, this place looks barely lived-in. You should appreciate that I'm helping make this place homier with the smell of fresh-baked cookies."

"Do *not* close that oven," I ordered.

"Jeez, G. You've got control problems, did you know that?"

Why was I arguing with her? She was clearly a mental patient in her previous life, which made me the insane one for thinking I could win an argument. Better to just kill her now and make my life easier.

The elevator chimed, and both our heads swiveled to Timothy, who was regarding us with an uncertain look in his eye. "Am I interrupting something?" he asked, clearing his throat.

I realized how close I was to Vivien, gripping her arm. Stepping back from her, I said, "No." My tone was gruff. Timothy's eyebrows rose.

Vivien narrowed her eyes at me as she shut the oven door on the catastrophe she tried to claim was a baked good. She gave me a triumphant, toothy grin.

Perhaps she wouldn't be so smug if I threw her over my knee and laid a hand against her backside.

Taking another moment, Timothy regarded us, perhaps trying to read the tension in the room. "I received notice of your meeting tonight," he said slowly. "Shall I get you both ready?"

Waving my hands at her. "Do something with her," I said, stalking off to my bedroom where I needed to change, now covered in flour myself.

Because if I stayed any longer, *I'd* do something with her, and I wasn't exactly sure what that would be.

11

Despite my protests, Timothy insisted there was no time for baking and pulled my big gourmet cookie out of the oven. He wrapped the mound with plastic and placed it gingerly in the near-empty fridge, assuring me it would stay there until I was ready to bake it. Then Timothy led me to the spare bedroom where I'd found all the women's clothes before.

When I crossed my sticky arms, I realized too late they'd glued themselves together. I pretended not to notice. "So what is this meeting?"

Timothy peeled himself away from his tablet long enough to pin me with a wide-eyed expression of awe. "The Oracle. She wants to meet with you and the master."

Nerves fluttered under my skin at the mention of an Oracle. "Can she help me figure out who I am?" Though I was hesitant to meet any more supernatural beings, I could hear the hope in my question.

Timothy shrugged. "I don't know. The Oracle called the master directly. If you are going with him, you must have been requested."

He set down his tablet to pull out two dresses from the wardrobe. "The meeting will be held at one of Sinopolis's exclusive clubs. Would either of these suit you?" The dress in his right hand was long and flowy, with a silvery sheen of rainbow colors. The one on the left was barely a slip of a dress in shimmery champagne. Both were sugary confections that would brand the wearer as instant arm-candy.

Unsticking my arms with a little effort, I propped my hands on my hips. "Now Timmy. We've only known each other a short amount of time, but do I look like a rainbow kinda gal to you?"

In truth, they were both gorgeous gowns, but the idea of having anyone tell me what I should wear made me want to don a trash bag and tape sponges to my feet for shoes. I bet his majesty would blow his top if I did.

Timothy pursed his lips thoughtfully as he rehung them. He'd seemed to catch on that I would be a tough customer. I almost felt bad for him.

A black sheen grabbed my eye. I pushed past him to rub the black fabric between my fingers. "Now this one. This just screams me."

Timothy paled, unknowingly giving me confirmation that I'd discovered the perfect attire. This getup would shock better than any trash bag.

GRIM COULD HAVE STEPPED off the cover of *GQ* magazine and then walked right onto the glossy pages of a *Playgirl*. The man didn't even have to peel off his clothes to rev up a girl's engine. His majesty had left the top few buttons on his fresh, black shirt open, exposing a tantalizing strip of caramel-colored neck. The charcoal-gray suit had an expensive-looking sheen that made me want to stroke it.

Speaking of strokes, his majesty looked to be having one as he regarded me. His jaw practically hit his chest as he pinned me with a horrified stare.

"You like?" I asked, spinning around.

"Absolutely not," he growled, his voice echoed with layers of many voices. The air crackled with menace and power. If I hadn't been so sure he needed to take me to this Oracle chick, I might have worried he'd kill me on the spot. Instead, I smiled wider.

The supple latex laid against my body like a second skin. The body suit had strips of fabric cut out from armpit to ankle on either side. Hot again, from all the blood I drank, I appreciated the spaghetti straps. I'd foregone panties to avoid unseemly lines. I mean, I was going for tawdry, not trashy. Though I doubted his highness appreciated the distinction.

After finding more than a couple dough chunks in my hair from my attempt at baking, I'd washed and dried it again. Now it fell over to one side, fresh and voluminous. I re-wrapped the strap of leather around my neck again, preferring how it covered my scars.

Timothy had also led me to the vanity in the bedroom. It was equipped with more makeup than I knew what to do with, but I'd given it my best shot. Black, smoky eyeshadow made my green eyes pop. Add a little blush, bronzer and some lip gloss, and I looked less...dead.

Earlier in the lobby, Grim had been all "why would you wear *that* in public?" and I didn't appreciate his judgment. So I took my fashion to the next level. If he wanted me to go anywhere with him, he was going to have to take me looking like a dominatrix.

"What?" I pouted as Grim looked increasingly incensed the longer he gawked at me. "You don't like the shoes?" I glanced down at the black patent peep-toe heels. The footwear was one of the two concessions I made on Timothy's behalf, the other being a gold arm band that clasped around my bicep.

Grim pointed at me but looked at Timothy. "Take her back in there and the next time she comes out, she'd better be in appropriate attire."

"If it was good enough for some sex kitten you've already nailed, why don't you like it now?" I taunted, batting my eyelashes at him.

A flash of confusion shot through his eyes.

Like he didn't know what I was talking about. I bet he hand-picked whatever bold gal wore this getup to come back to his penthouse for a sexy romp. I had no feelings about that whatsoever.

Timothy grimaced. "I'm sorry, sire, but she is as stubborn as you are."

Timothy shot a nervous look in my direction. I'd given him a taste of my feral side. When he tried to press the issue of what was "appropriate" I went off on him, asking where he got off, thinking he could tell me what I could or couldn't wear. I dropped words like "misogynist pig," and he backed up fast and quick. I later heard him talking to himself, while I dried my hair, about not being paid enough for his job.

Grim started toward me. "Then I'll dress her myself," he said, storming my direction. I flashed my fangs at him, ready to duke it out.

Just try me, buddy.

I needed a whip, or a crop, or something to go with the clothes, and to smack Grim in line so he knew who was really in charge here. Yes, I was technically his prisoner, and yes, I was supposed to be bait, but that didn't mean I couldn't take my own shots.

Timothy stepped between us at the last minute. "Unfortunately, sire, there is no time. Your meeting is imminent and if you wish to make it, you both must leave now."

Grim's fists were closed, shaking by his sides. I wanted to push him. Make Mr. Control blow his lid.

Why was tempting Death so...fun? Maybe I was a few fries short of a happy meal?

I recalled cackling like a maniac in the morgue, covered in blood. Yep, I was definitely this side of crazy. I tacked on death wish to the list of things I knew about myself.

Though knowing Death looked like *that*, who wouldn't wish for him?

Instead of tearing me to pieces for flaunting my Mistress Vivien costume, Grim passed by me, walking into the elevator. He smoothed back his thick, dark hair. I watched the tension transfer from his fists to his jawline.

I patted Timothy on the cheek as I flounced by him, joining Death. As the doors closed behind us, I thought I heard Timothy mutter a prayer.

12

I was pleased to find the line for my club, Wolf Town, was staggering, per usual. The club-goers waiting had likely started lining up mid-afternoon, but many were still eagerly peering up at the well-muscled doormen, anxious to get in. That is until Vivien and I arrived.

Despite Vivien's outrageous attire, I made sure Vivien stayed glued to my side, considering she looked like a walking felony. And she was sorely mistaken if she believed she was likely to get another shot at escape.

All eyes turned toward us as we strode past the line. Waves of awe and lust washed over me, while in others, I could sense cloying envy and reluctant respect. No one approached or called out at us, which was how I preferred it. I made sure to exude cold indifference to discourage any from advancing. Yet the reactions were also intensified by the presence of my escort.

With a glance at Vivien, my eyes drank in the sight of bared strips of flesh along the side of her bodysuit. Arousal shot through me in a furious torrent. I ground my teeth so hard I tasted blood. The urge to bend Vivien over the nearest railing and rip off that provocative outfit was driving me to near madness. Which was why the only way I could fight off the lust that pounded through every fiber of my being was by smothering it with anger.

Did I care that eyes from the throng also caressed her curves, the sway of her hips, as they imagined wrapping their hands in her hair while pounding into her without mercy?

My thoughts were interrupted before I could answer my own question.

"Grim, Grim Scarapelli." A man's voice called out my name with a familiarity he had not earned.

I stopped, forcing Vivien to pause as well.

At the front of the line, a man waved to me. The well-known actor's lips spread in an affable grin. My distaste for the man returned with immediate effect. I had to suppress the sneer that threatened to surface.

"Hey," Vivien said, recognition in her tone, "isn't that the actor in that movie that's coming out, *The Red Room?*"

"Bradley Hansen," I confirmed. Then looking at Vivien, I said, "You remember this second-rate actor, but you don't recall your own name?"

She shrugged, "I also remember the lyrics to Britney Spears' "Oops I did it again," that Raphael was the hottest ninja turtle, and to never eat yellow snow."

"It doesn't snow in Vegas."

"I never said it did. I was merely pointing out how smart and worldly I am."

Before I could ask what a ninja turtle was, Bradley redoubled his efforts to wave us over. "Hey Grim, any way you can tell these guys who I am?" He hooked a thumb at my doormen with a derisive snort.

Oh, I would help him, alright.

"Holy shit, that's terrifying," Vivien said under her breath.

"What?"

"Your smile. Like a shark who just spotted his lunch."

"This will only take a moment," I said, leading her over to the actor. His entourage consisted of two men and three women.

Satisfaction settled in the actor's eyes as we approached. The women, poised around Bradley, shifted their attention to me. They each shot me seductive glances full of promise. Many more in line goggled at me as well.

I was accustomed to this. I could practically taste it on the masses in Vegas—a death wish. Part of me surged up to greet their desire and rip their souls from their bodies. People came here for indulgence and pleasure, giving up their cares and letting go a little. But there was a dark side to letting go. Many tourists flirted with the line, if not crossed it, during their stay in Sin City. Perhaps it was one of the reasons I felt so at-home here.

These girls were professional. They knew how to make Bradley look like fun, which was probably how they'd secured a spot at his side. I disliked women being treated like commodities, even if they were amenable to such arrangements.

Giving Vivien's arm a warning squeeze, I released her to approach Bradley.

"Tweedle Dee and Tweedle Dum here don't think I am the right element for this club," Bradley said. "Can you believe it?"

The bouncers, Jerome and Nick, remained stone-faced even in the wake of Bradley's insult. They would act with the utmost courtesy until it was otherwise necessary. After Timothy's initial screenings, I personally interviewed and selected every staff member for Sinopolis. They were generously compensated, treated with respect, and in return they were each accountable for their professionalism and duty. I was rarely disappointed.

Vivien stayed rooted where she was as if waiting for something to happen. I really didn't have the time to stop, but I couldn't help myself.

"Mr. Hansen, when was the last time you stayed with us?" I asked, my smile widening. Only one man shifted, his eyebrows knitting to meet each other with worry. Perhaps he saw what Vivien had.

Bradley dropped his hand once he realized I wasn't going to shake it, but his smile didn't wane. "Yeah, it's been a year since I've been able to get back here."

"Has it been a year already?" My surprise was as fake as his veneers. "Oh yes, I remember. You had several young ladies with you then as well, one of them I recall in particular. What was her name again?" I pretended to think, dropping my hand to hover at about five feet. "Madeleine. Cute little French girl as I recall."

Some of the sparkle left Bradley's eyes. "Oh yeah? I hang out with so many people, I don't recall." He brightened, composure regained. "But I'm sure you're right, big man. So what about getting us in tonight? I'd be happy to lend you another lovely lady for your other arm since you're one short and I'm one too many."

He leaned to the side to leer at Vivien. My blood boiled, and my teeth clenched so hard I was surprised they didn't crack. I desired to rip his head off and punt it into the crowd where they could bat it around like a volleyball. But he deserved even worse than that.

I threw my arm around Bradley, leading him away from his companions. Our backs were now to everyone but

Vivien, who watched the scene with interest. "Yes, I recall. You called her *Mad who wants it bad,* didn't you?" My voice was deceptively light, but all good humor drained from Bradley's face.

My words grew increasingly chilly as I went on. "The cleaning staff discovered her in a near-destroyed suite. She was left behind as if she were a piece of garbage."

To Bradley's acting credit, he seemed positively befuddled. The picture of innocent concern. "Listen, man—"

I didn't let him finish. "She was strung up, covered in maple syrup and vodka. Strangled in what looked to be an overzealous sexual fervor."

The scene stayed with me. To have such a reprehensible thing happen on my grounds was unacceptable. I craved violence and retribution on that poor girl's behalf. And I would get my chance.

"That was two weeks after I was in town," Bradley protested. "The girl was up in drugs and all kinds of shit. Who knows who did that to her. I hear you though, it's tragic."

My hand on Bradley's shoulder shifted, fingers elongating into black talons. Vivien took a step back, her eyes wide. Bradley had yet to notice.

My voice dropped lower. "I know what you did, Bradley. And one day, not too far from now, I suspect, we will meet again. When that time comes, I will hold you accountable for all your wrongdoings and make sure you pay the ultimate price for them. You will leave this club." I enunciated my instructions, leaving no room for confusion. "You will inform these ladies you are no longer interested, and you will take greater pains to live a more ethical life if you know what's good for you."

Bradley visibly bucked against my preposterous

suggestions, but when he opened his mouth to retort, he stopped cold. I allowed my death mask to flicker through. Bradley gasped as if the air had been sucked out of his lungs. A horrifying visage of bone and utter, sucking darkness, I forced Bradley Hansen to face his own end, and the utter oblivion every human feared to their core. Then he turned to see the long, sharp black claws drumming on his shoulder. The sound that emerged from his throat was an animalistic screech of pure terror. Any trace of bravado or strength had fled America's so-called sweetheart.

Bradley ran as fast as he could, stumbling and falling a couple times. His two buddies followed. One of the women had been reapplying her lipstick when she noticed he'd hightailed it. She zipped up her purse and ran after him. The other two ladies stood in line, uncertainty lingering on their faces. I hadn't lowered my voice when I spoke of what happened to Madeleine, and it looked as if these two were no longer sure of who they should follow.

I flicked a now-human finger to the guards to let them in. "Ladies, I suggest you enjoy a drink on me, and seek out better company." Though it was likely my wishful thinking, there seemed to be new wisdom in their eyes, as they trotted into the club.

Vivien had chosen not to flee the scene, though a fresh fear was stamped in her eyes. I'd scared her. If she knew all I was capable of, she would be frightened to death. I almost smiled.

I took Vivien by the arm once again and led her by Jerome and Nick into the bright lights and thumping bass of Wolf Town.

13

Colored lights strobed and music pulsated like a living heart all around us. Grateful Grim had made dinner for me before heading out, but the smell of adrenaline, arousal, and excitement-filled blood permeated my senses, surrounding me, begging me to take a sip. It was an adult Disney World in here with the collective beat of all the people who were dancing, throwing back shots, and having a grand ole time.

Grim released my arm, to guide me with his hand on the small of my back. Though he appeared relaxed, I could tell his muscles were coiled with readiness under his suit. He was prepared for me to bolt. His vigilance was annoying. Mainly because I would totally make a run for it, given half a chance. I had to get back to the castle hotel to search for that guy who recognized me.

As soon as I got my moment, I planned to take it. Or I thought that's what I would do. I missed the perfect opportunity to sprint off when Grim was having his tête-à-tête with Bradley. Yet, despite my urgency to track down my lead, I couldn't tear myself away.

The instant I laid eyes on the actor, my instincts sang *Scum Baaaaaag*. I caught every word they exchanged. It was a wonder Bradley landed any roles when he couldn't lie his way out of a paper bag. What he'd done to that French girl was beyond disgusting and straight-up evil. I half-expected Grim to tear him to pieces right there. Savage one moment, and then the picture of manners and restraint the next, I could see Grim taking off his suit jacket and placing it over the pool of Bradley's blood for the women to walk across so they wouldn't stain their fuck-me pumps.

And the way his hand shifted into that of some demonic creature was bone-chilling. His fury wasn't focused on me for once, but standing so close to barely restrained violence caused fear to hammer down my spine shouting "run, you idiot!"

Grim directed me up a set of stairs that almost escaped my notice. Another bouncer let us pass before barring the entrance to anyone else.

The landing at the top overlooked Wolf Town. Modern, eggplant-colored couches made a U-shape around a couple end tables. There were already drinks on one of the glassy surfaces, what looked like a Manhattan and a glass of red wine. Something told me Timothy had something to do with the drink choice and preparation.

I realized we were in the VIP section connected to an entire balcony that wrapped around the second story of the club. While Grim's box was raised a little higher than the rest, as if anyone should forget that he is king here, the other boxes were taken up by high rollers, celebrities, and exuberant, sparkly dressed girls in their twenties with questionably older men. *Blech.*

You're dressed up like a dominatrix hooker, my internal voice reminded me.

I batted it away with the explanation that this wasn't the same thing. I wasn't vying for attention. I was lighting matches under Grim's shoes to see how high I could make him jump.

Okay, so I wasn't vying for everyone else's attention. Just Grim's.

It was quieter up here, since they directed all the speakers and base down at the dance floor packed with squirming ravers.

"Is it true what he did?" I asked, though I already knew the truth.

Grim's face hardened. "Yes."

"How did you figure out it was him?"

He sighed, a deep, weary sound that made me realize how old he was. "When it happened on the premises of Sinopolis, I handled the sorting of Maddie's soul myself. She told me everything."

"How come that bastard isn't in jail?"

"Unfortunately, hotel surveillance only shows a nondescript man wearing sunglasses, a baseball cap, and a sweatshirt with the hood up coming and going from that hotel room. Bradley's manager produced an alibi that placed the maggot halfway across the country. They claim he left Vegas a full day before she was murdered."

I clenched my fists as anger vibrated through me. "Why didn't you just smoke that guy? Aren't you Death? Can't you touch him and reap his black soul, then let me stomp on it?"

Jaw tensing, he said, "That's not how it works. I don't go around haphazardly killing people."

"Sure, you do." There was a hysterical edge to my voice. Grim turned to give me an inscrutable look, but I didn't care. "You sent that poor crying woman to her death."

"You saw that?" His face darkened. "You have no concept

of what you witnessed. I'm not an avenging angel. I am not
Santa Claus. Can you fathom how much time it would take
to punish every wrongdoer for their sins? I do, because that
is my every day. Looking into the eyes of people who wish to
plead their case to me, I give each one their due consideration. The workload is immense and never ending. I'm not
jumping at the opportunity to actively reap souls. When
their time comes, I will handle them." He turned away,
ending the conversation.

I wasn't sure why I got so riled. Did I really expect him to
murder that actor right there in front of everyone? Still, the
idea of that guy walking around, breathing, made me furious. If I weren't a prisoner, I might have gone after him
myself and wiped him off the face of the earth. Even with
how amazing human blood tasted, I doubted I could
stomach drinking from that monster. There was no part of
him I wanted in my mouth. Not even if I was starving.

Grim scooped up his Manhattan and walked over to the
edge of the balcony, looking out over the crowd with his
other hand in his pocket, as if a king surveying his castle.
The roar from the crowd below doubled and the people in
the other VIP lounges all raised a glass to him. The power
he possessed was frightening, but there was something extra
scary about watching how he looked over his dominion.

Did these people sense that Death himself was watching
over them? Did they secretly worship death? Is that what led
them to this club? So they could lose themselves in vices
and escape the humdrum, even if it led to darkness?

Or maybe I was the one scared of losing myself to darkness. It wasn't the thirst, or Grim's prediction, it was the
being standing mere feet from me. Despite his promise to
kill me, I felt tied to him—a growing sense of trust which
was straight-up cuckoo clock insane. Still, it didn't keep me

from wanting to be near him, taking him at his word, and wanting to reach out to him as he stood there seeming so alone and a little sad.

I picked up the wine. Though I couldn't say for sure, I didn't think I'd been big on fancy wines in my previous life. I pegged myself for a cheap beer kind of gal. But for a girl who now preferred to chug hemoglobin, I found the wine to be exquisite. It coated my tongue with rich spice and mahogany, and I tasted the soil in Spain. Despite the delicious aromatics and flavor profiles, something about the red wine made me deeply uneasy. My gut clenched hard enough to force me to set the glass back down on the table.

The visceral, almost painful reaction to the wine confused me. I enjoyed the flavor, but it also repelled me. Not because I wasn't able to enjoy other beverages, it was the red wine in particular. The paradox hurt my head, so I let it go.

I stood a few steps behind Grim, relishing the club as it pulsated with life. Part of me wanted to slip away to dance until I couldn't think straight. But we weren't here for funsies. I wondered if Grim had ever gone down below and lost himself to the music. I dismissed the absurd image as soon as I imagined it. He was more of a tango kind of guy; likely to favor measured, precise steps to enact out intense, fiery passion.

Grim stepped back, so he was next to me. "That woman you saw me kill..." He trailed off.

I wasn't sure I wanted to hear what he was about to say.

"She had already died. What you witnessed was my judgment of her soul. That's what I do." He gave me a sidelong glance. "Most of the time, my reapers can sort the souls and send them to their rightful destinations, but some call for me to make the assessment myself."

I was still swallowing the part about how I'd seen the woman's soul. I believed her to be there in flesh and blood. "What did she do?" I asked, my voice low.

"She poisoned her stepdaughter, slowly, over time. She put it in the six-year-old's morning cereal. The woman wanted the man for herself and was jealous of the child."

I blew out a breath. "That is some Snow White shit right there." How could people be so despicable? Did I know people like that? Was I one of them?

"Indeed. Yet the rest of her life, the woman dedicated her life to helping others, fundraising and making sure villages in Africa had clean drinking water. She impacted the lives of hundreds of people, which is why they brought her to me, to make the final judgement."

He took a sip of his Manhattan, his eyes sliding to me. "You think I chose wrong. That I was too hard on her?" Grim paused, then added, "The father never fully recovered. When his little girl passed, a part of him died with her. He's still limping along through life believing he lost the woman who had saved him from drowning in grief."

There was genuine curiosity in his question, underlined by weariness. Did he worry he'd made the wrong choice?

I shrugged, but then considered it. "As a newly minted bloodsucker, as you so lovingly put it, I have wrestled with this question many times over the last couple of weeks. What is one person? I told myself if I nabbed one person and drank my fill, I'd never do it again. Killing one person wouldn't make that much of a difference in the big picture. What is one little puny human versus how much it would mean to me?"

Despite my cooling temperature, I heated under his scrutiny. "But even when I was starving, alone in the sewers, sucking on rats, it didn't sit right. I'm not an animal, and I am the one who decides what I will or will not do."

"Do you really believe you can? Fight your nature?"

I shrugged. "I now know vampires exist, that Death has a face." I said the devastatingly gorgeous part silently to myself, *and that he has a conscience, so I know anything is possible.*

Grim didn't reply, just kept those liquid amber eyes fixed on me. I lifted the Manhattan out of his hands and raised it to him. "Here's to believing I control my fate." I chugged the remaining bit. Feeling emboldened, I asked, "Now can we talk about why you have so many women's clothes in your penthouse?"

He raised an eyebrow, taking the empty glass from me and setting it down.

"Are you super into women's fashion or is it just a revolving door of chicks at your place?" I tried to smile, though part of me seriously wanted to know.

"The latter."

I tried to act like I wasn't just kicked in the gut, but it hurt. For all that is holy, I was jealous of the endless parade of women who got to sleep with Death. If I didn't think I was nuttier than a squirrel before, this proved it.

"As you pointed out, the place is barely lived-in. I don't require much, if any, sleep. My people keep a close eye on the guests, including anyone who has over-imbibed, fallen in with the wrong company, or needs refuge. Timothy can set them up in the penthouse and bring them clean, comfy clothes when they are ready to leave."

"That's a lot of ladies' clothes," I said, still skeptical.

The moment he trapped me in the elevator with his body played on repeat in my mind. His tailored jacket dipped toward his waist, emphasizing his broad shoulders. I could feel the hard ridges of his abs even through our clothes. I'd been surrounded by the scent of freshly turned soil, from a greenhouse. Or a grave, I corrected myself.

And his cologne was a mix of lilies and musk. Lilies, the funereal flower. Who knew Death would smell so tantalizing? Was this a vampire fetish thing?

Grim shrugged. "I know their clothes are sent out for cleaning and they have the option to take their partywear with them or have them delivered."

"Hmm," I said, turning my attention to the crowd below. The jealousy drained out of my big green balloon, but I was still wearing some rando's clothes. He had no reason to lie, but for some reason I wanted him to prove it.

"Did you think I was bedding women by the masses?" The mirth in his voice made me look back at him. There was a knowing smile on his face.

Before I could answer and wipe that smug smile off him, his gaze trained on something past my shoulder.

"She's here."

14

The Oracle strode up the stairs to my private lounge. I stepped forward to greet her. We kissed both cheeks, while Vivien looked on in awe. Bianca looked every bit the goddess she was. Voluminous blonde hair falling over her model-thin shoulders. Her bronze skin glowed even more vibrant than her emerald dress that was a mix of glitz and high fashion.

"Grim." She said my name with fondness I reciprocated.

Despite Bianca's glamorous visage, worry tightened the skin around her eyes. Manicured hands fretted with the matching satin clutch she'd brought.

I made the introduction, opening a hand to the vampire. "This is Vivien."

Bianca's breath caught and her blue eyes rounded as she took in the ostentatious vampire next to me. Her sight far exceeded mine, as Bianca was clairvoyant, and I wondered if Vivien's sekhor aura was as drugging to her as it was to me. Even Timothy, the most even-keeled of our kind, shot Vivien the occasional hungry look.

I stilled, watching and waiting to see what would

happen. The likelihood that Bianca would kill Vivien herself was high. Not because Bianca was apt for such carnage, but because of the danger sekhors posed. It occurred to me, Bianca might think the risk of keeping Vivien alive for any amount of time, even as bait, was too great.

The two stood staring at each other, and I found myself tensed, on high alert.

At last, Bianca held out her hand. Vivien hesitated, then took it. Bianca's face broke into a friendly grin. "I'm Bianca. Nice to meet you."

I relaxed my shoulders. *What the devil was I worried about?*

Then I realized what had me worried. I'd been poised and ready to fly in swinging if Bianca attacked. I had instinctually prepared myself to protect Vivien.

Because I need her to draw out the master, nothing more, I insisted to myself. When I ended Vivien, it would be because I had cleaned up this whole sekhor mess, and she would be the last tie I'd need to sever.

But the prospect of killing her caused knots to tighten in my chest. The idea of anyone else hurting her caused those same knots to twist with acute violence. Every fiber of my being forbade it. Never had I felt the need to spare anyone before. Why now? Why her?

Because she could be your other half, your life mate, your sekhor. Even thinking such thoughts was forbidden. I was grateful when the two women interrupted the madness churning inside me.

"So you're the Oracle?" Vivien asked, letting go of Bianca after a brief shake. If I didn't know any better, I would have said Bianca made Vivien self-conscious. But the vampire was shameless. Then again, I detected jealousy when she asked about the women's clothes in my penthouse.

Bianca laughed airily and blushed. "Yes, well, we all have our talents." She reached out and gave my arm an affectionate squeeze.

We sat, and a server appeared moments later with fresh drinks and champagne for Bianca. Vivien sent the red wine back and asked for a beer instead. That caused the corner of my mouth to twitch. We did not start conversation until he'd returned with her order.

"Oh my," Bianca breathed, still riveted by Vivien.

Vivien squirmed in her seat. "What?" she asked.

"I haven't seen a sekhor in...quite some time," Bianca explained. To her credit, she kept her eyes on Vivien's face and not the blatantly erotic getup she was wearing.

It took a great deal of willpower to keep my own gaze trained on her face. A mere glance, and I struggled to forget the milky flesh of her exposed hips, or the way the tight bodysuit pushed her breasts up.

"But you saw her, in your vision?" I prompted after clearing my throat and my thoughts.

Bianca's voice dropped to a serious timbre. "Yes. But first, I have to ask." The glass shook in her hand as she brought it to her lips for a sip. "Does...the Original still slumber?"

"Of course she does. The first thing I did was check." My tone was gruffer than I intended, but to assume I wouldn't check to see if the Original was still secured was to presume I did not know my duties.

Vivien opened her mouth to ask, but I held up a hand to stop her in her tracks. She shut her mouth in what I could only assume was deference to Bianca because she'd never done so for me.

"I don't know how this happened." I gestured to Vivien,

who frowned. "All I know is I'm the one left cleaning up the mess. And if I don't contain the situation soon, we could have a real problem. My reapers are out looking for the trail of the vampires as we speak. The vampires leave death in their wake; I don't understand why my reapers are taking so long to find the trail."

Bianca shook her head. "You won't find the vampires like that. They aren't leaving bodies behind. When they feed, they are turning." She closed her eyes as if going inward to see something or remembering a past vision. "They are being careful not to leave a trail. Everyone bitten is being turned. They knew you would hunt them, and the master is being careful."

Except when he left a pile of bodies to lure us out then planted a new sekhor in their midst. I'd torn apart the sekhors I'd encountered so far, but if they were amassing in numbers, even I had to admit I could not fight an army on my own.

As my frustration mounted, I ran a hand through my hair. If what Bianca was saying was true, the master vampire was not a random generation. Someone had groomed and informed him. It was the only thing that explained such calculated moves. Someone else was behind all of this. "Then how will I find them?" I asked, hoping this was the true reason Bianca wanted to meet.

"You don't need to find them. They will find you," Bianca said to Vivien.

The beer bottle stopped halfway to Vivien's lips. She resembled a deer caught in headlights. "What?"

"The master wants you," Bianca said to Vivien.

"He sent others to come fetch her," I confirmed.

Vivien set the bottle down with a clack. "But why me? What did I do?" Then she frowned at me. "Fetch me? Really? I'm not a ball for a dog to retrieve."

I didn't take the bait, though she wasn't helping my frustration. "Why her? Why is she important?"

Bianca tilted her head at Vivien. "This one is different. She was made different. She was never supposed to be, and the master wants her back."

Vivien and I exchanged a look. "Different how?" I asked.

Bianca played with the fabric of her dress. "That is not clear to me, but that will soon become apparent. All I can see is that the master will come for her. She is the only one who can draw him out."

"So it's a dude?" Vivien asked, though her voice was higher pitched than normal.

Bianca's eyes glazed over, looking past Vivien. "Yes. The master is a man. He is impatient. He wants you back. And he will do anything to get you...even if that means making you come to him."

"Pffft." Vivien made a rude noise that startled Bianca. "I don't do anything I don't want to do." She turned to me and raised her eyebrows in challenge.

"I can testify to that," I said with a grimace. Vivien rolled her eyes next to me.

I had half a mind to lay her over my knee and take my hand to her backside to see if I could smack out some of that attitude. The image in my mind turned sexual as I considered the sound my hand would make against her perfect, spandex-covered rear.

Bianca's eyes became vacant, and her eyes turned white as her second sight made itself known. She grabbed my arm, and I leaned in close, ready to hear any wisdom she could impart. Her whisper was so faint, I had to strain to listen. "The arm. The Original's arm. Something is there...or it is missing. The Original is missing something."

Bianca slumped forward onto my shoulder. I caught her,

helping her to sit back in her seat. Vivien jumped up and crossed over to a table where there was a pitcher of ice water and several glasses. She poured some and hurriedly brought it back. I murmured a thank you as she handed it over. I helped Bianca sip some as she roused from her faint. She blinked and clutched my arm as if needing to borrow strength. I followed her gaze to Vivien.

"What did she say?" Vivien asked, her expression tense as if dreading the answer.

"Oh dear." Bianca straightened, seeming more cognizant now. "I hoped we would have more time, but I must take my leave. It's better I return to Paris, straight away." With slow movements, I helped her to her feet and waited until she was steady enough to let go.

Bianca nodded to Vivien with genuine warmth in her eyes. "I'm so glad I got to meet you. I'm still a bit unsteady." Then turning to me, "Grim, would you be so kind as to escort me?" There was a gleam in her eye that told me she needed more than a stable arm.

I shot Vivien a pointed look to let her know I would be right back and not to try anything. She snorted while folding her arms, then turned to observe the dancers below.

Bianca was silent until we reached the bottom of the stairs. "Grim, you must not let her out of your sight." The gravity in her voice told me to not take her direction lightly.

"I don't intend to," I said. I waited for more information, but she kissed my cheeks again and then took her leave.

Bianca must have seen something to make her warn me so. Ascending the stairs, I wondered if she foresaw Vivien escaping?

Vivien was still at the balcony, leaning over the edge, elbows resting on the railing. Her derriere stuck out in a casual repose. *There was something different about her than the others.* Was that why I felt so drawn to her?

The surrounding air changed. Time slowed around me as I walked over to the balcony, compelled by a familiar force I'd not felt it in centuries.

My expression must have been strange because Vivien's brows wrinkled when she turned toward me. "What's wrong?"

The pounding, rhythmic club beat gave way to a sultry tune with a crooning woman. The song made one think of sex and cigarettes in the Riviera.

Below, the crowd unconsciously parted to reveal a woman at the bar. No one appeared to notice the blue spot-light now trained on her as the rest of the lights dimmed. Either arm rested along the bar behind her, affording me the perfect vantage to observe her form. She was utter and divine sexual perfection. Hair cascaded down her shoulders in obsidian waves. A golden dress hugged her curvy form. The train of shimmering fabric flowed out at her feet, a gleaming waterfall. My mouth went dry.

"Whoa, who's that?" Vivien breathed, in open awe of the arresting woman.

The woman kept her dark eyes averted, allowing me to admire her profile and long elegant neck. An exquisite turquoise necklace adorned her décolletage, the perfect pop of color to make her bronzed skin sparkle under the magic spotlight.

I swallowed hard, trying to keep my composure. Now I knew why Bianca had run off in such a hurry. I was about to start down the stairs to the waiting woman when I remembered Bianca's last words.

"Do not leave my side, and absolutely do not speak," I

said to Vivien, pouring every commanding ounce I had into the words.

She didn't spout off threats or buck against my direction. Neither did she confirm that she would obey me. Vivien simply followed behind me as I made my way down the stairs. I slipped my hands in my pockets, passing through the parted crowd. The club goers were raving and conversing in slow motion, unaware of our motions.

The woman still didn't look up. Why would she, though? She was used to being addressed first.

"What are you doing here, Qwynn?" My voice was low, but easily heard over the sultry music.

Qwynn lifted her head as if surprised by my presence.

"Oh Grim, is this *your* club?"

"It is," I confirmed, though I knew full well she was aware of her surroundings.

A smirk pulled at her sensuous lips, a wicked twinkle in her eye. "I should have known. The decor alone screams your taste. It's positively enchanting."

"What do you want, Qwynn?" I asked, grateful my hands were already in my pockets. Anything to keep them off her.

She slid a finger across the counter. "Oh nothing, just a drink. Perhaps a chat with someone interesting." She looked up at me from under her lashes in a move that had been practiced and perfected over a millennium. It had galvanized men to throw themselves at her feet, abandon their loved ones, and start wars, simply to be gazed at in such a way.

"If that's all," I said with forced indifference, turning to go. I thanked my lucky stars that Vivien obeyed, standing nearby but keeping quiet.

"Well, since you're here..." Qwynn said, stopping me. She picked up a cosmopolitan that appeared next to her and raised it to me. "Join me in a friendly toast before you go."

"I'm not drinking tonight," I said, removing one hand from my pocket and straightening.

"That's not what I saw." Her dark eyes touched on the spot where I had been, watching the crowd below with a Manhattan in hand. "Come on, just one drink. What could it hurt?"

Everything. It could hurt everything.

I gave a curt nod. A glass of cognac appeared in my free hand.

Gliding toward me with all the predatory swagger of a panther, she raised her glass. "To history," she said, with a triumphant smile. The smell of expensive perfume, forbidden fruit, and sex wrapped around me.

Our glasses touched with a resonant clink that drowned out the crooning singer. At the last second, Qwynn's eyes flicked to Vivien as we drank.

"I miss you." Her finger skimmed the rim of her glass before dipping into the pink liquid. The pad of her finger disappeared in her mouth as she sucked the alcohol off it.

"Bored with your latest plaything already?" I asked.

She pouted. "They mean nothing to me, Grim. You know that, don't you?"

I didn't bother to respond.

"Is she yours?" Qwynn asked in a silky voice; her inquiring eyes landed on Vivien. I caught the slight twinge of hunger there. She was also drawn to Vivien's bright light. In another second, that spark of interest had all but disappeared, and Qwynn remained disaffected by Vivien's effect.

My expression remained stony. "Is who my what?"

"Is the dominatrix to your left, who is drilling holes into my forehead, your plaything?" Qwynn slowed down her words to make sure I heard each one before popping a cherry into her mouth, making a show of wrapping her tongue around it first. I remembered the things that tongue could do. I couldn't forget if I tried.

With a quick glance, I confirmed she wasn't wrong. Vivien looked ready to jump on Qwynn and pound her into hamburger meat.

"Purely business, I assure you."

"Perhaps a pet, then?" Qwynn asked, her eyes now glowing with power.

"Careful, I bite," Vivien said from behind me. Then she let out a yip-yip, and growled like a dog.

The urge to laugh took me by surprise, but I stifled it.

Qwynn didn't take her eyes off me, but ire flashed in them before she could hide it. Vivien had cut through her shield of cool, aloof power. Vivien's powers of antagonism were impressive. I already knew that, though.

Qwynn shrugged, then said, "Good to see you, Grim."

I only granted her a slight raise of the head.

Time sped up as music pounded around us again. The dancing mob resumed their enthusiastic writhing, and Qwynn was gone. The partygoers stepped in to fill the gap she'd left behind. I removed my other hand from my pocket and took a deep breath. I drained the remaining contents of my drink.

"So who the hell was that?" Vivien demanded.

"It doesn't matter," I said, making my way to a tall, round table at the edge of the dance floor. I set the empty glass down. Vivien followed.

"She was powerful, like you, like Bianca."

"Yes," I confirmed, not wanting to talk about this any longer, but Vivien, of course, persisted.

"But they can't reap souls?"

"No, they are...they have different powers." I turned to face Vivien. "Qwynn is not someone to trifle with."

"Why? Because she might pull out my hair and scratch my eyes? Or because she's your ex?" She folded her arms, daring me to say otherwise.

I opened my mouth, but no sound came out. How did she do that? Take me by complete and utter surprise?

As if reading my thoughts, she waved a hand. "Please, it's obvious she wants you back. I'm not an idiot." She pushed her hair back behind her ear in a vulnerable gesture that was unusual for her. "What happened between you two? And what kind of gal dates Death?"

"The kind who shouldn't be messed with," I reiterated, shooting a warning look at Vivien. "She wasn't here for me. She was here for you."

Vivien drew closer. Her presence erased the remnants of Qwynn that lingered around me. "What? How can you tell?"

"I picked up a few key things about my ex-wife, so I know she was here to check on you, not me."

"Wife," she repeated in a lower tone, as if absorbing that fact.

A scream interrupted us, somehow piercing through the cacophony of the club. The music stopped and the crowd parted again, this time in a panic. A man dangled in the arms of the large, muscular vampire. He was gushing blood all over the dance floor, his throat torn out.

15

Bruiser was back, and it looked as though he'd found a snack. After all, I'd kept him from chowing down on Miranda, so the poor dear must be hungry.

All hell broke out, as shouting people ran every which way in a mass of confusion.

My stomach somersaulted, and I wasn't sure if it was from the abject look of terror on the victim's face or if it was the tantalizing smell of hot, human blood calling to me. The victim dropped to the ground like a sack of potatoes and Bruiser strode over to the convulsing man. The club lights accentuated his broken, blunt nose.

Part of me hoped his brain would overload again, and his violence would drain away like it had the last time and he'd turn right around to go back to where he came from.

He bared his teeth at me with promise.

Or not...

Grim stepped in front of me and his power whipped out in a mantle. Most everyone had cleared out, leaving us supernaturals to duke it out. When Grim spoke, his voice was layered and sonorous, like when he yelled at me about my Mistress Kitty outfit. "You come into my club, harm one of my guests, and think you will walk out alive?"

Bruiser grabbed the nearest object, a speaker the size of a compact car. He launched the sound equipment, and I watched it sail through the air before colliding into Grim. Both Grim and the speaker disappeared as they smashed into the far wall as fleeing club goers dove out of the way.

My heart clenched.

Before I could try to help him, a welcoming party of three blonde, twenty-something girls with blood-red eyes stepped in, and hissed at me like a pack of aggravated mongooses. They could have been the Swedish Olympic gymnast team from their fair features, compact muscle, and tight-fitting spandex uniforms. No. They were wearing too much glitter, and their outfits...

Two of them broke into impressive flips and twists befitting a gymnastics competition. Aw blood clots, I knew where I recognized them. Someone had turned performers from Cirque de Soleil into vampires. I'd seen the twisting trio on billboards.

At least the master hadn't turned Blue Man Group and sent them after me. Those dudes creeped me the hell out.

"Call me crazy, but I would love to start a braid train with you gals," I said, in honest awe of the girls' flaxen locks.

They charged.

"Guess that's a no, then?"

I dodged the first one with a last-minute sidestep, letting her momentum send her tumbling behind me. When the second girl came at me, I grabbed her arm. With a twist, I flipped her over. She landed so hard on her back, the floor cracked under the impact.

A feral grin curled my lips. The vampire strength had not gotten old yet.

The third blonde flipped over my head, then scored a punch to my midsection. If I had still needed to breathe, it would have knocked the wind out of me. My stomach smarted from the blow, but I was still standing. Haha, suck it, gymnast barbie!

When I took a step back, my ankle rolled, and I went down like a clown on a banana peel. Damn peep-toe heels. I knew I should have gone with combat boots. My ass took the brunt of the fall, pain radiating up my tailbone and spine, but my ego was far more bruised.

The third blonde wasted no time, scrabbling on top of me, holding down my arms. A second blonde grabbed my legs. I squirmed and jerked, kicking and punching as best I could, but their grips were like iron.

"Pineapples, pineapples," I cried out. Didn't they know the universal safe word? "No means no. And pineapples means hell no," I elaborated for their sake.

Still, they refused to loosen their grips despite my helpful lesson in consent. The last blonde approached, pulling out chains from the back of her tight pants. *Whoa. Where had she been hiding that thing?*

"If that's been up your crack, I don't want it touching any part of me, you hear?" I said, dead serious. She ignored me and wrapped the cold metal around my wrists.

Ew.

The three vampires flew off my body as if blown away by an explosive wind. I tilted my head to find Grim was back on his feet. Darkness hovered around him like he'd opened up a black hole. Gold arced and sparked from his eyes. His hands morphed again, elongating into black nightmarish talons. The skin of his face roiled and shifted as if he were about to transform into something else. His smile turned my blood cold.

I wasn't sure if I wanted to invite whatever transformation he seemed on the verge of, but I was grateful the big scary monster was on my side...for now.

With ease, the blondes flipped back onto their feet before rushing Grim.

Grim's clawed fist connected with the first vampire, sending her reeling across the room. Then he clobbered the second, sending her smashing into the bar with a crash of glass. He grabbed the head of the third blonde, and with a sharp, violent twist, he tore her head clean off.

Whoa. So that's one way to kill a vampire. Is that how he intends to finish me off?

When I got to my feet, another hand closed around my arm.

"You're coming with me," Bruiser growled.

"For the last time, I'm not going to prom with you. You'll have to ask some other lucky girl. I suggest checking out the coma patients at Sunrise Hospital."

"The master wants you."

The possibility of going along with him and getting the answers I needed flitted through my mind. It took all of half a second to dismiss that idea. I would get answers, but it would be on my terms. The master would have to get his "thrills" somewhere else.

I threw a punch, aiming for his nose, but he caught it. "You think you can handle this, bitch?" Bruiser asked, his sour breath fanning across my face. Then he looked me up and down, as if undressing me with his eyes while dragging his tongue across his fangs. "Though maybe we can stop and have a little fun along the way, seeing as you are begging for a good humping in that slutty getup." He directed my hand to his junk, and I grimaced as he slid my knuckles against a rising bulge. And they said chivalry was dead.

"Hey, ya big creep, this outfit is not a sexual invitation. I dress for my own damn self." I left out the part about wearing the skintight suit to drive Grim crazy. "You like it so much, buy your own catsuit and prance around."

Pitted against Bruiser once again, I wondered how likely I was to tear his head off like Grim had done to gymnast barbie. Examining the thick neck on the meathead, I did not like my odds. So I threw my knee into his groin. He doubled over with a groan of pain, releasing me.

Grim was still tangoing with the twins who'd gotten smarter about staying out of his reach, so I'd have to finish big boy off on my own. Stilettos had proven to be a detriment in a smackdown. I needed to ditch the footwear. I kicked one off, then the other.

Not realizing my own strength, the shoes didn't just somersault into the air, they careened like missiles. The first one ended up embedded in the far wall, and the second one landed heel first, right in Bruiser's eye socket.

Whoopsie doodle.

With an enraged scream, Bruiser grabbed the shoe and ripped it out of his eye socket with a wet sucking sound. Blood gushed down from his now mangled eye socket. Murderous rage flamed in his good eye as he stalked toward me. While I wasn't a girl to back down from a fight, murderous rage came off Bruiser in white-hot waves. I'd bet my left boob Bruiser juiced, explaining the throbbing veins on his bald head. Not my right boob. That one was my favorite and I'd never put her on the line.

I backed up, wondering did vampires get 'roid rage? I couldn't decide if it was the perfect time to ask or not.

Then, like the last time I encountered Bruiser, his face drained of all expression despite the near-black blood still oozing from his eye hole. It was as if both times he crossed a violent threshold that was too much for his tiny brain to compute, which tripped a switch that turned him off before he exploded. Bruiser turned and hightailed it out of the club.

"Oh no, you don't," I said, sprinting after the surprisingly fast vampire. I'd seen this bastard twice now, and while I didn't fancy him dragging me to the master, I intended to tie Bruiser down and demand some answers of my own.

Keeping up with the lunkhead wasn't the problem, but the streets were teeming with humans, making for a crappy obstacle course. Content to smash his way through the crowd, Bruiser barreled through like a wrecking ball. I wasn't as willing to throw people into oncoming traffic and was therefore losing ground.

At least I didn't tire or lose breath as I chased him. I could keep this up all night. Would I be able to stay on his ass until dawn? We'd already passed by four hotels when I heard it.

Come to me.

It was a thread of a thought, barely perceptible, yet it stuck out like a nun in a whorehouse, because the words came through in a man's voice.

Bruiser had gotten some distance on me and cut left.

I missed you.

The voice was louder, clearer.

Now, now, I told myself. This was a bad time to go insane. *We are very busy, Vivien. No time for mental breakdowns.* I turned the corner down a less crowded street. Bruiser was nowhere in sight, but I kept running.

Something pulled at me, urging me on.

I slowed my sprint to a jog.

No, you must come to me.

"Yeah, no, I think I'll pass," I said out loud, although there was no one but me.

The schizophrenic voice in my head did not get the memo I was not interested.

You'll come when called. I made you.

The magnetic pull doubled, almost yanking me off my feet. I stopped altogether, digging my heels in. I focused on the scrape of asphalt against my bare feet. Bruiser gave good chase, but I suspected he was leading me somewhere specific.

"I'm not your damn dog, and my mama made me, wherever she may be," I said through clenched teeth. My muscles tensed, fighting the invisible force that urged me to continue. I stepped back and gripped a railing to a staircase that led to an underground bar and grill.

No one told me where to go. No one would make me do anything I didn't want to do.

No? Then perhaps you'd rather feed?

A couple of laughing girls passed by. I could tell they'd been dancing and drinking vodka, and a thin sheen of sweat still covered their skin. A heady mixture of perfume, excitement, and adrenaline wafted into my nostrils.

The thirst hit me full force, and I doubled over with a gasp. It was as bad as when I'd jolted awake in the morgue. Every part of me screamed to close the short distance and rip out their jugulars, spill their fresh blood into my mouth. Need demanded I fill the empty, cold expanse inside me.

Checking my torso for the rabid dog that was trying to chew his way out of my body, every atom of my being insisted if I didn't feed now, I would die. My body would eat itself from the inside out. I didn't know if that was true, but reality was fast slipping away.

The satisfied smugness of the master resonated through my mind, infuriating me. It was almost as if I could feel his hands puppeteering me from wherever he was. He squeezed and pressed, stoking the thirst inside me until I thought I would lose all control.

I stilled, afraid a single movement would trigger me to bound across the space between me and the girls who were fast putting distance between us. *That's it, run away, girls. Get far away from here.*

Just when I thought I was safe, people spilled out onto the street, most wearing the same pink shirt with a pop singer's face on the front. A concert had just let out. So much blood, excitement and exhilaration hit the air, I groaned as it washed over me. I stopped breathing, to cut off all my senses.

The metal railing bent with a screech of protest under my crushing grip. My fingers wrapped around so my nails dug into the edge of my own palms. Blood welled from the cuts, trickling down my wrist. This was a losing fight. The master had me in his power and it wasn't a matter of *if* he would break me, but when. Hopelessness welled in me, only weakening my defenses faster.

Grim appeared, his face a furious mask. "Did you think you could get away?"

I grabbed his lapels. "Get me out of here," I said, my voice ragged and desperate.

Hesitance replaced his fury, as if he were trying to figure out if I was trying to trick him. A pounding vein drew my attention, and my head swiveled, homing in on the exposed neck of a man walking with his girlfriend. My body shook with need. I was so cold. Frozen to my core and the warmth of that couple could save me.

Unlike the walking blood bags, tempting me with their presence, I had no desire to sink my fangs into Grim. Whatever lay beneath his skin did not entice. For that, I was grateful. Who would have guessed I'd find safety in Death's arms?

"Right," Grim said with some understanding. He grabbed my arm and dragged me back farther down the street, away from the crowd. I let go of his lapels and grabbed either of my arms with bruising force.

This isn't you, I tried to tell myself. That was a hard argument when I didn't know who I was and was ready to flip and go full feral demon.

It is you, said the master's voice. *It's what I made you for. We can share it all.*

You can take a frosted fuck off a cliff, I shouted back in my head. Despite my clever, creative, and crude comeback, the thirst was blocking my every rational sense until the primal drumming in my ears was all I heard, urging me to hunt and feed.

Grim ended a call. I wasn't sure who he called or what he said.

"I can't believe I'm going to win this bet." His voice suggested he was bored.

His words somewhat penetrated the bloodlust. "What?"

"Timothy and I made a bet. He bet that you were a vampire of your word and wouldn't lash out and hurt anyone because he claimed you were too stubborn to give into the thirst. While I said at the first sign of weakness, you would crumble and jump on a human like a rabid, wild animal."

I hated him. I despised his condescension and superiority as he looked down his handsome nose at me. And most of all, I hated the safety I found in his company. He was the only one who couldn't tempt me into murderous violence. Well, his blood didn't, but the way Grim treated me pushed me to the edge. Still, I decided if I would jump over that cliff or not.

"You're not Death," I growled. "You're the devil. Sent here to torture me."

A bemused smile lifted one side of his sensual lips. "Funny, I could say the same about you."

I was about to launch into all the ways I planned to torture him—one involved a car battery and a watermelon —when a sleek black limo pulled up to the curb. It now blocked the way between me and all the people. Exhaust from the engine cut through the scent of tantalizing blood as Grim walked over and opened the door.

Earlier I would have cut off my arm rather than go back to be his little vampire bait, but now there wasn't anywhere safer than under his watch. I stomped my way to the limo and pretended not to be grateful to climb into the rear of the long vehicle. A closed window separated us from the human driver.

Grim's phone rang. He answered, bringing up video of Timothy's face. "Did you receive the car alright?"

I could have sworn he meant to ask "in time" but that might have been me projecting.

"Yes, thank you, Timothy," Grim said, sparing a quick glance at me.

"Please tell Ms. Vivien I already have a mug of blood warming up for her, and I instructed the driver to bring you up through the back entrance via the garage."

"Thank you, Timothy." Grim's words were gruff, then he ended the call.

The grip the master had on me was slipping, and I could

feel his frustration through our psychic connection. Each passing minute we drove in the opposite direction of wherever the master was, the more I gained control over my body, though the thirst remained. I was so cold, so hungry, I wondered if ice crystals had formed in the marrow of my bones.

Don't fight what you are, the master's words snaked through my mind one last time.

I didn't bother answering, instead opting to lean my forehead against the glass window and shut my eyes. At least now, I knew I wouldn't end up murdering anyone.

"What did you bet?" I asked.

"Pardon?"

"What did you and Timothy bet for?" I finally turned to look at him.

"If Timothy wins, I have to take a week-long vacation. If I win, he has to dress up as a French maid and serve me dinner."

"Hmm. Well, sorry to disappoint, but you chose the wrong horse in that race."

"It appears so." Despite his admission, I didn't detect genuine disappointment, which didn't suck either. He didn't want me to feed on someone to win a bet. Classy guy.

"But there is plenty of time for you to prove me wrong," he added with cold knowing.

I laid my head back on the seat, trying to calm the torrential sucking feeling inside me. "Why don't I want to drink your blood? Do you not have any?" I asked to distract myself more than anything.

When he didn't answer, I lifted my head. Grim had gone so still, he could have been one of Madame Tussaud's wax figurines. His dark eyes were fathomless. I could have fallen into them and still not have known what he was thinking.

Fingers interlaced on one knee; his pose rivaled Rodin's *The Thinker.*

What wasn't he telling me? There was something important—let's be real, more than one thing—he was keeping from me. When I asked about his blood, I brushed up dangerously close to something he didn't want me to find out.

A wave of thirst pounded through my body. I wasn't in the master's control anymore, but I still needed to feed. He'd set me off, and distance wouldn't restore my equilibrium. Only a pint or two of life-giving blood would do that.

"Let me guess." My voice came out as a rasp. "You run on caffeine and souls of the dead?"

Grim's brows drew together in concern for a moment before disappearing. He regarded his cuticles with indifference. "Did you ever consider that my blood is too rich for you?"

"Come on, maybe you should donate to a good cause? For mere droplets a day, you too could help a starving vampire in need." My Sally Struthers impression was lacking, but I gave it my best.

He leaned in. "This doesn't sound tax deductible."

"Blue bloods," I joked, though my throat felt choked off by razor blades. Swallowing hard, I closed my eyes. "Will I die if I don't feed?"

"Yes." He said it as if he were a doctor, giving a diagnosis, not wanting to mislead the patient about their certain death.

"That's what I like about you, G. You don't pussyfoot around." I said it with levity, but I meant it. For some reason, I knew I couldn't take it if Death was a liar. But no, he didn't hide behind riddles or half-truths. With him, it was all or nothing.

Sharp prickles stung behind my eyes. I would not cry in

front of Death. I refused. "Would you reap my soul if I died, right here?"

"No."

When I met his gaze again, I saw past his usual cold, hard superiority; pity was stamped in his eyes. I hated it. Was it because I wasn't good enough for him to bother with, or because I didn't have a soul anymore? I didn't like the idea of being soulless, but all the vampire lore was clear on vampires being devoid of one. I'd argued with myself still. If I had a conscience, didn't that mean I still had a soul? So, if Grim wouldn't reap my soul it was either because I didn't have one, or because it was too broken to collect.

"That's fine," I said in a disaffected tone. "I saw your Yelp. A lot of one-star reviews, G. Would not recommend. Reaping only half done before Death stepped out for a sandwich. And one guy said you reaped him while he was still on the toilet? For shame." I was blabbering. I didn't care. Every atom squeezed in vice-like pain, demanding I feed. It was pure agony.

Grim pulled out his phone and began typing.

"Am I boring you?" I wanted to punch him. Wipe away that dumb impassive expression on his face. If I expired right here on the floor of his limo, I knew he would simply pick up his feet and continue to text whatever sex bunny was dying to jump in his bed and add another dress to his already impressive collection.

He had said the closet full of women's clothes had been Timothy's doing, but at least a couple had to be his conquests. I saw the way people gawked at him. When I'd first set eyes on him, I remembered how his being smashed into mine like a wrecking ball. The need to fall in front of him and beg him to take me right there warred with the need to run like hell from his out-of-this-world intensity.

I couldn't grasp why I wanted Grim to care about me. Maybe because no one did? Because I was alone and insignificant.

The limo stopped and instead of getting out, Grim held up a hand, signaling for me to wait. I'd graduated to shivering. The cold inside of me was biting.

He rolled down the window, and a hand stuck through it with a thermos. Grim opened it and handed it over to me. "Drink," he commanded.

I didn't consider whether it was a good idea. I simply grabbed the thermos and drank. Hot, human blood slid down my throat and I let out a sound half between a mewl and a moan.

I hated that the master had control over me. I hated that I needed blood. And I hated that I didn't know what Grim was thinking as he passively watched me.

16

I was familiar with pain. I witnessed it with such regularity, I was dullened to its nature. But watching Vivien jerk in pain and wrestle with her thirst, I found myself sharing her distress.

I folded my hands to keep myself from doing something I never did. Comfort her.

Yet, I was tempted to move to her side, hold her to me until the shaking subsided. Perhaps say something reassuring, though I'd not know what to say.

The sekhor shivered and groaned as she drank from the thermos of blood.

Vivien did not realize how dangerous her question was about feeding from me. If she knew the truth about my blood and what it would do to her, who knew what she would do?

Though at every turn, she surprised me. Vivien was doing everything she could to fight her nature, to protect others.

When she finished, she melted back into the seat with evident relief. A bit of blood ran from the corners of her now ruby lips. Then her eyes flew open, and she sat up as if remembering where she was and had to protect herself from any sudden threat. There was a silent accusation in her gaze, perhaps because I'd taken her back to Sinopolis, yet again.

"Relax." I instructed. "We are going to sit here for a couple minutes until I am sure you won't leap upon any of my hotel guests or staff."

She sagged against the seat again. "Didn't your mother teach you it's not polite to stare?"

Ah, so that's what that look was for. I'd witnessed her at her most vulnerable. She wiped away the remaining blood from her lips with the back of her hand.

"My mother had little to do with my upbringing," I said. "So she can hardly be to blame."

"Is your mom the reason you have such shit taste in women?"

I frowned.

"Whoops? Did I step into that one?"

"From a purely psychological point of view, I'm sure one could draw a conclusion that ties the two together." I hated to admit it, but Vivien echoed a musing Timothy had once uttered. It stayed with me, much to my dismay. One hardly wished to draw similarities between one's lover and one's mother. Thankfully, she didn't press.

"I'm surprised you aren't with Qwynn right now," she said. The way she said my ex's name made it seem as though she'd sucked on a lemon.

Tension coiled into the muscles along my back. "What makes you say that?"

"I mean, aside from the fact that she looks like...well, that. The woman looks like she was ready to blow your mind ten ways from Sunday. Have you grown bored with spectacularly gorgeous, willing women?" Her glib tone gave way to a quiet observation. "You looked like you couldn't wait to get your hands on her."

Her perceptiveness surprised me.

"You are right. It took everything in me not to reach my hands out and..." Resignation and, dare I say, disappointment flashed across her face before I finished. "Wring her neck."

Vivien's brows shot up, though she remained melted against the seat.

"She is a destructive succubus who is a mere shell of a being. For a long time, I believed there to be so much more to her. I believed her to possess...soul." Unable to meet Vivien's probing, curious eyes, I plucked a piece of invisible lint off my pants. "I was wrong. The woman is a vacuous wench."

Vivien sat up straighter, seeming more herself. "Whoa, she did a number on you. How did she pull one over on you? Aren't you the guy who judges souls?"

My lips pulled in a tight, wry smile. "Qwynn has perfected the craft of homing in on a subject and making them feel they are the center of the entire universe before she drags them down into her hole of pleasure and sin." I cleared my throat as Vivien canted her head with interest. Before she could ask about Qwynn's sexual prowess, I went on. "But sometimes I wonder if I didn't see in her what I wanted. I chose to ignore the parts of her that didn't match up to my ideal. And she let me indulge in my fantasy of who I wanted her to be."

Vivien went quiet, lost in thought. I was on the verge tapping my foot to layer some kind of sound into the limo to distract from my sudden discomfort. Why was I telling her all this? How did she continually find new and different ways to get under my skin?

"So, what did she do that was so horrible?" Vivien asked, at last.

"It doesn't matter anymore." I said, straightening my wristwatch.

Vivien leaned forward, propping her elbows on her knees and offering a generous view of her cleavage as it strained against her near-cutting latex neckline. "Clearly it does, if you want to strangle her, and can't bring yourself to say out loud what she did to you."

"It was a long time ago." My tone was firm and authoritative.

"If it was so long ago, then it doesn't matter if you tell me."

"It is unsavory to bring up the past."

"It is unsavory to drink blood, but I've been able to savor a lot these days—"

"She ate corpses," I said loudly, talking over her to stop this inane bickering.

Vivien blinked. "She what?"

Lowering my voice to a normal volume, I said, "You have to understand, I fancied myself irrevocably in love with Qwynn. She was everything I'm...not. She is spontaneous, passionate, and she knows the dark arts of pleasure. She took me by the hand and led me into indulgences I would never permit myself. Soon, I was addicted to all manner of vices. Above them all, my love for Qwynn had turned to obsession." My tone lowered. "Which made it all the easier for her to deceive and manipulate me."

I leaned forward and ran the backs of my fingers along her bare arm as I spoke. "I not only judge souls, I protect the bodies of the deceased. The body is a temple for the soul and must be treated with respect even in death."

Vivien shivered as I continued to drag my knuckles up, up, up to her shoulder. My index finger lightly traced down the column of her neck. Our gazes locked. Though her eyes were red with bloodlust, they were still expressive and bewitching. Her pupils expanded as if trying to drink me in.

My arousal made itself known, straining against my pants. The silky texture of her skin begged to be touched, tasted, licked, and teased for days on end. My gaze fell to her side. Those strips of exposed flesh were finally too much temptation for me to resist. I lowered my hand and brushed my thumb against the skin bared by her breast. She didn't stop me. Her fingers were wrapped tight around the thermos while she refrained from moving a muscle.

"The body deserves worship in all fashions. From nourishing food, to plenty of water. It protects the soul from the elements, a complicated machine, yet it is also a delicate system." My voice lowered, becoming husky. "It needs and craves touch. It can process countless feelings, textures, pressures."

My eyes were riveted to the journey of my thumb as it slid ever so slowly under the edge of tight fabric, toward the mound of her breast. As I did so, Vivien's hips bucked an inch.

The movement brought me to my senses. What was I doing?

You are seconds from ravishing her in this car.

I ignored Vivien's mewl of loss as I sat back, folding my hands in my lap, covering up the hardness there. I returned to my explanation. "Cannibalism is one of the highest atrocities."

"Which explains why you aren't huge fans of sekhors."

Vivien rolled her shoulders back as if trying to also come back to her senses. But I could see the stiff tips of her breasts through her suit and her thighs clenched hard against one another.

I nodded my head in assent, focusing back on her eyes. The red had receded, and they were sparkling green once again. "To sekhors, people are nothing but a meal. But even people have committed atrocities against the dead. In the past, people would grind human remains into tinctures to make what they thought was medicine. It was abhorrent, and I did everything I could to stop it. The practice finally died out with new medicinal knowledge of the eighteen century." With a deep inhale, I steadied myself for the next part. "I could have done more to stop people from such atrocious practices, but I, myself, was lost. All my time was spent worshipping Qwynn and playing in her den of sin. Then, in the Victorian era, I'd gotten wind that people were purchasing mummies and holding private parties to unwrap them while everyone watched on. And then they would dine upon the flesh of the pharaohs."

Vivien's nose wrinkled. A line formed between her brows as her eyes seemed to drink in every horrifying detail I shared.

My earlier arousal was chased away by sour memories. "I attempted to discover the culprits and put a stop to it, but they evaded me time and time again. Then one day, Qwynn insisted I pause my investigations for one evening to attend one of her dinner parties. Another one of her extravagant affairs."

Only the richest, most decadent guests were allowed to attend. Qwynn hired servers to walk around naked, save for priceless jewels and gold paint that covered them from head to toe. The house had become widely known as the den of inequity, and I remembered how Qwynn threw her head back with a throaty laugh when she heard. Then she commissioned a plaque for the house, officially naming it so.

That night, the wine was exquisite and opium filled the air until every room was dense with the haze. I walked through that party with liquid, sluggish movements and a fuzzy head. I observed our guests as if walking through a dream. There was nothing but the finest suits and dresses, save for the ones who'd chosen to disrobe and fuck like dogs on the antique furniture. There had even been a caged pair of lions in a corner. One of the big cats had melted to the bottom of the crate, blinking sleepily, while the other paced the short enclosure, periodically roaring in frustration. The bystanders squealed and laughed riotously whenever the lion snapped at them through the bars.

Everything about that night had crystallized in my memory.

"And then came supper on covered, silver platters. The lids were removed, revealing thin strips of dried, grayed flesh." Even now the revulsion and the anger rose in me as strongly as it had then. "And Qwynn, who sat at my side, smiled at me with gleaming eyes as everyone delighted and descended with vigor upon the flesh. They thought it would grant them long life and continued status, a lie Qwynn had concocted to make the horrendous practice fashionable."

Vivien let out a low whistle. "Damn. What did you do?"

"I ended the party," I said.

By the way Vivien's brows rose, I knew she'd guessed the manner in which I had done so.

Violence had overcome me. I'd upturned the long dining table, smashing it on top of some of the diners. I lost complete control while servants and guests screamed and fled the house in terror. All except for Qwynn, who had remained seated, her expression one of mild inconvenience whilst chaos erupted around her. I wanted to kill her.

"Of all the stunts she had pulled over the years, that was unforgivable, and she knew it."

Vivien put the thermos aside, leaning in. "Why would she do that?"

"She claimed I needed to prove that I loved her more than anything. If I'd eaten the flesh of the dead, it would prove that I loved her more than my duty. When I didn't succumb to her request, Qwynn accused me of neglecting her, casting her aside for the true love of my existence."

Vivien held up a hand, her forehead wrinkled. "Let me get this straight, she was mad you loved your job more than her? The job of reaping souls?"

"My duty is sacred and vitally important to the well-being of this planet, and I believed there may have been some truth to the matter." Even now the accusation cut through me. Though I knew enough now to attribute Qwynn's string of paramours to a bottomless pit of vanity, I still couldn't shake her recrimination.

"What a selfish biatch. Did she expect you to quit your job to feed her grapes, stroke her hair and tell her how pretty she is all day, every day? Even if you had done what she wanted, she would have eventually gotten bored. No, she's just an entitled, unhappy tramp intent on using others like playthings."

Even as she said the words, a sense of validation settled over the memories that still had power enough to wound me.

"You sound like you have experience with this."

Vivien shrugged. "I wouldn't know if I did. But I can tell you that your ex is a selfish narcissist. Maybe she's even behind this whole vampire thing. Have you thought of that? She just happened to be at the club right before Bruiser and his butt-face squad ruined the party."

I shook my head. "She may have the tongue of a snake but she wouldn't get anything out of bringing vampires back to power." I could see Vivien was about to protest so I added, "Not to mention, the audacity and cunning it would take to pull off this kind of plot is beyond her ability. She may be a liar and a manipulator, but a mastermind, she is not. There is a bigger game here; I am just not sure what it is yet."

"Hmm," she said, unconvinced. "And I think you don't want to believe she's involved because you want to avoid her at all costs. I'm simply saying we should keep an eye on her."

As I studied Vivien, I realized now I'd believed her to share many qualities with Qwynn. I'd thought both were wrecking balls, intent to smash my world in order to pursue their own needs. And while Vivien had every opportunity to cause harm to humans, to trap souls by creating more sekhors, she had no such designs. Now that I had seen them side by side, they were as different as night and day.

But what they shared was far more dangerous. The ability to draw out a part of me that craved pleasure, play, and refuge from my never-ending duty.

There was a knock at the tinted window, saving me from my thoughts. I rolled it down and Timothy handed over the pair of heeled boots along with some folded clothes.

I set them on the seat next to me, and said to Vivien, "I will step out so you can change."

"Wait, what?" she asked, sliding down the bench closer to me.

"We have one last stop to make before the dawn comes. Your attire is not appropriate for the next venue." I pressed the button, sending the window back up with an electric buzz.

"We don't have time for me to pop inside to change clothes in a bathroom or something?"

"The fatigue you must be feeling by now should indicate to you that daylight is fast approaching. There is no time. I cannot let you leave my side, and there is one last place we must go." I opened the door and stepped out.

Vivien moved to where I had been seated. She stared up at me with big green eyes. For the bloodsucking bane of my existence, it surprised me how she could both look so earnest and wanton in that tight suit that pressed her breasts up for my consideration.

I swallowed, clearing thoughts of running my fingers along her inviting flesh, or leaning down to capture her lips in a hot, demanding kiss.

"We are going to visit the Original." At her blank looked, I clarified. "We are going to see the very first vampire."

17

Timothy did not join us, mentioning he was still dealing with the cleanup at Wolf Town. I wondered about all Timothy had to do. There was not only the cleanup, but there were terrified partygoers to deal with, and then the cops. He seemed more inconvenienced than overwhelmed by his task, though. He somehow still made the time to prepare that thermos of blood and deliver an outfit to me.

I appreciated the clothes Timothy provided, the same heeled boots I'd worn before along with a red halter top, leather jacket, and jeans. He'd even thrown in a belt with a big buckle of sparkly ruby-red lips.

Despite being the coldest hour of the night, I still didn't need my jacket after my snack. We'd driven off the strip for fifteen minutes on a road that wound into a deserted stretch of land. The building was tucked away out of view.

I raised an eyebrow at Grim as I closed the car door behind me. "This is where the first vampire is?"

Instead of responding, Grim held out a hand to invite me to go first.

"Lion's Den Care Facility? Did the Original come here to get treated for his blood addiction?" I let out a nervous laugh. "Maybe I should check in next?" After coming so close to losing control earlier, I was only half-joking.

Grim tried to hide his smile, but I saw it anyway. The glimpses of his smile did funny, fluttery things to my belly. I chalked it up to him being sinfully sexy. I wondered if he looked delectable in order to help people deal with the transition of death. Like here, you have to die, but at least this devastatingly handsome man will send you to the afterlife.

I'd also seen his scary side, though, and it was enough to make me change my shorts. The idea of another escape attempt entered my mind before it drove right on by in a Bugatti. Grim was right. There was only a little over an hour until dawn left, and I could feel lethargy settle into my body. I was already anticipating passing out and sleeping like the dead for two straight days. Pun intended. Trying to fight off, run away, or outsmart Grim was not in the cards for me right now. I had to bide my time.

Grim pressed a buzzer and within minutes, a male orderly showed up and cracked open the glass door. He was in his early thirties with a round face, twinkling brown eyes, and a smile any girl in her right mind would drag home to Mommy and Daddy. The shiny nametag read Kabir. His eyes lingered on me a moment, his smile intensifying before he saw Grim. Uncertainty flickered across his face as if he were considering the need to be nervous. He had no idea.

"Can I help you?"

"We are here to visit my aunt," Grim explained.

Kabir looked back and forth between us. "You are a little early for visiting hours. You'll have to come back at ten a.m."

"You can make an exception." The imperious chill of Grim's words demanded Kabir obey.

Death had a short fuse for patience, go figure.

The orderly's mouth thinned. "I'm afraid you'll have to come back at visiting hours tomorrow."

Grim took a menacing step forward. "Listen here you—"

I pressed a hand against Grim's chest. "Give us a minute," I said to Kabir, sending him a flirtatious wink. That twinkle returned to his eye as I led Grim off a few paces from the door and out of earshot. I did my best not to notice the firm, hard muscle of his chest. Tingles spread across my palm, shooting up my arm and warming my body.

Turning to Grim, I whispered, "Do you always try to get your way like this?"

"I will make him let us in," Grim said, his jaw hardening. Gold flashed in his irises. I wondered if he'd look half as dangerous without the scruff of dark hair around his sensual, magnetic mouth. The heat traveled from my hand to my arm, then pooled in my belly.

I snatched my hand back like I'd touched fire and said, "The bulldozer method is not always best. Sometimes a lighter touch is needed."

His lips thinned. "Says the sekhor who dressed like a sex toy and flung her stiletto into the eye of her opponent."

Instead of answering his ridiculous and entirely accurate accusations, I held up a hand, silently telling him to wait. I walked back to the door where Kabir was on the other side, playing on his phone. When he saw me approach, he cracked it open again, a little more than last time. He shot a wary look over my shoulder in Grim's direction.

"I'm sorry, I still can't let you in," he said, with a genuine apology in his tone.

I raised both hands. "Of course, you're just doing your job. A couple of weirdos show up in the middle of the night on your shift and hassle you, I wouldn't let us in either. But you see that guy over there?" I asked, pointing at Grim. "I don't want to put you in any danger, but that guy is with the mafia. Someone threatened his aunt, and he was so worried about her safety, we rushed right over to make sure she's okay. He won't rest until he's set eyes on her."

I couldn't tell if Kabir was buying my bull and crap story, but as he eyed Grim, I knew he could at least swallow the prospect Grim was in the mob. In that black suit with an imperious yet menacing demeanor, he absolutely looked like he'd cut off some fingers with his expensive cigar trimmer.

Kabir's eyes fell back on me. "I wish I could, but I can't. Visiting hours are from ten to three tomorrow."

As a last-ditch effort, I put my hand on his wrist to keep him from stepping away from the door. "Kabir, it's of utmost importance. We need to see his aunt. Please help us out." I gave his wrist an extra squeeze. Suddenly, I was locked in on his eyes, his essence, his very being. It was as if I'd sucked him in on a tractor beam I wasn't aware I had until now. His tension seemed to melt away and his jaw relaxed.

"Sure," he said, before opening the door and inviting me in. His eyes turned vacant, and his response was monotone and strange.

What the hell was that?

Still, I wasn't about to argue with getting my way. I shot a nod over my shoulder to Grim and stepped inside. Even as Kabir led the way to the front desk where the sign-in sheet was, I felt a tether connecting us.

I wonder...

"We don't need to sign in," I said, shooting him my sweetest smile.

Kabir nodded. "I'll look up her room number. What's the name?"

Holy blood bags, it worked. I was using vampiric mind control over Kabir. If I had known about this ability sooner, I could have made my life a lot easier the last two weeks. I could have waltzed into a hospital or a butcher shop and *suggested* they give me some blood instead of feeding on dirty vermin.

"No need," Grim said, now at my side. "I know where my aunt is."

I followed him through the swinging doors and down the halls wallpapered in sweet bluebells that smelled of talcum powder.

"What did you say to make him so enamored and pliable?" Grim asked as he strode beside me. There was a stiffness to his tone. If I didn't know any better, I might have thought him jealous.

Death, jealous of you getting attention? He plans on using you as bait and then killing you. You are nothing to him. Get that through your crazy brain.

"Honey and flies, and all that. You would know. What happened to that magnetic charm I've seen you blast on the unsuspecting masses? Are you cranky? Do you need a snack too?"

Grim made a sound somewhere between a snort and a scoff.

I wasn't about to tell him I just used mind control on good ole Kabir back there. I wasn't even sure how I felt about it yet. Maybe I had made it up? Still, the orderly didn't come running after us. But if he did chase us down, I'd get my chance to try out the line "these aren't the droids you are looking for."

Grim stopped in front of room #7000 and opened the door. The rhythmic beep of a heart monitor was the only sound in the rest room. A raven-haired woman lay asleep in the bed. She might have had tanned skin at one time, but it was pale now. There was a regal elegance to her nose and cheekbones. Her body was slim and cheeks sunken, but I could easily imagine her muscled and lithe. She was one of those women who could have been twenty or forty years old.

Grim noticed I was hovering near the door. "The Original won't be waking up. She's in a coma. She has been for quite some time."

My shoulders dropped, and I relaxed. I was getting weaker with every minute we approached dawn. I wasn't looking to tango with some big bad power. I needed a timeout.

"So this is the first vampire." I laughed nervously. "Do I call her Mom?"

Grim walked over to the other side of her bed, looking down at the woman with what I could only guess was a tinge of sadness, maybe remorse?

"How long has she been here?" I asked.

Grim looked up as if startled from his own thoughts. "In this care facility? Maybe ten years, but we have to move her from time to time to make sure the staff doesn't get suspicious."

"How old is she, really?"

"Five thousand years old."

I struggled to swallow that.

"Bianca said something happened to her arm," Grim murmured, gently lifting the Original's wrist.

"If she is a vampire, doesn't she need blood in her coma state? And aren't you worried about her getting fried?" I asked, gesturing to the semi-open blinds that would let sunlight in when the sun rose. She also had a heartbeat, which baffled me, but I knew if I bombarded him with too many questions, Grim would snap shut like a clam.

"No, the Original is," he paused, seeming to struggle with how to respond, "different." Again, there was that nostalgic look in his eye. He knew her. Probably from five thousand years ago. What a trip.

"Another ex?" I asked. My voice came out softer than I meant it to.

Looking up at that, he said, "What? No, but I guess you could say we are related."

I nodded, though I understood even less. Death had a family? I mean, he had an ex-wife, an assistant, and a friend who was an Oracle, so why not?

"Why is she in a coma?"

Grim's dark gaze cut across the room. "She is too dangerous to walk this world."

"Then why don't you..." I wasn't sure why I paused, but I got the sense this was a personal matter.

"Kill her?" he finished for me. "She is the Original Sekhor, and she can't be killed. But it's best she remain in slumber." He ran his fingers along her arms, slowly, surely. Watching the pads of his fingers glide along her forearm made me shiver. They were strong, sure hands, with elegant fingers. I could see them performing complicated surgeries or sliding along naked flesh with expert use of pressure.

"Are you cold?" he asked without looking up.

"Yes," I said automatically. But temperature had nothing to do with that zing that shot up my spine while watching him. I'd been imagining how his delicate ministrations would feel on my arm and elsewhere.

"There," he said, pointing to the inside of her elbow. "Do you see it?"

Coming to stand on the opposite side of the bed, I

directed my attention to the spot next to his finger. "Looks like a slight bruise from a needle. So what?" I gestured to her other arm; it was hooked up to a bag of saline and god only knew what else to keep her kicking. Or laying, as it were.

He shook his head. "No, this is what Bianca saw. Someone came and took the Original's blood."

"How many people know where the Original is?"

"Only Timothy, myself, and a few trusted others." When he raised his head, there was a storm cloud of fury in his eyes. "Someone came here and took her blood, then made a master vampire with it."

"That's how you make a master vampire?"

His tone snapped like a rubber band. "You will not speak of this to anyone."

I stuck a hand on my hip. "Who am I gonna tell? Vampire Groupies R Us? In case you haven't noticed, I'm not a fan of my new brethren."

He was not amused by my quip and muttered something about eventually killing me anyway.

To distract him from his eventual homicidal plans for me, I walked around the room. Suddenly, I swayed on my feet as a dizzy spell hit me. About to smash face-first into the floor, I reached for the wall, hoping to catch myself.

Next thing I knew, Grim was at my side, holding me up. He'd circled me in arms of steel, though there was a gentleness to the way he handled me. "We need to go," Grim said, his words clipped. "Dawn is coming."

I nodded, fighting the urge to sink into him. When I tilted my head up to meet his gaze, I found concern written on his face. And underneath that, a growing hunger. Entranced by his whiskey-colored eyes, I watched a heat begin to build in them, as I became even more aware of our proximity. I'd laid my hands along his arms, and his hard-muscled shoulders radiated heat. My stomach somersaulted and my mouth watered. Pure power and dangerous energy radiated off him, causing liquid heat to pool down between my thighs. We'd already established I was crazy and had a death wish.

The desire to kiss him was so overwhelming, it beat off all other thoughts with a bat so it could take up residence as my sole focus. I wondered if he tasted as good as he smelled. Grim said he'd once fallen into a pit of vice and pleasure, and that was exactly where I wanted to be, peeling off that suit and feeding a different hunger he'd stoked in me.

His hand moved to slowly thread up into my hair, while the other pressed against my lower back, pressing me against him. My mouth dropped in an "o" when I felt the length of his arousal straining against my thigh. My mind couldn't quite wrap around the size of his hardness, while also comprehending that Grim's thoughts mirrored mine.

If anyone struck a match anywhere in the vicinity, the whole place would blow.

Pushing away from him, the angel on my shoulder gave me a standing ovation while the devil threw her pitchfork at the angel in hopes of nailing her pious halo or an eyeball.

Grim was right. We needed to go, before I did something I'd regret, like tear my clothes off and ask him to take me next to a coma patient who happened to be my vampire ancestor and might also be potentially related to Grim.

That did it. Jets officially cooled.

18

Once we entered the penthouse, I was surprised to find a sleek black dog sitting at attention. It looked exactly like the one I'd seen in the morgue, and in the underground chamber, except this one's eyes glowed gold.

Grim rubbed his forehead. "Yes, yes, work does not wait."

The dog caught sight of me and growled, a low rumbling sound, then streaked toward me. A yelp caught in my throat. In a split second, I realized I wasn't willing to hurt a dog, even in self-defense. My bits could grow back, but I wasn't so sure about poochie.

I shielded my face, preparing to be mauled. Two paws landed on my chest. The dog was light enough that he didn't knock me to the ground; instead he looked into my eyes with expectation.

"Um, good dog?" I said, lowering my arms and smoothing a hand over his head. The dog closed his glowing eyes, as if reveling in my touch.

"What is the meaning of this?" Grim asked in an affronted tone.

"I met your weird dog at the hospital right after I woke up a vampire." The dog dropped back down to all fours. I got down on my knees to hold him against my body and pet his side. He was a nice supernatural pooch. "You really should get control of your pets. If someone else saw him at the hospital they'd have a conniption fit."

"Not you," Grim snapped at me before looking at my new furry friend. "Explain yourself, Assilem."

The dog turned his head away from me to regard Grim. Since when was Fido not a good enough name for a dog?

"I know she can see you; she is undead," Grim said. "What I want to know is why you believe this behavior is appropriate while you are on the job. What do you have to say for yourself?"

"Hey crazy man," I said, waving a hand while continuing to pat the belly of the dog with my other. "Are you addressing the dog? Because he can't talk."

Grim's eyes flashed and my senses warned me of danger. Maybe it was the long night, or the fact I was petting his weird dog, but he seemed at the end of his rope. If I pushed any harder, he might snap and kill me now.

"That is not a dog," he said, as if explaining to an insufferable, dumb child. "Assilem is one of my reapers, and while he should act with dignity and mind his duty, he seems to think it appropriate to beg you for belly scratches." He wrinkled his nose and said the last words as if he'd sipped vinegar. Grim paused again. "Yes, I know you are always on the job." It took me a moment to realize he was talking to the dog again.

Assilem had rolled onto his back while I rubbed and patted his stomach with vigor. As tired as I was, it was satisfying to pet the reaper's soft fur. It was the best thing to happen to me, short of a hot, fresh meal. Turned out, fur therapy was just as effective on supernaturals.

Timothy chose that moment to join us in the penthouse. Despite the madness of the night, he looked as pristinely put together as ever. It didn't appear as though he'd had to deal with a mound of bodies, a mob of terrified guests, and the authorities. Forget blood. Whatever he was drinking, I wanted some of that.

Timothy stopped in his tracks when he saw us, Grim bearing over me, snarling, while I sat on the floor snuggling Assilem's adorable face off.

"What is happening here?" Timothy asked, his tone suggesting he knew to approach with caution. The way his face turned red suggested he was halfway between busting out laughing or making a hasty exit out of the tension-filled room.

Grim ignored his question, his attention still directed at the reaper. "I don't care what Nire told you, this is completely unacceptable."

"Who is Nire?" I asked, struggling to follow.

Grim's eyes narrowed as they met mine. "Another one of my reapers you have apparently met and wooed with your degrading treatment."

"Degrading treatment? You mean the dog I petted in your dungeon?" When Grim's eyes glowed for a split second, instantly incensed, I amended, "The *reaper* I met in your dungeon?"

"Yes, he has conveyed your propensity for affection and now my reapers are all abuzz with this need for pets." He curled a lip. Timothy took one look at Grim's expression and disappeared farther into the penthouse.

I grabbed Assilem's face and gave it a thorough petting

before dropping a kiss on the top of his sleek black head. "Do they not normally get affection? Who could keep their hands off such a sweet doggie?" I said to Assilem in a baby voice.

Timothy returned with a glass of scotch. The aromatics on the air told me it was aged far beyond my years. "No human can see the reapers," Timothy hurried to explain, handing the glass to Grim, who took it with an approving grunt.

Grim swirled the scotch. "They aren't stray dogs who need to debase themselves like common canines. They fetch the souls of the dead, then sort and deliver them to their appropriate destination." He sipped his drink and closed his eyes as if the liquid were ambrosia, helping to ease his troubles.

Try as I might, I couldn't help but watch him. I'd never seen Grim do anything but volley back and forth from glower to death stare. But for the first time, as he drank, I saw pleasure smooth his features. Seeing him like this felt too intimate, like I was intruding on a private moment.

Girl, you are being held captive in his penthouse. You have enough reign here you could fish out his underwear and pull them on your head and dance around if you wanted. He's just wetting his whistle.

I hugged Assilem closer to me. "I thought sorting souls was your job? Why are you forcing these sweet puppers to do your job? That's animal abuse." Then I remembered, "Oh that's right, you only take the extra special cases, like the Supreme Court. Even so, it's a crime you don't give your sweet little reapers some love and affection." Assilem pushed himself further into my arms.

Timothy opened his mouth and looked back and forth

between Grim and I as if expecting World War III to break out.

Instead of flying across the distance between us and ripping my head off, Grim let out a long-suffering sigh and pinched the bridge of his nose.

Yay for the effects of brown liquor on the beast.

Then he snapped his fingers and pointed to his side. Assilem turned to give my cheek a friendly lick before trotting over and dutifully sitting at Grim's side. Grim drained the rest of the glass and placed it on the countertop with a clink.

"Refrain from treating my reapers as common canines or I will put a leash on you," Grim warned.

Not bothering to get off the floor, I popped my knees up and rested my arms across them. "Kinky, G. Where was that when I was wearing that getup in the club earlier? Would have totally completed the look."

A choking sound had us turning to Timothy. He hid his face behind his tablet, pretending to be absorbed, though he was fighting back laughter.

Gold arced from Grim's eyes this time. He pointed a finger at me. "You will stay here. You will not leave until I return. So help me, if you do, I will rip your head off like those other nasty sekhors."

With impressive agility, I kicked my legs out and landed on my feet. I saluted. "Aye aye, captain."

Grim didn't give me a second look as he stalked off to the elevator, but Assilem shot me a longing gaze even as he followed his master.

Once they'd gone, Timothy dropped the tablet, his face redder than before. Only after the elevator closed and descended did Timothy speak. "I wonder why you feel the need to aggravate him so?"

I shrugged before walking over to one of the sleek gray couches and flopped on it. I shut my eyes and said, "I may be here acting as bait, but he doesn't control me. If Grim thinks he can keep me from petting an adorable dog, reaper or not, he needs a reality check. And maybe he should see about getting the rod removed from his sculpted ass."

You should volunteer. You would love to get your hands on his bare ass.

The memory of his exploring touch in the limo sent heat shooting through me again. I'd wanted him to go further. Hell, I wanted him to go all the way. The rough, firm pad of his thumb so close to my nipple had almost made me lose my damn mind.

Timothy made a humming sound. He was unconvinced. "Yes, well, I'm not sure what reality you live in, but I can see you have a total disregard for order. Grim prefers things to be in order. Without his tireless efforts, the world would fall into chaos. I guarantee you he does not forget that for a single second," then he muttered, "though sometimes I wish he would."

I propped myself up on one arm. "Is he even capable of relaxing? I would think he'd combust into black confetti the second he tried."

Some of the mirth drained from Timothy's eyes. "I understand you had a run-in with Qwynn?"

"Oh yeah," I said, dropping back onto the comfy couch. "What a piece of work she is."

Timothy nodded. "The master is a dedicated being to his core. Even though she hurt him, he loved her beyond reason. Part of me believes it's because she brought out his desire to play. But what they had was toxic, and it almost destroyed him on several occasions. He doesn't allow himself any enjoyment lest something terrible should happen if he were to relax."

"That's a bit extreme. What he described was obsession, not love or true play. Qwynn doesn't respect him. Sounds like she ran him around on a leash until he broke it off. He's got to know it's not always like that."

Not that I knew. I didn't remember anything, but common sense told me there was a billion kinds of love out there, and Grim thought there was only one kind. Or maybe that he was capable of only one kind, which made me feel sorry for him. I wonder what his highness would think of my pity.

Timothy pursed his lips. "Yes, well, she had a millennium to ruin him."

Millennium. If Qwynn wasn't a vampire or Death like Grim, what was she? What was Bianca? Even Timothy set off my radar for "weird." Discomfort squirmed in my belly like a pack of worms. I didn't like the idea of Grim being with that harpy. He deserved...better.

What is it of my concern what he deserves? He can be with whoever he wants. He's death for crying out loud.

Still, I told myself that nobody deserved to be manipulated and betrayed like that. Qwynn was determined to wrap him around her finger like a plaything. Qwynn didn't care about Grim. And if Timothy was right, that mattered to Grim.

"Why are you telling me all this? This is super personal stuff. Aren't you worried I'm going to spill to the wrong person or use this information?"

He didn't respond for a long moment. Then he said, "I suppose there is safety in confiding to strangers."

The only reason anyone confided to a stranger was

because they didn't believe the stranger would be around to remind the secret-teller of their sins.

Timothy didn't tell me because I was some rando he'd never see again. He could tell me because these secrets would die with me. When all this was said and done, Grim still intended to twist my head off like a bottle cap.

My stomach clenched, even as I closed my eyes and set my hands under my head. I was cold again. Tempted to grab one of the fluffy throw blankets, I wanted to cocoon in it for warmth, but I refrained. I needed to be frosty for anything. It was the same reason I wouldn't sleep in the guest bedroom. I needed to stay near the exit to be aware of anyone coming or going.

"You really care about him," I said, trying to sound indifferent, but my voice came out scratchy.

"So do you," Timothy said, before leaving me to sleep like the dead.

19

The soft chime of the elevator had me fighting to open my eyes. My instincts recognized it was the middle of the day and my body fought to remain in a deep, dreamless sleep. If Grim thought he could rouse me to play bait, he would have to carry me to where he kept the large box and stick he could set me under.

Images of Grim throwing me over his broad muscled shoulder triggered a warming sensation in the pit of my stomach. In my half-sleepy state, I fantasized he was about to whisk me off to his ginormous bed with the black silk sheets.

Before my thoughts got too X-rated, the smell of a stranger hit me. I bolted up on the couch and met the muzzle of a familiar gun.

"Miranda, was it?" I asked, peering past the barrel to the equally familiar face. "Pleasure to see you again. I'd offer you a drink, but you might shoot me." I really wasn't looking forward to getting shot.

Her dark kinky hair fell over one eye as she glared at me with precision focus. She'd come armed to the gills, wearing a chain with several crosses on it, a necklace of garlic around her neck, and a wooden stake was holstered at her side. She'd ditched the security uniform and instead wore a black, long-sleeved Under Armor shirt and army-issue fatigue pants, with her combat boots. Her dress was as tactical as her steely gaze. She was here on business.

"Wait, how'd you get in?" I glanced at the elevator. Security here was as tight as they come.

"All emergency responders know how to override an elevator."

"You're with the fire department?" I asked, skeptical. My eyes crossed, returning focus to the gun. Would a bullet to my skull kill me? I mean, Grim ripped off heads, and that did the trick. Maybe zombie rules applied with a head shot?

"No." She shrugged one shoulder. "But I can get in and out of anywhere."

"Security guard school?" I asked as casually as if I were inquiring about how old her kid was.

"Army," she said, confirming my initial suspicion.

"Ah," I said, keeping my hands up and tone light. "So did you come to kill me? Kind of rude to shoot someone who is just trying to get some shuteye."

"Give me one reason why I shouldn't kill a bloodsucking vampire?" Despite her resolved expression, there was a real question in there.

"Because I saved your life? Because I kept your kid from being squashed by a couple of drunk assholes? Because I'm too pretty to die?" My answers tumbled out. *So much for keeping cool.*

There was a flicker of hesitation in her eyes, but her trigger finger never relaxed. "Why does the owner of Sinopolis want you? Why is he keeping you up here? Are you some kind of bloodsucking pet to him?"

I made a face. That was the second time I'd heard that. "I'm no one's pet." The words came out gruffer than I intended. She pulled the hammer back on her gun.

I became cognizant of the blood pulsing through Miranda. It sang to me, begged me to open up a vein and drink. I was always ravenous right when I woke up. There was the familiar pinch of hunger in my stomach, and if I didn't feed soon, some bad shit was likely to go down.

"Excuse my tone, I'm...hungry. And if you don't mind, I'd like to grab myself a drink, so I don't embarrass myself." I tipped my fingers toward the kitchen.

"Not gonna happen," she said, bringing up a cross with her other hand. The bottom was sharpened into a stake.

I used the opportunity to flinch from the cross. A smile of satisfaction formed on her lips. I grabbed the gun as quick as a lightning strike, disarming her. Terror took place of her surety, as Miranda realized the cross did nothing and I now had her gun pointed at her.

"Yeah, sorry, the cross is a bogus myth. I tried it out first chance I got. Same goes for the garlic, though I have to say I haven't tried the wooden stake in the heart. Seemed too risky to test—"

She kicked the gun from my hands, and her arm sailed through the air with the makeshift stake, directed at my heart. I caught her wrists before she could jam it in my chest.

"Whoa, whoa, I didn't say I wanted to test it." The scent of her adrenaline fanned the flames of my hunger.

No, I am not a monster. I will not hurt her.

With vampiric strength, I pushed her, sending her flying backward, only to land ass-first on a couch. I'd planned for a soft landing, but the couch slid five feet and right into a podium displaying a three-foot-tall glass pyramid. It smashed into the ground with a tremendous explosion of glass. Or was it crystal? Diamond wouldn't do that, right? Grim couldn't be too mad if it was crystal. I think.

Miranda's dark eyes widened as she regarded me from across the room. I picked up the gun and wooden stake before walking over to the kitchen. I set them on the counter with a loud clack. Okay, so I slammed them down. I grabbed a blood bag from the fridge and ripped off the top like a juice pouch. The cool liquid chilled the mug as I poured it in, then I stuck it in the microwave. As soon as the timer finished with a loud beep, I pulled out the cup and poured into a goblet. At the last second, I pulled out a cherry and tiny cocktail umbrella like I'd seen Timothy do. As I took a long sip, I realized it did taste better with that little extra pizazz. My ache abated as warmth spread through me.

I was about to take another drink when I turned around and saw Miranda was still on the couch, blinking at me. "Sorry," I said with an apologetic shrug. "I get hangry."

She got off the couch and edged her way toward me. Or she was trying to get closer to the elevator to make a getaway.

I continued to talk as if this were totally normal, and she hadn't tried to impale me two minutes ago. "The truth is, I'm super relieved you came to me. I was going to come find you."

Her chin tensed and her eyes narrowed.

I rolled mine. "Not like that. I need your help with the security camera at your hotel. There was a guy who recognized me before he tore off like a bat out of hell. I need to find out where he went."

"What do you want with this man?"

"Funny thing about my being turned into a vampire, I

don't remember who I am." I took a seat at the counter, hoping it would put her more at ease.

"Vampire amnesia?" she said, with more than a trace of skepticism.

I shared about the two weeks of my vampy existence, up until I met Grim. That I needed to figure out who I was, and that runner was the only link to my past. I hoped she'd understand that I was a good vampire who just needed to drink blood like she needed water.

Or I hoped she understood. She could have been just biding her time to get the gun back to put a bullet in my brain after humoring me.

"Why does Grim Scarapelli want you?" Miranda asked.

It was one thing to spill my own tea, but I wasn't about to knock over Grim's teapot. "He's...helping me."

"Seems like he is holding you captive."

I set the mug down on the island. Miranda was way too damn smart. She'd seen me and Bruiser go vamp and was handling the info about the undead tolerably well. I could attribute her keeping cool under unexpected circumstances to her military training. Still, I didn't think telling her Death himself ran the hotel next to hers was a pill she could swallow.

"It's a...reluctant alliance. Grim's a..." I tried to think of something. "A vampire hunter. And you got a good look at big and beefy," I said, referring to Bruiser. "Unlike myself, that fang banger doesn't mind chowing down on the innocent." I waved my hands in the air. "More evil vampires are sprouting up all over Vegas, like a bunch of daisies. And Grim is intent on stopping them."

"So what does finding this man in the hotel yesterday have to do with hunting other vampires?"

A woman of focus. I hated that. Mainly because I didn't

have the same superpower. "Um, nothing?" I got up and walked around the counter, feeling safe enough to be in closer proximity to Miranda. To her credit, she didn't back away from me. She stood like a brick house, daring anyone to blow her away.

"So why should I help?"

"Because..." I didn't have a good answer. "You're a nice person?"

She made the sound of a buzzer.

I squared off and put my hands on my hips, bracing myself. "What do you want?"

I hoped it wasn't to shoot me in the face.

"I want information," she said with a resolute glint in her eyes. "I want to know about the vampires. If something is happening in my city, in my hotel, under my nose, I need to know."

Oh, Grim was *not* going to like this. But Miranda was the only lead I had to finding out who I was.

I pretended to think about it, then said, "Get me info on the guy from yesterday, and I'll share with you what I know."

I held out a hand to her. She looked at it as if considering whether this was a trick or if maybe killing me was still the way to go. Then she grasped my hand and gave it a firm shake.

"By the way," she added in a nonchalant tone. "You have a blood mustache on your lip."

20

One case turned into three, then twenty, and by the time I'd judged the souls brought to me by my reapers, the day was almost gone.

Reluctant to return to the penthouse, I did a walk-through of Sinopolis. I greeted each staff member by name and checked in with them about their wellbeing.

As I completed my rounds, I had to ask myself if I was avoiding Vivien. Bianca's words about not leaving Vivien's side returned to me. But the sekhor was in the second most secure location on the Strip. I didn't believe she'd take kindly to being kept in the special chamber adjoining my "office" under the hotel.

After seeing Vivien's effect on my reaper, I was struck by how much she was altering my routine. It was my job to keep things in order, and a trail of chaos followed Vivien everywhere she went.

I'd given Assilem a stern talking-to on the way back down to the antechamber, but I wasn't sure the reaper was listening. He started scratching his ear in the middle of my lecture. Insolent wretch.

Though I had to admit, I too had been tempted by Vivien's touch. More than once now. The pull she had on me was maddening. At least, she was likely to still be asleep with the sun still up for another hour.

Stepping into the penthouse, the smell of burning hit me in the face. Vivien was in the kitchen again and smoke escaped out of the oven's edges.

Taking in the disaster, I removed my hands from my pockets. "Dear god, will you not be satisfied until you've burned down the entire hotel?"

Vivien's back was to me. She didn't react to my bellowing. As I drew near, I found her staring at a corner of the kitchen, eyes glazed as she dug a steak knife into her palm. My skin prickled. She'd cut a word into her flesh and was finishing the last letter. It read, *Mine.*

The master had a hold of her. He was controlling her and sending a message. *Dammit to hell.*

Yanking the knife from Vivien, I threw it across the kitchen. It clattered and slid into the wall. Next step, I had to keep the kitchen from burning down. Grabbing a towel, I opened the oven to pull out the massive dough ball. I threw the smoking, charred mass, pan and all, into the sink and ran water over it to keep the smoke alarm from going off. It would be more than inconvenient if the hotel's sprinkler system triggered. I returned to Vivien, grasping her shoulders and giving her a slight shake.

"Vivien. Vivien, come back to me."

Eyes glazed with a faraway look, she remained locked in a trance. Though she did not need to breathe, she was making quiet, panting sounds. I wrapped a clean towel around her hand to stop the bleeding. Tempted to drag her to the bathroom to dress her cuts, I reminded myself she was a sekhor and her wound would heal in minutes.

"Vivien, don't think you can sidestep what you've done to my kitchen. There will be punishment," I scolded. "Perhaps I should force you to scrub the oven, or maybe I'll bend you over my knee and take a hand to your backside."

I'd said the last part to provoke her, but she remained distant. Fear raced through me. Had I lost her? Could the master fully hold her consciousness?

No, she was too strong for him. She'd proven her mastery over her will too many times for me to believe I'd lost her.

I continued to talk as I guided her toward the living room. "Why oh why didn't I take one of those vampires who attacked us as a hostage? Then I could have disposed of you and pumped them for information on the master. But no, here we are. I get to babysit a vampire who can't be left alone without trying to destroy everything around her."

In truth, I'd already beaten myself up for my hasty destruction of the sekhors last night. But the need to get to Vivien and protect her had driven me to kill all of them, leaving no one to lead me to the master.

After I guided Vivien to sit on the couch, I held her arms and searched her face. Did she need blood? Should I throw a glass of ice water on her face? Perhaps stick by my word and give her a sound spanking?

The urge to kiss her until she snapped out of it seized me. I leaned forward until there were only mere inches separating us. Every fiber of my being demanded I lay my lips on her slightly parted mouth until she responded. Yet I did not allow myself to kiss her.

Holding myself there, on the edge of the cliff, I wrestled with myself.

"You'd miss me," Vivien finally uttered, though there was still that faraway look in her eye.

I let out a small sigh of relief. Then I asked, "What do you mean I would miss you?" My tone was cold and imperious. I'd learned how that attitude got a rise out of her. And I refused to admit that she had scared me.

Vivien blinked as her eyes focused in on me. "I'm the only sekhor you can handle. Any other would eat you alive." The slight curve of her lips told me she was coming back to me.

My shoulders dropped as I relaxed, but I remained far too close to her. My gaze flitted down to Vivien's mouth before returning to her dazzling green eyes. There was a ring of gold around her pupil that was responsible for the brilliant shade of sea glass. Entranced by the striations in them, I couldn't help but inhale the scent of sugar and leather wafting off her.

"Thank you," Vivien said, visibly swallowing. "For keeping me from cutting my hand off."

When I unwrapped the towel from her hand, I rubbed my thumb near where the cuts had been. They were almost entirely healed now, the only evidence remaining were bright red, angry lines. I wiped away the remaining blood with the towel.

"Not to say you wouldn't serve your purpose without a hand, but Timothy would be less than pleased if I asked him to come clean up after you. He's already pinched about last night's massacre."

"He was inside my head," Vivien said, cutting off my levity. Her expression was more serious than I'd ever seen it. Eyes solemn, her lips a firm line.

"You aren't scared, are you?" Even as I said it, I didn't believe it. This vampire, this woman, wasn't afraid of me, or anything, except maybe hurting someone else.

"I won't let him control me." Her voice was low, and her

expression haunted. It made me wonder about her past. Vivien didn't recall her previous life, but past traumas imprinted on the psyche and body. Someone had likely controlled her before, and she did everything she could to keep it from happening again. She seemed to view even her own instincts and needs as something to fight off.

We were the same in that. Neither of us wanted to let go of control. While I viewed Vivien as complete disorder and chaos, she had her own code that the master had tried to break. Not because she was, herself, a control freak. No, Vivien had decided who she was and acted according to that decision. And she had decided she wasn't a monster.

A wave of feeling for her came over me. Despite her need to incense me, she made me feel more alive. Her glow drew me in.

I iced against the onslaught of emotion. This was a sekhor. There was no future for her. I could not permit it. Even if I deigned her existence acceptable, the others would never allow it. Vivien was dangerous, and she did not know half of the danger she posed.

The placid expression I wore while making judgements snapped into place. "Then don't. The more you allow him in your head, the tighter his grip will close around your mind. If he takes you entirely, I'll kill you on the spot."

I expected her to jump up and lay into me with scathing remarks about how she'd fight me tooth and nail before letting me kill her. Instead, she looked down at her now-healed palm and closed it into a fist. "Good."

Uncomfortable with her agreement, I changed the subject. "You haven't yet asked the question everyone asks when they meet Death."

"Maybe I don't want to know."

"Everyone wants to know."

"From what you've implied, my options are limited."

"True..." Her lack of curiosity surprised me.

She turned to better face me, as if preparing for some test. "Alright, then, if it bothers you so much. We can run your usual script. So Death," she said in clipped words, as if she were a reporter conducting an interview. "I'm dead. What happens now? Is there a heaven? Is there a hell?"

My lips twitched. "Yes and no. There is indeed a heavenly, abundant afterlife. But if a person hasn't lived an ethical life, their soul will be destroyed."

Her pupils dilated and nostrils flared. I knew she was thinking of what she saw in the antechamber. What I'd done to that woman. I wasn't sorry for my actions, but I regretted having Vivien witness the judgment.

In her normal voice, Vivien said, "An ethical life? Sounds like a math problem that would give me a headache and make my stomach hurt."

For a second time, my lips threatened to curve upward. "More or less, that is the sum of it. My reapers often sort the souls to their rightful destination, but like I said, there are many instances where my final judgement is required."

"So Death," she said, continuing with her interview voice, but it was softer now. Vivien looked out the window, but not before I caught a vulnerable look. "Seeing as I'm an undead bloodsucker, what has happened to my soul now that I'm a sekhor? Or rather, what happens now that I don't have a soul and where did it go?"

I studied her a long moment. The way her eyelashes swept down, how she bit the inside of her cheek as she pretended not to care about the answer. Her fingers toyed with her ankle. The urge to reach out and touch the hair that had fallen on her cheek was so strong, I had to curl my fingers into my palm.

"You did not lose your soul," I said at last.

Those lashes swept back up as she met my gaze. My stomach dropped. What was she doing to me? Was she controlling my mind? No, I knew the answer. She didn't have hypnotic abilities, that was impossible.

"When you were turned into a sekhor, your soul became trapped inside your body for all eternity."

"Frozen inside," she whispered to herself.

"Crystallized. I'm not sure you are aware of the glow you emit. Your soul has undergone incredible pressure and like a diamond you now emit a supernatural shine. And yours is..." *Entrancing? Magnetic? Irresistible?* I cleared my throat, choosing none of the words that immediately came to mind, and went on. "Being a sekhor has irrevocably changed you and I cannot dislodge your soul from your body to escort it to the glorious afterlife."

"But you can't destroy it either?"

I shook my head. "No, but I can destroy the vessel and with it the soul perishes."

"Huh," she said, now looking off at a corner of the room.

"What?" Indeed, I wanted to know what she was thinking.

"When I was changed, the master robbed me of any shot at this glorious afterlife you speak of. I'm deciding how I feel about it. Not that I'm sure I would have gotten in anyway, seeing as I don't know who I was before all this."

"Perhaps it's best not to dig into your past?"

She snorted. "Right, because if I found out I was some Mother Teresa type, I'd be super pissed I'd lost my shot at a cookie-filled heaven complete with pool parties and male go-go dancers."

Catching the look on my face, she glared at me. "Okay yeah, knowing what we know about me, unlikely I was out on mission trips. But maybe I was a nice baker who gave out free cupcakes to little old ladies, or people who were down on their luck?"

"So you agree, it is a bad idea to dig into your past?"

"What? No, that's not what I'm saying. More than ever, I need to know who I was. And then when I find this bastard who changed me, I'll make him pay. Because he either robbed me of my chance at the glorious afterlife, or I'm a sadistic psycho and it's in my nature to seek revenge. Hello, my name is Vivien. You stole my afterlife. Prepare to die." She squinted at an imaginary foe and made jabbing motions with her hand.

I shook my head. "Perhaps you were simply mentally deranged." I stood to go but paused. "If you insist on digging into your past, I think you should be aware of something."

"Oh yeah?" She looked up at me, expectant. For a moment, she seemed almost childlike, eager to know what I'd share but afraid of what she'd learn.

"You may have gained vampiric strength and senses, but you do not gain other inherent skills."

She blinked at me.

"Meaning, if you were a baker, you would indeed remember how to construct a cupcake. For all that you have tarried in the kitchen, you haven't paid attention to your natural affinities."

"Like what?"

My eyes touched on the elevator. "Why did you know how to seek an emergency key for the elevator? Why do you know how to fight?"

She frowned. "All the other vampires we've encountered can fight."

I nodded. "They can. The master is choosing specific kinds of people to turn. He isn't turning homemakers, or computer programmers. He wants an army." I pursed my lips for a moment. "But soldiers are a dime a dozen when you can make them. So, why does he want you so badly?"

She shrugged. "A winning personality gets a person a lot of attention. Not that you would know."

"If you mean vexing me past my breaking point, then yes, you are indeed winning."

Vivien shot me two thumbs up. We were back where we started. She was an antagonistic dissenter, and I was her jailer. As soon as we found the master, this tentative alliance would be over, and I'd end her as if she was nothing. I paid no attention to the tightening in my chest that accompanied that last thought.

"We know he wants you. We'll take you out tonight, and he'll surely send someone to get you. This time we'll be prepared." I sounded back in control. This was business, nothing more. "Get cleaned up and meet me back out here in ten."

Vivien sauntered up to me, an unidentifiable gleam in her eye as she entered my personal space. I froze, not trusting myself to move. My instinct was to set a hand on her waist and draw her closer.

With a lascivious smile, Vivien stuck a finger in her mouth and slowly dragged it back out.

Every thought I had halted in its tracks as I focused utterly and completely on her. The slide of her finger against her lips caused me to stiffen below the belt, my breath turning shallow. A deep, ancient, animalistic hunger made itself known inside me as I dipped my head closer.

Gods, did she know what she was doing? When that perfect nail emerged from her wet lips, I was seconds away from crashing my mouth over hers and showing her what it was like to feel true hunger and craving. I had a mind to drag her to my bedroom, tie her up and give a taste of the painful desire she evoked in me. I would make her beg and plead for me to satisfy the pleasure I stoked in her. Yet I would deny her release until she was screaming for me to break her.

Then she stuck her cold, wet finger right into my ear hole. I jerked and reached for her wrist, but she'd already flounced away, off to the guest quarters.

I took it all back. Killing her was the only logical conclusion.

21

Thanks to Miranda, my personal GI Jane, I had gotten less sleep than normal. After she woke me up, I couldn't fall back asleep. Thus my foray in the kitchen during the daylight hours. Between the necklace and my gut instinct, I had been certain I was a Betty Crocker type. It bummed me to learn I wasn't Ms. Baker extraordinaire, but Grim made it sound as though I was closer to a ninja. I didn't hate that idea either.

Vivien, vampire, ninja princess. On the prowl to fight the big bad master vampire, kick some butt, and save the day.

I pondered if that was too long to fit on a business card as I got ready. I changed into a red halter top and black leather pants and freshened up. But even after splashing some cold water on my face, my head was still fuzzy from being up during daylight hours. Or maybe the fatigue was from the master vampire probing my brain like a collegiate ET studying for his anatomy final. I hated how he pulled my strings like a puppet. I knew he was in there and I'd tried to stop him. But his grip was so strong, I had reached for the knife and cut away.

As Grim and I stepped out into the lobby of Sinopolis, I wondered if coffee was still something that could get the hamsters in my head off their fluffy butts and turning the wheel again. I hadn't asked him where he was taking me.

But that didn't seem right. How would he know I cared if I didn't endlessly badger him? I was about to ask about our destination when I stopped in my tracks. Grim continued a few more steps before he realized I'd halted. Ice cold dripped into my stomach.

Closing the few steps back to me, Grim said in a gruff tone, "We need to go."

"Something's...wrong." I swallowed hard, unable to better convey the strange feeling that held me captive.

The lobby blurred, bringing certain elements into focus. Through the overwhelming scents of lush greenery and flowers, I detected a whiff of copper. It was blood, familiar blood. Twisting around, moving as if I were in water, I saw the two figures standing still by the front doors while everyone else walked by, not noticing a thing.

"Oh god, Miranda," I breathed.

I felt Grim next to me.

Bruiser was there, holding Miranda West in front of him. Despite the anger and hate radiating from her eyes, she remained motionless. To anyone else, he must have appeared to be an affectionate boyfriend the way his body pressed against the back of her. From the vantage point Grim and I had, Bruiser's mouth hovered mere centimeters from her neck, ready to tear it out. Even if I streaked over with superhuman speed, the sekhor would have plenty of time to kill her.

The broken boxer's face curled into an evil grin. He knew he had me.

Next to me, Grim's power whipped out like a cloak,

surrounding me in the same feeling I'd had the first time I met him. Like I was standing on the edge of everything and nothing. It made me feel as though the floor were falling out from under my feet as an all-consuming blackness closed in on me. I focused in on Miranda's deep frown, grounding myself in her fear.

Screams erupted around us, but they weren't because of Bruiser. He'd yet to make a move. From the other side of Grim, a man pulled a gun out from under his designer jacket, a wild look contorting his face. It was Bradley. From the dark circles under his bloodshot eyes, and the smell of bourbon that wafted off him, America's sweetheart hadn't been right since his last encounter with Grim at Wolf Town.

"You," the actor stuttered. "You're a monster. And you can't take me to hell if I send you there first."

Fan-freaking-tastic. Fratboy gone loco.

The smirk on Bruiser's face told me this wasn't part of the plan, but he was amused.

Grim held up his hands, though I doubted he was as concerned about his own safety as he was everyone else's. "Bradley, listen to me—"

Bradley did not, in fact, listen. The gun went off with a crack and more screams echoed throughout. Then Grim was there in front of him in a flash. His death mask flickered as he grabbed hold of Bradley. No, not Bradley...his essence. A ghostly likeness to the actor shimmered and grew brighter under Grim's hold. With a sickening crack, Grim separated the actor's soul from his body. The scream was shrill and deafening, but it didn't emerge from Bradley's open mouth. The soul itself was screaming in pure agony, as if it were being tortured. Bradley's eyes were round, horror-filled orbs, and I knew he could also see what Grim was doing to his spirit.

Bruiser spoke, drawing my attention back to him. I heard his words from all the way across the lobby. "The master wanted me to pass along another message for you."

Bruiser's fangs sunk into Miranda's neck. Her eyes flew wide, revealing the whites of them. The scent of her blood filled the air as he punctured her skin. My stomach rolled, then dropped.

"No." The word came out no louder than a murmur as I focused in on Bruiser, who was staring right at me. I harnessed the same power I'd used to glamour the orderly, connecting to the sekhor across the lobby. Like a seatbelt clicking in place, I locked on his mind. Bruiser stopped right before he was about to rip out her throat.

I could taste Miranda's blood on the air, but I put all my focus onto the oversized vampire. Confusion flickered in his eyes as I forced his head to lift away from her neck. He had planned to make a big graphic show of killing her, right here in the lobby in front of all these people. Make sure I saw her die in a horrific spectacle.

Apparently, the master wasn't satisfied with sending a girl flowers. He wanted to woo me with bloodshed and violence.

Something pushed against my mind, trying to loosen my hold on Bruiser. "Oh hell no," I ground out between my teeth. "You leave her alone."

The master's voice invaded my mind. *Release my servant. Let him extinguish your false ties. Come to me. We belong together.*

I didn't respond because the concentration it took to hold Bruiser was physically draining me. It felt like trying to ride a bull that was doing everything it could to buck me off. I dug in my proverbial heels and held on for dear life. If I didn't, Bruiser would kill her in an instant.

Bruiser's hands tightened around Miranda's arm until I heard an audible crunch. She grimaced and groaned. Still, I was winning. Bruiser's face was ever so slowly but steadily moving farther away from her neck.

This was what the master had done to Bruiser and Milky-eye. They'd gotten too violent, so he grabbed hold of their minds and stopped them. But he was stronger or had more practice than me.

I was beginning to fatigue. My concentration wavered and my body felt like it was being buried under tremendous weight. If I just let go of Bruiser's mind, I would be free of the strain.

No. I had to save Miranda. She was the only one who would help me find that guy, help me find my past. And wouldn't you know, I was too damned stubborn to let anyone take away my chance of finding what was mine.

When I forced Bruiser's grip to loosen with one last push, Miranda didn't miss a beat. She cut loose and ran like hell until she was at my side.

Not wasting any time either, Bruiser lunged at a woman who'd gotten too close. I tightened my grip around his mind, and he tripped. The woman dodged out of his way.

Panic welled in me. There were too many people. I could sense the bloodlust in this hateful vampire's being. Hunger wasn't driving him. He *wanted* to torture, maim, and hurt those around him.

I used my power to turn Bruiser around. The first set of automatic doors to outside opened. As he walked through, he began to bellow out curses. The master pushed back, hard. Searing pain pressed into me as I refused to let him go. I dropped to one knee, feeling the weight of a hundred bricks pressing down on me. Something dripped from my nose. Crimson droplets now decorated the tile floor.

Bruiser halted. Another step and the second set of doors would open. There was just enough daylight left to smoke his ass.

Let him go. The voice instructed, shock and disappointment brimming under the surface.

You first, I shot back in my head this time.

Bruiser lifted a foot, then set it back down where it started.

Blood bags.

I was tiring. The master was winning. I wanted to tell Miranda to get away from me. The open wound on her neck, coupled with her pounding heart, drew me in like a magnet. It siphoned my focus away from Bruiser.

Then Grim's power was there. It whipped out and gave Bruiser a "push." The doors opened and Bruiser flew into the sunshine. His scream stopped short as his body caught fire instantly. The drumming in my ears drowned out the cries of people panicking.

I needed blood. The hunger gripped me so hard, I was glad I was already on the floor. Yet I could not tear my eyes away from the flaming mass of a being.

My throat dried up as I watched. If I walked out into the sun, the same would happen to me. Not that I couldn't die. I knew I could, but seeing it made things so much more real. I didn't want to die like that. Screaming in fire.

Finally, Bruiser's body fell to the ground, a smoking charred mass.

Timothy was suddenly on the scene along with several of the hotel staff, directing people and trying to control the situation.

Then I was dangling in the air. At first, I thought the master had managed to scramble my brains, or maybe the hunger left me lightheaded. But with a quick glance down, I confirmed I was several feet off the ground.

"You are the master," Grim snarled in my face. His eyes shone gold. Maybe it was because I exhausted myself trying to control Bruiser, but I found myself thinking there was an elegant beauty to Grim's fierce expression. I wanted to touch the flexing muscles at his jawline and run my hand through his dark hair. A few locks now dipped over his forehead.

Was this the part where he ripped my head off? Would that be better than burning to death? Quicker, probably.

His accusation penetrated my fuzzy brain. "I'm not the master."

Over his shoulder, I spotted Bradley's body on the ground. His face was a frozen homage to the horror of his last terrifying moments.

"Oh really?" Disgust shone in Grim's eyes. "Then how did you control that sekhor's mind? Only a master can do that. You are slipping out during the day somehow and turning people, aren't you? You are the one responsible for all this."

I didn't have the energy to fight Grim's rage. Miranda stood off to the side, her hand clapped over her neck. If she removed her hand, allowing her blood to hit the air, I was likely to turn into a shivering mass of want. I was already so cold. My teeth were chattering. With my fangs out, I was liable to accidently chew my lip off.

"Sire," Timothy's voice broke in. "Perhaps we'd better take this scene to a more discreet location."

Grim didn't respond, only continued to stare at me with burning hatred and...betrayal?

It stung. Worse than I thought it would. Grim's opinion of me mattered. I yanked his chain and worked to raise his blood pressure, but I was hurt he thought I lied to him. I wasn't a liar.

Timothy's voice snapped like a whip this time. "I've already got my work cut out cleaning up this mess. If you wish to dispose of the sekhor, I beg you to do it in another location."

Next thing I knew, Grim was dragging me behind him.

"Ms. West, it's best you come along too," I heard Timothy say to her.

Grim directed us to a wall of mirrors. I caught sight of my blood-red eyes, and sallow, pale face. I really did look pathetic.

The Master of the Dead revealed a secret door in the wall of mirrors. We entered a private gambling room that was empty. Cigar smoke, expensive scotch, along with sweat, power, and fear lingered here. Fortunes had been made and lost in this room.

After forcibly throwing me into a chair, Grim paced in front of me. "You thought you could make a fool of me? You think I don't know the master can control minds? Well, think again." He leaned in close, fangs elongated in his mouth, as his eyes glowed as bright as the sun. Looking into them burned. Goosebumps stiffened all along my body so hard, I wanted to run a hand over my arms. But I got the sense if I made any sudden movements, he would end me right there.

"I don't know what you are talking about. I only learned I could control someone's mind at the care facility. That's how I got us in. I put a whammy on Kabir I didn't know I possessed. I haven't used it again until just now to save Miranda."

The master made it clear he wanted me, but now he was trying to sever any other ties I had. The patent characteristic of an obsessive psychopath. Getting Miranda out of the way meant I was more likely to go to him. He was willing to do anything necessary to isolate and corner me. I shivered, my stomach performing flip-flops.

Grim still looked on the verge of tearing me into itty bitty pieces. To show him I wasn't afraid, I glared right back. But I was scared. I was terrified. I didn't know what this life, or unlife, was. I had no damn footing, and I felt whiplash from trying to keep up with everything, while continually pulling away the numerous hands that kept wrapping around my throat. Not to mention, without blood I was as helpless as a baby, and I despised my dependency.

Everything was all messed up. Whatever my life had been before, it had to be better than this. Screw what Grim said. I'd learn to bake and open up a shop that operated only at night, of course. As long as I was kicking, I'd make plans and live on my terms.

"Ms. West, if you would be so kind as to sit over there." Timothy directed her to the opposite corner of the room.

Miranda squared off her stance, despite holding onto her neck with one hand while her broken arm dangled at an awkward angle. "I don't know how, but she just saved my life, not once but twice. I will not let him hurt her."

She must have missed what Grim did to Bradley Hansen. Or maybe it was like the reaper dogs, and she didn't see him rip that guy's soul out like I had. It had probably appeared as though Bradley collapsed.

"Yes, but if you continue to stand close to her with your open wounds, you could only cause more problems," Timothy pointed out.

Not backing down from our glaring match, I spelled it out for Grim. "I'm not the master. I don't know what's happening. Yes, I fought the master for dominance over that broken-nosed behemoth, but if you hadn't pushed big boy out the door, I might not have won the fight. Believe me, I don't want that creep inside my head, trying to push me around anymore."

The glow ratcheted back from his eyes, leaving them a molten brown. My gaze continually dropped to the fangs that remained. They weren't like my sharp vampire incisors. His were thicker, more menacing. My fangs pierced, where his teeth would mangle and tear like an animal's.

When he spoke again in a rough tone, the hairs on the back of my neck rose. "The only way you could have such power is because you have received blood from the first."

Some of my haughtiness drained from me. "What?"

He put his hand on the arms of the chair, leaning so close I could feel his hot breath and was instantly surrounded by his scent. My body almost surged forward to meet his heat. I wanted to wrap myself up in it, in him.

"You have taken blood from the Original. The very first sekhor. You say you don't remember who you were, and maybe I say you've been lying this whole time. You've been manipulating me."

"Into doing what?" I shot back, finding my fight. I wasn't going to sit here and be accused of something I didn't do. "How could a little vampire possibly manipulate Death into doing anything? And what would I want from you?"

I felt more than saw Timothy shift. Grim's expression emptied as if worried I would read something in his face. They both knew something I didn't. "As far as I've seen, all you need to do is rip off vampire heads like screw caps and it's no longer a problem. So why would I bother to come to you? Why would I work so hard to find out who I was? Why would I ask Miranda for her help only to have her killed before I could get the information I needed?"

Grim straightened, leaving the air cold and empty where he'd just been. Straightening his lapels, his eyes returned to amber brown. But he closed his mouth, so I didn't know if all of him had returned to normal.

"Yes, there is the case where Ms. West broke into my penthouse. We've yet to address that, haven't we?" Grim said in an icy tone.

I stood up. "You knew about that?"

Then I realized he also knew the master had been controlling the sekhors. When I mentioned Bruiser's sudden lobotomy, Grim had changed the subject. Not because he wasn't interested, but because he already knew how powerful the master vampire was. Damn it, how had I missed that?

Timothy rolled his eyes with a slight, delicate snort. "You escaped once, you didn't think we would watch you?"

I crossed my arms. "I'm surprised I didn't get a spanking for that one. You seem to want to punish me for everything else."

Grim's head swiveled around, another flicker of gold ignited in his eyes. I dropped my arms. Okay, maybe not a good time to piss him off any further. But I was cold, hungry, and exhausted after using my woo-woo mind-control magic.

"Well, why don't we see what Ms. West has dug up, shall we?" he said.

I didn't know if it was his tone that skated near major danger or if it was something she saw in his face, but tough-as-nails Miranda, who rarely backed down from a fight, took a step back.

22

At first, I'd been against investigating Vivien's past, but now I could see it was unavoidable. Perhaps I should have looked into her history the moment I decided to use her as bait. Discover why the master vampire wanted her so badly.

Then why didn't you, fool? my internal voice berated me. *Because you didn't want to get any closer to this sekhor than you have to? Because you already feel drawn to her and don't need cause to bond with her anymore?*

I strode behind Miranda, who moved at a fast clip considering what she'd just been through. Timothy called for a doctor that would meet us at Camelot, the neighboring hotel, to see to her wounds, but we couldn't wait any longer for information. Timothy had procured a bandage for Miranda's neck, and made a makeshift sling out of a shirt he grabbed from one of our gift shops. Then my aide peeled off, with the assurance he would rejoin us shortly.

I refused to let go of Vivien, holding her arm with bruising force, though she didn't let on that my grip bothered her. She set her jaw and hadn't looked at me since we'd left the high-roller room. Timothy had provided a pair of sunglasses to hide her red eyes and she struggled to keep up. The thirst was consuming her.

If she thought she could make me feel guilty for accusing her of being the master vampire, she was mistaken. I owed her nothing, certainly not trust.

I was angry. Angry with myself for not paying better attention. I was also angry with Vivien for getting Ms. West mixed up in this matter. It didn't help that Bradley had forced me to take extreme measures with him. I'd reaped him before his time, one of the most excruciating punishments I was capable of. But he'd forced my hand.

"I don't know why you are all pissy," Vivien grumbled. "I'm the one you accused of lying and being a master vampire. If you had told me about the mind control powers, we could have put two and two together."

"And why didn't you tell me about how you wooed the orderly so expertly when we went to see the Original?"

She shrugged, her bottom lip jutting out in a pout. "I wasn't a hundred percent certain it happened. Part of me insisted I'd made it up, and he just changed his mind about not letting us in."

Not liking the logic she presented, I changed tactics. "You got Ms. West involved in this mess. She is human and not to be embroiled in supernatural matters."

She made a rude sound. "Miranda is her own person, and she got into this herself. She could have run for the hills, but I don't think that's her personality. And no, I don't like it any more than you do that the master targeted her. If she'd died because of me, or worse..." Her words drifted off as she delved into the imagined horror of it. Then she said, "I want the master dead too. But I don't want to meet him on his turf, which is why every time his goons come, I end up running. His power is increasing, and I'm not so sure I'll win if it comes to another battle of wills."

"He's turning more people, creating a horde. Their power feeds his."

"Well, let's get one thing clear. I'm not looking to turn a bunch of people into vampires to fight him. You got that? When the time comes, you are going to do the dirty work and take him out."

"Agreed." We exchanged a look, our eyes lingering far too long. Her glow pulsated around her like a warm beacon, inviting me forward, but I resisted. I would always resist.

The tension rocketing back and forth between us had drained. She may be a master vampire, but she didn't truly know what she was. She hadn't lied or manipulated me. I shouldn't take comfort in that, but I did.

When we arrived at Camelot's security office, Miranda used her key card to open the door.

A Hispanic man with a pencil-thin mustache and keen gray eyes swiveled around in his desk chair in front of the wall of security cameras. The room was smaller than my closet. The boy I'd seen with Ms. West before was sitting on a bean bag in a corner, playing on a tablet. Both jumped to their feet when they saw the state of Miranda.

She held up a hand, the bloodied one, which didn't help their distress. "Javier, I need the room."

Still, neither of them budged. Javier's eyes moved to each of us, quietly assessing. He was no loaf-around security man. I could see him gleaning the information we each presented and assessing the threat we posed.

Pity, I might have to kill him. I didn't have time for anyone to get in my way right now.

"These are friends of yours?" Javier asked, an underlying thread of skepticism in his voice. When he stood, his hand went to his gun. He was ready to pull it if Ms. West even hinted it was necessary. It surprised me to find my neighboring hotel employed such vigilant staff. I'd have to compliment the hotel owner when I saw him next.

Miranda explained. "They are here for a delicate security matter, and I need the room." When he still didn't soften his stance, Miranda said his name in a coaxing tone.

"Does Mr. Landis know about this?" Javier asked, finally dropping his hand from his firearm. He was referring to the manager of security.

There was little I didn't know about the neighboring business.

"Nope," she said, locking him in with a steady gaze that conveyed she had no intention of informing anyone of our visit. There was deep trust and camaraderie between these two.

With a sharp nod, Javier relaxed his stance and walked past me, shutting the door behind him.

"So I'm guessing he doesn't get paid enough to tattle," Vivien said.

"We did two tours in Fallujah together. I got him this job," Miranda explained.

The kid moved toward the door. "No, Jamal," Miranda said. "I need you here where I can keep an eye on you."

The kid looked up at me with apprehension. I tried to smile. He took a step back. Kids could usually sense something was different about me. In their bones, they knew death was near, no matter how I tried to blend.

A knock at the door distracted us. I opened it, ready to unleash my full fury to get whoever it was to leave. Timothy stood there with a placid expression, holding a travel mug.

"Very scary, master," he said drolly.

I opened the door wider to let him in. He passed the

mug to Vivien, who shot him a hopeful smile. "Jeeves, did you bring me a special juice box?"

Timothy winced. "Jeeves?"

"How about Alfred, then? Any better?" she asked.

Timothy wrinkled his nose.

I grabbed the cup from her. "Apologize."

"That's really not nece—" Timothy protested, but I cut him off.

"Now," I said, putting steel into the word as I addressed the sekhor.

Vivien opened her mouth as if to say something further antagonizing, but she then seemed to think better of it. Turning back to my aide, she said in a chastened tone, "Sorry, Timmy. Thank you for this." She nodded toward the travel mug I held.

"Was that so hard?" I asked, handing the drink back. She swallowed down the contents while managing to glare at me through the sunglasses she wore.

The child let out a giggle, then snorted.

"Hang out over there with your iPad," Miranda directed Jamal. When the kid didn't move, she barked with an authority scarier than any military tone; she used her mom-voice. "Move it, young man."

Jamal started, then settled back into his spot on the bean bag.

"I'm not leaving my son home alone with everything that's going on right now," Miranda explained. "Here, he can entertain himself with either me or Javier around."

"Single mom?" Vivien asked in between sips.

"His father died in action three years ago." Miranda delivered the line with practiced efficiency and no small amount of pride. Still, I saw the flash of pain in her eyes.

I wondered if I had judged her husband's soul, or

perhaps one of my reapers had sorted him. Jamal was staring at me again, as if sensing my thoughts.

"Don't worry, kid," Vivien said, catching his look too and nudging me in the ribs with her elbow. "He doesn't bite. And neither will I." She pulled down her sunglasses to wink at him. A smile tugged at the corners of the kid's lips in response.

Miranda sat down at the computer and typed. Vivien wasted no time plopping down in the empty seat next to her, setting the sunglasses on the counter. Her eyes had returned to their normal sea-green hue.

"I think I found your guy," Miranda said. "It will just take me a second to pull up the footage."

While we waited, Vivien spun around in the chair. With every rotation, it let loose a pitchy squeak, but that didn't keep her from doing it. The rusty scrape wore on my nerves.

"Will you stop that?" I said on the fourth spin.

"What are you gonna do if I don't?" she said, looking me dead in the eye, breaking eye contact only long enough to complete another full rotation.

Several ideas came to mind. Not all of them were family-friendly.

"Here we go," Miranda said, pulling up the video of me dragging Vivien back to Sinopolis. Again, the man halted in his tracks with obvious recognition before sprinting off.

Vivien set the travel mug down, having finished it. Color had returned to her cheeks, and her eyes brightened with interest as she leaned forward, mouth slightly parted.

Miranda zoomed in on the guy's face a little more. Any closer and his features would be too pixelated, but it was enough. Blunt nose, small eyes, and light brown hair. He wore board shorts and a Hawaiian shirt.

Vivien whispered something.

Miranda saved me the trouble of asking. "What was that?"

"Skip," Vivien said, louder this time. "His name is Skip."

"How do you know him?" I asked, tucking my hands in my pockets. "A former lover, perhaps? That would explain why he ran for the hills."

Vivien shot me a glare, while Miranda's eyebrows rose, a smile playing at the corner of her mouth.

"No," Vivien protested. "Or, I don't know. I don't think so, but I don't know where I know him from. I just know his name is Skip."

I came up behind Vivien, set my hands on the back of her chair and leaned in to get a better look. While the personnel were excellent here, they could use larger monitors.

Focusing on the man on the screen, I considered his connection to Vivien. I hadn't been kidding when I suggested he was a former lover, but I had also learned to assume nothing about anyone. There were a million and one reasons he could have recognized her and ran. He hadn't been a vampire, of that I was sure. He lacked the ethereal glow sekhors emitted.

As I pondered the implications, I realized Vivien had stilled. When I turned my head, she did the same until we were staring into each other's eyes. My breath halted. Tension crowded the air between us, practically smothering me. Those complex green eyes flicked down to my lips as she swallowed.

Vivien's lips were mere inches away again and the magnetic pull between us was so strong, I had to grip her chair harder to keep myself from closing the gap between us. In doing so, my knuckles grazed her exposed back. Her skin was silky smooth and the leather and vanilla scent curled around my senses again.

Visions of whirling her chair around and crashing my mouth against her lips sent a flood of heat through my body. Not only did I want to taste her, I wanted to suckle and nip down the column of her throat, to the top swell of her breasts. Then I'd tongue her nipples through her shirt until they stiffened into peaks through the fabric. I would lave her skin and most sensitive parts with my curious, probing tongue until I had her begging for release under me.

Vivien's pupils expanded, nearly swallowing me whole.

Miranda broke through my intense fantasy, keeping me from acting on any of my insane thoughts. "I used the cameras to follow him back to his room," she said. "Tenth floor, room 1009. Skip, here, packed up in a hurry and high-tailed it out in less than ten minutes. He paid for the room in cash, and booked it under the name Raoul Duke."

"Fake name," Vivien announced loudly.

"If my name was Skip, I'd use a fake name too," Miranda said, still studying the screen.

Vivien closed her eyes in concentration. "I know that name, Raoul Duke." She snapped her fingers with a triumphant smile. "Wait, I know. That's the name of Johnny Depp's character in the movie *Fear and Loathing in Las Vegas.*"

"Yet you don't remember your name," I pointed out.

Her glowing victory darkened into a scowl.

Miranda went on. "I caught housecleaning in time, and kept them from entering until I came and got you."

I stayed behind Vivien's chair to keep from alarming anyone with the rock-hard erection I now sported. I tried to focus on Miranda's words, but all I could think of was if this were any other situation, I'd easily seduce any woman who held my attention and take care of my *problem*. I treated my needs with the same efficiency I gave to brushing my teeth. But with Miranda and Jamal in the room, I needed to focus entirely on business and neglect my sudden and urgent needs.

Rolling my shoulders back, I reminded myself how I managed every day. I pushed aside my own wants to see to my duties, and that was the only way it could be. Qwynn taught me the dangers of choosing pleasure over duty. And Vivien posed the same danger my ex-wife had. I could drown in her, forgetting everything else.

"We should check out the room," Vivien said, pressing her hands on the desk and standing with sudden nervous energy. I backed away so the roller wheels on her chair wouldn't scuff my shoes. She was likely invigorated by the mug of blood she'd drained.

When I caught Timothy's eye, he was watching me with a strange expression. Did he sense my mounting attraction to the sekhor?

It was likely. For a moment, I wondered if my aide would tell the others, or worse...no, I couldn't think of *him* finding out about any of this.

Timothy turned his gaze back to the monitor, and I did the same, trying to ignore the churning in my stomach.

Standing as well, Miranda said, "I'm coming too."

"Ma'am," Timothy interjected, "the physician will be along to see to your arm. I think you should wait here and let them go on without you."

Miranda's mouth thinned. "You patched me up fine enough for the moment. If you think I'm going to miss a chance to figure out what the hell is going on around here, you're dead wrong."

My aide and I exchanged a look. It was obvious there would be no changing her mind.

With a sigh, I submitted. "Bring the boy as well. I don't want him unattended after the sekhors targeted Ms. West."

We made our way to the door. Behind me, Miranda asked Vivien, "Sekhors?"

"Another name for vampires," Vivien clarified.

Timothy had fallen into step next to me while Jamal trailed behind his mother, headphones lodged in his ears.

"Sounds kind of...lewd," Miranda said under breath.

Vivien perked up. "That's what I thought." Then hushing her voice in case Jamal could hear, she said, "I thought he was calling me a sucky whore when he first said it."

A snort came from beside me. I shot Timothy a dark look. He made sounds as if he were clearing his throat.

THE SHEETS WERE RUMPLED, half-pulled off the hotel bed. And the room reeked of cheap liquor, unwashed male, and the skunky scent of weed. Unlike the suites in Sinopolis, the room in Camelot was as generic as any other three-star hotel. Cheap sheets, decent-sized television, but the room had an excellent view of the strip. I crossed the room to close the curtains so Vivien could enter without bursting into flames.

Vivien wasted no time going to work checking out the room. Her motions were practiced and methodical as she pulled back the sheets and checked all the drawers. She went through the room with single-minded focus. I don't think she was aware she had seemed to fall into some kind of routine.

"What are you looking for?" Jamal asked. Miranda had washed the blood off her hand and her fingers curved around his shoulder to keep him close by. Timothy stood outside as the rest of us crowded the room. We'd call him in if we needed him.

"Anything that can tell me either where he was before, or where he might go," Vivien said absentmindedly. She didn't realize she was doing it again. Returning to some unconscious habit the way she did when fighting vampires. It was tied to her past, and I felt we were close to pulling on the right thread so the whole thing would untangle before our eyes.

"Can I help?" Jamal asked Vivien, before looking up at his mom.

Vivien paused, opening the drawers. "Sure, kid, go check out the bathroom and note any personal items he might have left behind, then come back and tell me what you see." Just as he was about to disappear, she stopped him. "Make sure to lift the lid on the toilet tank and let me know if anything is in the tank."

Just as Vivien shut the closet, no personal effects left behind, Jamal emerged from the bathroom with a report. "No personal stuff. He even took the hotel soaps. I lifted the tank like you said and there wasn't anything except for some pieces of duct tape stuck inside."

Vivien grinned, then patted Jamal on the back. "Good going, kid." She disappeared into the bathroom. I followed her in, Jamal on my heels.

Miranda relaxed while her ten-year-old shot her a giant goofy grin of pride.

I folded my arms, waiting for Vivien to reveal the source of her excitement.

Ceramic scraped against itself as Vivien pulled the top of

the tank off and set the lid onto the bathroom counter. Wadded towels littered the ground and counter. "Well, at least we can guess why he ran," Vivien said, pointing at the duct tape.

"What does it mean?" Jamal asked. Indeed, I was also curious as to her excitement.

There was a shining gleam of victory in her eyes. "Some guys love room service but hide their valuables in the toilet tank."

"Why not use the room safe?" I asked, pointing toward the closet. Safes were standard with rooms in this hotel.

"Hotel management can still open the safes," Vivien said, "but he wanted whatever he was packing to be completely undetected. And be in a safe spot where no one would find it."

"You think he was moving drugs," Miranda said.

Vivien made a finger gun and pointed it at Miranda. "Exactly." Then turning to me, she said, "Do you think I'm some kind of cop? Maybe that's why Skip ran? I could be some big hotshot police detective. Maybe I'm in narcotics."

"Yes," I said. "Because you are so excellent in situations where you have to follow rules and yield to authority." Despite her investigative skills, I doubted she was an officer of the law.

Vivien frowned. "Hey, I could be. I'm more like a Mel Gibson kind of cop. I probably have some tragic past which makes me crazy, but also crazy smart." She snapped her fingers. "I bet I even torture some poor schmuck who keeps trying to shrink my head, but I play with his instead."

Jamal lit up. "And your captain is always pissed off you've wrecked a bunch of cars trying to get your man."

"Yeah, yeah." Vivien nodded with vigor. "But I'm too good to fire, so they have to keep me on board."

Both were now egging each other on with their inane theories.

"Maybe you have a partner who helps cover for you too. Loose cannon cops always have some straitlaced partner who helps cover their butt."

"Time out." Miranda teed her hands, albeit at her side to accommodate her sling. "I think the only thing we can confirm here is that both you and my son love action movies. And this still doesn't help us find Skip."

"You're right," Vivien said, frowning again. She passed by us and went straight for the garbage by the dresser. Pulling out papers, she smoothed them on the desk. A wrinkle of concentration formed between her eyebrows. "You said he was here for how long?" Vivien asked Miranda.

"Seven days. He was booked out for thirteen but ran for the hills when he spotted you."

"This dude has a thing for Luiggi's Pizza Palace," she said. "The address is a little way off the Strip, and he has three receipts here and he orders the same thing every time. Dude has a habit, and that's how we are going to find him."

Jamal stared up at Vivien in wide-eyed wonder. "That's awesome. You are going to catch this guy using pizza?"

"Yep," she said. "And next time he orders a pizza, we are going to force *him* to deliver some answers."

"Awesome," the kid breathed.

I shared a look with Miranda. Without saying a word, we agreed her discovery was viable, and that we were in the presence of not one child, but two.

23

Grim and I returned to the penthouse where he made a call to the Pizza Palace. While they had an address attached to his phone number, Skip ordered from any number of locations. Grim used his skills of persuasion to convince them to notify him when Skip made his regular order. The trap was set, now all we had to do was wait.

I was glad Grim got on board with my plan to follow the bread crumbs of my past. But what the hell happened in my previous life that made a master vamp obsessed with me? Did I key his car? Turn him down for a date?

At least I knew answers were coming, and they would lead us to the master. So now we could kick back and relax until Skip ordered a pizza.

"Feel like wriggling on the hook for a bit?" Grim asked as he hung up.

So much for kicking back. Though I wasn't too shocked. Grim really wasn't the sit-back-and-wait kind of guy.

"Are you asking the bait how it feels? That doesn't sound like you," I said, laying the back of my hand against his forehead as if checking his temperature. Grabbing my hand, Grim held it against his chest instead of letting go.

Once again, I was caught in his special thrall like in the security room. The need to grab him by the neck and haul him down for a thorough, hot kiss until we both lost our minds was overwhelming. Warmth trickled down my stomach and flooded my southern region as I fell headfirst into those bourbon-colored eyes. I wanted him. Bad.

The moment he'd switched from blame mode to "do something about it" mode, the tension between us melted away. Yet the attraction seemed to be growing exponentially.

But I needed my freedom more. I stepped back. He released my hand. I wanted him to grab me again. I wanted to yank his crisp black shirt out from his pants and run my fingers up his abs to see if they were as carved as I imagined.

"Sure," I said, managing to not sound as breathy and bothered as I felt. "What did you have in mind?"

Grim's eyes swept up and down my body with a heat that took me by surprise. Suddenly, I wasn't so sure what he meant by "wriggling bait."

"Don't you think this bikini is a bit over the top?" I asked, standing next to the infinity pool. The night air was cool, but I'd drunk my way back up to a comfy body temperature again.

Hands on my hips, I twisted my pelvis so my rhinestone-studded bottoms would catch the outdoor lights. Reflected dots swept back and forth along Grim's face as I did so. The top was just as ostentatious. The blood-red bikini had so many shiny crystals on it, it looked as though it belonged in a locked case next to some royal tiaras. A matching jewel-encrusted necklace circled my neck instead of the tied leather I'd been using to cover up the scars.

Waltzing around the private pool and cabanas of Sinopolis, I was doing my part, dangling on the hook, waiting for any other sekhors to come knocking.

Come on, master dickwad. Come out, come out, wherever you are.

It was only midnight, and down below, the common pool for Sinopolis was thumping. There was a party with some famous DJ. Up here, you could hear the rhythmic thrum of the base and the roar of the crowd when the beat dropped. The sounds skimmed across my exposed skin. I could taste the life and excitement on the air, coming from below.

Grim assured me the private pool was a better location. If sekhors had gotten into club Wolf Town, there would be no difficulty crashing the private pools of Sinopolis. There were few people hanging around the private pool, primarily here to use the giant hot tubs.

Positioned on a lounge chair, Grim did not lie back. He sat with a leg on either side of the chair, watching, waiting.

While I was cavorting about in a bikini in the dead of night, his majesty deigned to remove his jacket, and undo two buttons on his black shirt to reveal an appealing amount of dark chest hair. I wanted to slip my hand in there and run my fingers through it and explore the hard muscle peeking out. I gripped my hips harder to keep from doing any such thing.

Grim scanned me with what I could only guess to be calculating indifference. "We want you to be noticed so the master targets you, and this attire is," he paused, "satisfactory."

Satisfactory? He might as well have said the F word. If he

had said I looked fine, I would have slugged him on the spot. Even I knew I looked like a glittering sex goddess. My auburn hair was pulled up into a messy bun, tendrils falling out and around my shoulders. The bikini perfectly offset the dip and tone of my long torso while accenting the swell of my breasts. Even the bottoms were the perfect fit to make me look bootylicious. I did draw a line at the kitten heels, however. That was far too obvious.

I'd pulled on the BDSM bodysuit to razz Grim before, but this time the outfit had been presented to me in a box folded in tissue paper. I wasn't sure if the gift was because Timothy and Grim now believed it was to my taste, or because my last costume had drawn out the baddies so effectively. Either way, I wasn't as comfortable in this getup. But I'd be damned if I let Grim get any hint of that discomfort.

Inwardly smirking, I wanted to see if I could crack his cool demeanor. Spotting a penny, I turned, then bent over to pick it up, giving him one hell of a show. Timothy had graciously arranged for a quick, in-house wax when I saw that bikini, so I knew his view was flawless.

When I turned around, I held the penny out to him. "Did you want this?" I asked, blinking innocently while putting emphasis on my last two words, implying more than the coin.

"No, thank you," he said, delivering the words with cool indifference. Despite his tone and hard jawline, his eyes glowed gold and his nostrils flared.

Gotcha.

I flipped the coin into the air. It perfectly arced in the air over to Grim. He reached out with lightning-fast reflexes and caught it between his thumb and middle finger. Then he fluidly pocketed the penny, his heated gaze still glued to me. Annoyance flickered in those molten amber eyes.

Was I some huge slut in my past life?

I considered it for a moment but then dismissed the thought. I wasn't letting my cha-cha lead me around indiscriminately. More than anything, my goal was to get a rise out of Grim. That implied I was an antagonistic little shit, as Timothy already pointed out.

Even if I was trying to seduce Grim, who the hell could blame me?

The air notably cooled as he broke eye contact, pulled out his smartphone, suddenly absorbed. Fingers flying as if he were orchestrating the movements of armies, I resented his sudden indifference.

Maybe he was ignoring me to play Candy Crush, simply trying to pass the time while I shook my ass out here. Who was I kidding? Grim probably hadn't even heard of the app. That would brush up too close to fun, which was something he didn't do. All work and no play made Grim a dull boy.

Sauntering back down the pool toward the hotel, I was tempted to start singing Disney tunes. Surely my innocent, slutty, damsel-in-distress routine would lure my stalker out.

A man who had been alternating between the hot tub and his lounge chair the last hour I'd been here caught my eye for the third time.

He was handsome, in his mid-twenties. Muscular and lithe, suggesting he spent a good deal of time in the gym, and judging by his bare chest, he shaved himself smooth. He had light-blue eyes and had given me a half smile every time I walked by, not bothering to hide he was watching me. I wasn't sure if it was because I had vampiric senses or if I was observant, but I could look at some people and peg them as

Richie Riches. There was something about their skin that was a little fresher, their teeth a little whiter.

When his eyes caught mine, his smile spread, revealing perfect teeth. *Uh oh.* He grabbed two drinks on the table next to him and approached. He smelled like expensive face creams and cornflakes.

"The waiter brought over two mojitos," the man said, flashing me another dazzling smile. It was underlined with just enough humility to not seem cocky. "I don't suppose you'd want the second one?"

Smooth. But the idea of taking a drink from a stranger put me on an edge so hard, I almost wanted to push him away from me.

"I just had a drink, so I'm not thirsty," I said, not technically lying. His blood beckoned but I'd had more than enough to resist.

With a bashful laugh, he looked down at the drinks. "Yeah, I suppose that was a pretty lame pickup line."

"Does it usually work?" I asked, honestly curious.

He set the mojitos back on the table by his chair. With a shrug, he ran his fingers through his dark-blond hair. "Sometimes."

There was something so neat and tidy about this guy. I'd bet he paid his taxes on time, never used the wrong utensil, and was excellent at making people feel at ease. It probably explained whatever high-paying job that afforded him access to the private Sinopolis pool. Oddly enough, I found him lacking.

You aren't in fear he might kill you any moment.

Great, I was comparing this pleasant, loaded dude to the scowly, all-business, master of death at the other end of the pool.

"I guess I thought, or rather hoped, you kept walking by in the hopes I'd say hello," he said.

"Oh, I was—"

Warm fingers caressed my bare flesh as a hand slipped around my waist. "Otherwise engaged," Grim finished for me. I turned to look up at him. His gaze was flat, dangerous.

The Ken-doll tried to keep his composure, but a pesky stutter snuck its way into his words. "Mr. Scarapelli, I'm sorry. I didn't mean to bother your—" His eyes flicked to me a moment, but he didn't finish that sentence. "I often stay at Sinopolis for business. I'm even part of your VIP guest membership. Your hotel is unparalleled in comfort."

I didn't blame the guy for his nerves. I'd nearly jumped out of my skin when Grim appeared at my side. As it was, I wanted to squirm under his light touch. My blood ran hotter than a moment before and I was suddenly lightheaded.

Do not lean into his touch. Do not, I repeat, lean into his touch.

Did the bastard think I'd fall over myself simply because he paid me attention? He seemed not to care for anyone or anything, which was why he was able to claim whatever he wanted when he put his full force upon it. And I was not unaware that he was currently marking me as off limits to the Ken-doll.

For the moment, I was grateful the bra of my bikini was so covered with jewels because my nipples tightened with an ache to be touched. Despite the greedy nerve endings of my hip insisting I push further into his palm, I somehow managed to keep control of myself.

Grim released the man from his pandering with a slight nod. "Glad to hear you enjoy our hospitality. This round is on me." His eyes touched on the two drinks. Then Grim started to lead me back to where he had been sitting. I tried to send Ken-doll one last friendly smile, but he seemed to be in his own head reviewing his lack of cool in front of the hotel owner.

Grim didn't remove his hand from my hip, but it was the light caress of a gentleman. Ever in control, this guy.

Licking my lips and trying to focus anywhere but on Grim's touch, I waited until we were out of earshot to ask my question. "Can you tell what kind of soul people have before you reap them?"

"Mostly," he said. "Though souls are in constant flux. In the moment of meeting them, I often know where they would be sorted, but they could change into something quite different within a few days."

"How about cutie pie back there?" I asked, wanting to know if he was as nice as he seemed.

Grim grimaced, then released my side, putting distance between us. Was he bothered by my prying into his reaping skills? Or the nickname I'd given that rando? Either way I was grateful he'd let go of me. My brain was on the verge of melting out my ears trying to resist jumping him.

Grim slipped his hands back into his pockets in that casual way models did to show off their designer trousers. "He would be granted access to the afterlife. He is a nice, bland, inoffensive man. Perhaps a bit selfish from being raised by wealthy parents and a bit naïve to the dealings of his business partners."

Suddenly antsy to get out of here and out of this exposing getup, I rubbed one arm. "It's been over an hour. Don't you think the master or one of his goons would have shown up by now?"

"Patience." Grim looked out over the edge of the landing and down to the party below. The masses writhed in the show of lights and deep well of techno music. It was the same posture he'd taken in Wolf Town. As if he were surveying his kingdom from some faraway tower with no small amount of burden and responsibility. I was struck with the need to lighten the invisible weight that I could almost see pressing on him. Who would have guessed Death could seem so...human.

"Have you ever been down there?" I asked, coming to stand next to him.

"On occasion, I will go and make a brief appearance at some of the larger events," he said.

I nudged him with my shoulder. "That's not what I meant. Have you been down there, dancing, drinking, letting loose?"

A smile tugged on one side of his lips. "Mingle amongst the masses?"

I rolled my eyes and gave him an actual push this time. "I mean have fun. Fun, Grim. Do you know what that is?"

Turning to look at me, his eyes darkened with either regret or distaste. "I have had lifetimes of experience with pleasure."

I understood what he was referring to. "I'm not talking about what you had with Qwynn." The way he'd described those times sounded like a hard metal trip of nonstop orgies and drugs. "Fun isn't only about vice. Maybe if you let go a little bit here and there it wouldn't be such a deep rabbit hole when you finally gave in."

Based on the slash of his mouth, he did not agree. And he certainly didn't seem to appreciate my butting in to give my opinion on how he lived his eternal life.

Looking back at the pool, I said, "When was the last time you went for a swim?" I walked over to the edge of the glittering, lit pool. The smell of chlorine and expensive vodka stung my nose when we'd first gotten here. But with so many tropical flowers planted around the grounds, they mellowed the sharpness of the initial odors.

Grim followed me over to the edge. "I often swim laps. Especially after a long day's work. I find it invigorating."

I sucked in my cheeks right before sticking an arm out, pushing Grim off the edge and into the pool. He barely pulled his hands from his pockets before he hit the water with a tremendous splash. I wasn't fast enough to throw my arms up to keep from getting half-soaked.

Grim's head emerged, sputtering with shock. Before he could get out with a burst of murderous power, I jumped. Grabbing my legs, I shouted, "Cannonball." I hit the water, an explosion in the tranquil atmosphere of the private pool.

Submerged in the water, joy and peace surrounded me. I let myself slowly sink, enjoying the sensation. Maybe immortal existence wasn't so bad if you could stitch your life together with more moments like this.

Finally, I kicked my legs and swam to the surface. Emerging into the night air, I pushed my now-loose, wet hair back. Grim's pristinely tousled black hair dripped in his glowering eyes. His lower lip glistened in a pout that was both menacing and adorable.

"Hey," I said, allowing the smile to blossom on my face. "I just learned I can swim." I pumped a fist in the air while continuing to tread water. "Awesome." Then before he could bum me out, I swam over and wrapped my arms around his neck.

The scowl Grim sported gave way to surprise, as I brought my face within inches of his. Despite the ruckus I'd made, the other guests were doing a fantastic job minding their own business.

"I bet I know something you've never done before in your whole existence," I murmured, licking my lips.

My motion captured his lust-filled gaze. "Never bet Death," he rumbled. "Especially when he owns a casino."

Fighting the smile, I said, "What should we wager?"

His hands finally rested on my bare ribs. His touch was infuriatingly light again. Need pounded at my center. I wanted him to press his hands against me, slide them over my breasts and then lower.

"The usual would entail your soul but..." He trailed off.

"Right, vampire," I said, with understanding. "Well, how about I collect my winnings later, then."

Then before he could say anything else, I gave into my impulse and kissed him. Our lips were already wet from the pool and slid against each other with a sensuous heat. I sighed against his mouth as he coaxed mine open. When our tongues met, fireworks exploded inside me. All rational thought slipped away as I drowned in the taste of him.

I was right. I could die like this. I wouldn't even be mad about it.

Grim kissed deeply, thoroughly, awakening every nerve ending in my being. The pressure of his lips promised sex that would flay the skin from my very body. There was raw, desperate hunger in his kiss, making me wonder when the last time was that he'd done this.

My legs found their way around his waist of their own accord. His hands dropped to my ass, lining up my sex to his hardness. A tortured moan escaped my throat as the underwater friction stoked the incredible need inside me.

More. Everything in me screamed for more.

When I pulled away, his dark hair fell into his eyes in a sexy disarray. Danger and barely restrained power emanated off his powerful body. Gold rolled over his irises. It terrified and excited me. I'd seen Grim's death mask, I'd seen him transform into a beast, and I watched him rip the soul out of someone with a violence I'd never known existed.

I wasn't sure if there was monster in this man, or a little man in the monster.

Either way, my demons wanted to dance with him.

"It appears as though I will be the one collecting any winnings here," Grim said. There was an edge, or maybe a promise, in his words.

I did my best to rein my raging need back in. "Oh, *that* wasn't what I was talking about."

He raised an eyebrow in question.

Then with a coy smile, I brushed my thumb over his full lower lip and said, "You're it." Then lifting my legs, I planted my feet on his chest underwater and launched myself away from him.

24

Vivien splashed away from me while laughing maniacally. Did she seriously just engage me in a game of tag?

I wondered what she would say if I told her I had played water games with Marco Polo himself? She would probably throw her head back and laugh, not caring how loud or who heard it.

Suddenly my only mission became to see if I could make her laugh with abandon. Sliding into a breaststroke, I sought to close the distance between us. While she could swim, she was not particularly elegant or fast, splashing heavily in her attempts to flee me. Even fully clothed, I'd easily overtake her.

Vivien glanced over her shoulder and caught sight of me. Her splashing doubled. My heart pounded with excitement, and it took a second to realize I was grinning from ear to ear. She squealed as I gained on her.

Diving under the water, I decided I would go for a sneak attack and avoid her splashing at the same time.

My fingers nearly brushed her bare back when something made impact with the water with a thunderous blast. I was about to start for the surface again when I saw a large, dark figure smash into Vivien's form.

I shot forward, buoyed by my power, and grabbed the assailant. We tumbled underwater, away from Vivien. I was unable to see if she'd gotten out of the pool as I grappled with a muscular individual who not only matched me in strength but in speed.

When I realized the identity of my opponent, I disengaged and was up and out of the pool in little time. I found a dripping Vivien, pale as a ghost now, her eyes were wide, pupils dilated with fear. Water also sluiced off my fully clothed form as the other man stepped out of the pool. I kept myself in between them, my stance rigid and ready in case he went for her again.

Similar in height, the other man was slimmer than me, but packed in muscle. His features were lighter than mine, and his left eye, marred with a ghoulish slash of scar tissue, glowed blue. "Anu," he said. "We must kill the sekhor."

"Anu?" I heard Vivien repeat to herself quietly.

"I need her, brother," I said, slightly bowing my head. If it came to blows, I would fight to keep him off her, but I prayed it wouldn't.

"Anubis, we have no time for this," he said, stalking forward.

My fingers elongated into demonic talons and my fangs lengthened. My skin turned black as silt as I stepped forward. I released my power as I broke out into my god-likeness that was over seven feet tall. Fabric audible ripped around my muscles form as I now resembled a hellish black dog beast on two legs. In my periphery, Vivien shivered. Some had described my power as standing next to oblivion.

It was disorienting and chilled most to the marrow of their bones.

My voice was gravelly, monstrous. "I do not wish to fight you, brother. You are as powerful as I, and a collision between us would undoubtedly result in collateral damage."

Straightening from his aggressive stance, my brother's mouth parted but he had no response. I knew I'd bewildered him, but it couldn't be helped.

"Anu, have you lost your mind?" he asked. "She is a sekhor. She cannot be permitted to live. If you won't end her, I will."

"I know what I'm saying does not make sense, but you must trust me, brother."

Fallon's gaze turned to Vivien, casting her in the glow of his blue light. I could tell he was debating whether or not to attack.

"So you don't trust me?" Indignation filled me. My power whipped out around me like a hundred asps, snapping at the air with fury. My muscles swelled, ripping through my shirt and pants. "Then you will have to go through me to get to her." My face cracked and changed into the full black muzzle of a monstrous jackal. I growled, showing off my teeth, eyes glowing. My voice became even more grizzled. "Is this what you want?"

Fallon straightened, and gritted his teeth. He pointed at Vivien. "You know what the others would do if they knew she was alive. They would not be so trusting."

I roared. "I am handling the situation."

Fallon lifted his chin and gave me a short nod, though his face was still twisted with displeasure at not getting to kill Vivien on the spot.

With that, I turned. Vivien stared up at me, her eyes round, genuine fear shining in them. I wouldn't give Fallon a chance to change his mind. I picked Vivien up in my arms and sped off. I took a secret route around the back of the hotel to a door that was hidden from everyone else. I threw it open and led us to an elevator that would take us to the penthouse. I had to duck down to fit in the elevator. Once inside, I set Vivien down.

I closed my eyes and took a deep breath, allowing my body to calm back into human form. My shirt was gone, and my pants were tattered. As soon as my claws receded back to the normal pads of human fingertips, I smashed the top button.

Emotions crashed against each other inside me. I couldn't think straight. Was it mere minutes ago we were in the pool splashing each other? Kissing each other until I'd damn near lost all control. I'd lost sight of the danger, and I was cursing myself for being so foolish. Hadn't I learned that fun, as Vivien called it, led to nothing but trouble and chaos?

As for Vivien, I avoided meeting her gaze, reluctant to see her fear or disgust at having seen my beast form. We rode the elevator in silence. Thankfully, the few guests had all vacated the pool area when Vivien an I had our interlude, and didn't witness the fight or my transformation. One less mess for Timothy to clean up.

Surprise registered on Vivien's face when the doors opened into the library of my penthouse, parting the bookshelves. While the elevator I'd used to ferry Vivien from the lobby of Sinopolis up to my abode only made three stops, the third being my antechamber, the secret lift that opened to my library ran on a far more complex route. And there was absolutely no chance I would reveal that to Vivien. It was grating enough that I was forced to use the back entrance, revealing it to her at all.

I headed straight to my bathroom, grabbing a towel to dab off any remaining pool water. I hung the towel around my neck and went to my walk-in closet.

"So are you going to tell me?" Vivien asked, standing in my doorway.

"Tell you what?" I asked, my tone stiff, as I went about shifting through my clothes.

"What you are?" Her tone was soft, careful, as if she feared I would turn around and bite her head off. She should be worried.

"I'm Death. You know this," I snapped. Anger and confusion writhed in me like live wires.

Why am I angry? I managed to count several reasons straight away.

Because I couldn't tell Fallon the extent of the sekhor problems. I was doing my best to deal with the matter quickly and quietly, but if he got the others involved, it would become a mess of catastrophic proportions.

And now it appeared as though I was keeping secrets rather than protecting my family. I didn't care about appearances, but I respected my brother and it seemed as though I chose a sekhor over him.

The next thought was far more disturbing. I *had* chosen Vivien over my brother. I needed Vivien so I could find the master, but it was more than that. I was no longer certain I could kill her.

The chilling realization came over me. No matter how I reminded myself of my duty, I had developed feelings for Vivien. I wanted her. I wanted to tear that bikini off with my teeth and work her from front to back until she forgot her name a second time. Even more so, she made me laugh. She was stubborn, rebellious, a loose cannon, while also observant, savvy, and unlike any one I had ever met. And I had encountered a staggering number of souls, yet she still stood out, a bright burning star amongst a billion meteors.

"If it doesn't matter, then you can tell me," Vivien said, a harder edge in her tone.

I turned to face her, emotions still boiling under the surface. There was hesitance in her eyes, yet she continued to push. It seemed to be her nature, the fool woman.

"You really want to know?" With all the deliberate menace of a predator, I closed in on her, yet she didn't recoil or back away. Instead, Vivien lifted her chin, her eyes conveying that she could handle anything I threw her way.

Well, we'd find out.

"I am a god."

25

A god?

I laid a hand against the doorway of Grim's massive closet to hold myself up, since my legs had magically been replaced by rubber. My stomach took an icy plunge as the gears in my brain did their best to turn faster. I imagined tiny people running around the pink matter in my skull yelling to each other in a panic.

How is she processing, Jenkins?

Doesn't look good, sir.

Dammit, Jenkins, start pulling all the levers. But for god's sake, keep away from the one that releases drool. We don't need her looking any stupider as is.

I'll try, sir, but we might have to give her all we've got.

Challenge simmered in Grim's eyes. Before, he had been a buttoned-up, repressed kind of scary. What unnerved me was I knew he could change into a terrifying, powerful being any instant, but I didn't know when or what would provoke it.

Now, he was entirely wild and primal. I preferred this

unhinged, ferocious side of him. Like I was looking into the beast's eyes, knowing exactly what I was facing.

"Okay, you're a god. The god of death." I repeated that in my head a couple more times and tried to maintain eye contact. "Your brother, is he a god?" I asked slowly. "And Bianca?"

Grim nodded.

I blanched. "Timothy?"

He nodded a second time.

"Your ex?" When had my voice gotten so quiet?

Grim fixed me with that penetrating stare. There was no need for him to nod again. I got the picture. I was in the midst of literal gods. My pea-sized brain was likely to explode if I thought too hard about it, so I silently named the Kardashians to keep from melting down.

A god. A god? Sure. It checked out. Because right now, I was one thousand percent convinced Grim was a sex god.

Every cell of my body vibrated in awareness at being near the half-naked master of death. Excuse me, god of death.

The suspicions I'd had about what he was hiding under those suits were confirmed. He had lickable, cut abs, and the most perfect, muscled arms. A tattoo covered his left shoulder and dipped down over his bicep. It was a skull in a pharaoh's headdress. His torso V-eed down into what remained of his pants, which rode dangerously low on his hips. Grim's state of undress didn't help my processing abilities one bit.

And Jenkins accidently pulled the drool lever. I bit my lip to keep it at bay.

"Your brother called you Anu," I said, sucking back saliva and trying to make sense of it all. It was the pieces to a story I'd once heard but couldn't remember.

Grim pressed a hand on the door jamb over my head, leaning in close. Chlorine and Grim's masculine scent invaded my space. "I am the god of the dead, also known as Anubis."

"The Egyptian god," I whispered. Things snapped into place. How had I not seen it before? His reapers were jackals. The form he'd taken by the pool resembled a giant, monstrous jackal. Hell, even his décor screamed a blend of modern and ancient Egyptian. The antechamber was something right out of a Mummy movie. The guy lived in a literal pyramid. How had I missed it?

I mean, you were turned into a vampire and forgot your own name. Maybe you get a break for not recognizing ancient mythology come to life.

Digesting the idea I was running around town with Death had already been a huge leap. I liked to think I handled that news shockingly well. But information was piling on in layers and I was struggling to keep up.

Despite the newfound revelation, a hundred more questions swirled around me. Any other person probably would have thought through their questions to pick out the most pertinent ones, but I blurted the first one that came to mind.

"What are you doing out of Egypt?"

Grim's dark, brooding expression gave way to surprise as he dropped his arm and straightened. "That's your first question?" Just like that, the edge of his beast melted away, and Grim was somewhere in between the wild and the restrained.

Oh blood clots. That was the dumbest first question. Why couldn't I have asked something else. But now that I'd asked it, I couldn't think of anything else.

He stepped back. "As the world has expanded, the gods

have spread far and wide, spending a great deal of time on different parts of the globe."

"Is that why Bianca more resembles a barbie than an Egyptian?" I asked.

Grim pulled on the ends of the towel around his neck, causing his arms to flex. My stomach leapt then dropped in a fantastic somersault. All my parts screamed yay, while throwing their arms in the air as if at a concert, screaming for an encore. Again, I became incredibly aware I was wearing nothing but a bikini. My hair dripped on his carpet.

Focus. You are in way over your head without layering in the intense fiery attraction you feel toward him.

"Because," Grim explained, "Bianca spent centuries in Europe and the Netherlands. We adapt to our environment over time, which includes our appearance and names."

I shot him a suspicious look. "So you chose an Italian gangster name because you hung out with the mob for a long time?"

His brows drew together.

Maybe not.

I needed to ask better questions. "Why don't gods like sekhors? You said immortality corrupts absolutely. If the gods are also immortal, then why is it okay for you to live forever, but not for me?" First came pride, followed by indignance once I realized how good my question was. I stuck my hands on my hips.

Grim's fingers flexed around the towel. "It is exactly as I told you. Humanity can be corrupted. As gods, we never had humanity to begin with."

I pointed a finger at him. "Aha! You are the one who is soulless, then."

Shaking his head, with a slight roll of his eyes. "No. We do not have souls. We are divine beings. It's not the same."

"Well, if you can live forever without turning evil, so can I. So to keep my crystallized soul from atrophying, I need to do the soul's version of push-ups. Maybe that means volunteering at the soup kitchen regularly. That would do the trick."

He shook his head, a frown tugging at his lips again. "It is difficult to explain."

"I'm immortal too, I've got time," I said, pointing at my wrist where a watch would be.

"Sekhors were once slaves to the gods."

My jaw dropped so hard, I was sure it hit the ground.

"Exsqueeze me?"

"For many centuries we lived in symbiosis, providing for each other. But the sekhors always turned power hungry and countless cities were plunged in fire and bloodshed. Finally, it was decided the sekhors could be no more. If they were wiped out, the destruction would cease."

That was it? The vampires were violent and cruel and so the gods exterminated them. I swallowed hard, finally meeting a pill I couldn't swallow.

A phone rang, causing me to jerk.

Grim crossed over to a set of drawers, opening the top. There was a lineup of cellphones on a velvet cloth. Picking up the one that was ringing, Grim answered, his eyes still on me. He didn't say a word, and I couldn't tell if he was trapped in the moment with me or if he was intently listening.

Even though the eight-foot monstrous form he took by the pool was pee-my-pants scary, he had fought his own brother off to protect me.

Because he needs you for bait.

Still, seeing him go all protective had made me feel things I hadn't quite processed. It had sparked something in me. Hope? I immediately tried to bat away the notion. What did I think? He was going to keep me alive and ask me to be his girlfriend? He was Death. The ancient death god, Anubis.

Then something new occurred to me. It should have been my very first thought, but the little dudes running my brain were working overtime as it was.

If the Original who was in a coma was a god, did that mean I was given a god's blood?

"Yes, thank you for letting me know, Timothy. We are on our way." Grim turned the phone off. "We need to go, now." His tone brooked no argument.

But I wanted to brook. I wanted to brook hard.

We weren't done talking about this. And next time there would be more clothing, less drool, and more answers.

26

Once the door opened, I dropped the pizza box, so it was no longer obstructing my face under the ball cap. "Hiya, Skip," I said.

Skip's eyes flew open. He tried to shut the door but a hand stopped him. Grim pushed his way into the apartment and I followed, kicking the door shut. It crunched in the frame behind me.

Right, vampire strength.

I needed to cool it. But excitement thrummed under my skin. I was finally going to get some answers.

Grim pointed at the La-Z-Boy recliner. "Sit."

Skip opened his mouth to protest, but Grim's eyes glowed like molten gold.

Skip's butt hit the chair so fast he almost sent the entire thing flying backward. His foot bounced in agitation. I grimaced. Socks with sandals. God, I hoped Grim was wrong and this wasn't my boyfriend. I'd just die if I found out I was hooking up with one of those socks-with-sandals guys.

Or, I mean, die again.

I set the ball cap and pizza box on a beat-up wood table. I'd changed into dark pants and a halter top again.

"You know her?" Grim asked, his voice reverberated with monstrous echoes.

Skip's wild eyes volleyed back and forth between us.

"Today, genius," I snapped.

Skip nodded.

"What's your name?" Grim's menace was palpable, rolling off him in heavy, black waves. All of it was directed at Skip.

"Dev—Devon Seward."

"He's lying," I said. I knew very little, but I knew I drank blood, I wanted Grim naked, and this dude's name was Skip.

Grim held up his hand at me. Oh no he didn't. Did he give me "talk to the hand"? 'Cause I might bite it right off.

"What's her name?" Grim asked next.

Confusion flickered over Devon's face, as if he were wondering if this were a prank of some kind. Skip, or Devon, looked back and forth between Grim and me, until he realized the punchline wasn't coming. "Jane," he stuttered again.

Something dropped to the bottom of my stomach. Recognition. Disappointment.

So much for fancying myself as a Vivien or Persephone.

"Last name?" Grim probed. Dark clouds of death continued to curl up and around his shoulders, choking the air. Even I felt the oppression of Grim's power.

"I— I don't know, man. I just know her name is Jane." Devon's voice was strangled, nearing hysteria. Tears leaked out of the corners of his eyes.

"How do you know her?" Grim dropped his scare-o-meter a couple levels. Good call, because it looked like it took all of Skip's focus to not crap his pants right on the gray leather seat.

Skip's words tripped all over each other as he cried, "She's a bounty hunter."

Every fiber of my being stilled as I digested that.

I was a bounty hunter.

Did that feel right to me? Searching inward, I thought of what Grim said. How I could fight, knew things only a sketchy criminal would. How I was able to track Skip by combing his hotel room. I'd even tracked down Chad when I needed information.

When I met Grim's eyes, he seemed to be waiting for confirmation from me. I swallowed, my throat suddenly dry. "Skip. You call someone who runs out on bail a skip."

Devon's words sunk into my gut, full of truth. I knew he was right, while the rest of my memories and my identity remained elusive.

Stepping forward, I took control of this inquisition. "Do you know me because you've tried skipping bail before, Devon?"

Getting a hold of himself, Devon shook his head. "No, I just know you've been tracking me down. My ex said you came by the house a couple weeks back and texted me a picture from her doorbell with the camera and told me you were trying to find me."

"Were you busted for showing up to the party with drugs, Devon?" I asked, putting my hand on either side of his chair like Grim had done with me. I wanted Devon to feel pinned down, small, and trapped. That was how Grim had made me feel repeatedly. I wanted Devon to squirm the way I had. I would punish him for my disappointments.

"Yeah, they text and I make room deliveries." Now that Grim wasn't the one in his face, some of Devon's attitude returned. "And you're hassling me for providing a service. If it weren't me, it would be someone else. You should keep your bitch nose out of my business."

Dark, soul-sucking power flared behind me when Devon called me a bitch. "Oh, you are going to be sorry you said that," Grim said in an airy tone. He didn't move, giving me ample room to work.

A line formed between Devon's bushy eyebrows as he peeked over my shoulder. "You going to sic the monster back on me?"

Grim chuckled darkly. "He thinks *I'm* the monster here."

It took Devon a second to turn his perplexed focus back to me. Opening my mouth, I let my fangs elongate and hissed in his face. The piercing shriek that came out of Devon could have cracked glass as he jumped up in his seat. I punched him out cold, shutting him up.

We stood there in Devon's shitty apartment in silence for a long moment.

"Jane," I said finally, before making a face. "Blech." At least there was no way my last name was also Doe. Right?

"It's enough to go off of," Grim said. "Between your profession and your first name along with this," he sneered at Devon's prone form, "young man, we have all we need to dig up the rest."

Meeting his level gaze, I asked the obvious question. "Why would a master vampire want a bounty hunter?"

"I don't know," he said. "But we'll find out."

I walked out of Devon's apartment with purposeful strides, though I wasn't looking where I was going. I felt numb. My past was about to be unlocked.

What, did I really think I was some big shot police detective? It didn't matter. But there was someone out there who missed me, needed me, was searching for me. Someone, or several someones, were up all night with worry, wondering where I was, and I would find them.

GRIM WAS RIGHT. It took little time for Timothy to uncover my identity. From the moment we pulled up to the address registered under my name, I understood why I thought I was a baker. I lived in an apartment directly above a business called "The Cupcakery."

I didn't have my key but breaking the lock was simple. I stood at the threshold, hesitant to enter. The smell of freshly baked cakes and sugar saturated my place. The moon was full and bright, lighting up the room so much I didn't bother turning on the light. I couldn't help thinking how the apartment was dead, like me. I didn't want to disturb that.

This was where I would find answers, maybe have my memory jogged. Or perhaps, the part of me that lived in this place had also died and no amount of rooting around in my past would return my sense of self. The urge to turn around and get back into Grim's car almost overwhelmed me. He'd driven here this time instead of using the limo. It would be too conspicuous in this part of town.

Despite my reservations, I forced myself to step inside. There was no walking away now.

Grim followed me in but stood by the door as if sensing I needed a minute.

It was a studio apartment with white walls and old appliances. A quick look in my fridge unveiled some expired yogurts while my freezer was packed frozen meals and ice cream. In the cupboards there was a cup of ramen and two mugs. One was in the shape of a unicorn with a chip out of one side. The other had a bunch of skulls on it and it read

"Death before Decaf." I side-eyed Grim, who raised an eyebrow. He could see it from where he was standing.

My rickety oak table had two mismatched chairs, and the full mattress sat in the corner on the ground. At least it was covered in bright purple flowered bedding. It was one of the most cheerful things I'd ever bought.

It was coming back to me. Memories returned to me with every step I took in my old place. A stack of paperbacks, fifteen books high, sat next to my bed in a precarious tower.

"No family photos," Grim said, his voice low and rumbly, somehow appropriate for the quiet of the room. He was backlit by the light on the stairs as he leaned against the door jamb.

"I don't have family." I touched the table illuminated by a ray of moonlight. Something in my chest twisted with sharp disappointment. "Or, not family I've talked to in a long time. My parents died when I was young. I went to live with my aunt and uncle. We didn't get along. They wanted me to act a certain way, to fit their perfect life, and I wanted to live on my own terms."

I waited for him to say something snarky, but he refrained. Must have damn near killed him.

Over the last couple weeks, I'd imagined every possibility from being a police officer, a scientist trying to cure cancer, to a baker with a husband and a couple kids.

The reality was small, grim, and depressing compared to all my theories. Worse yet, I was alone. No family, no friends. No one had missed me. I'd been missing for over two weeks, and no one was around enough to think anything of it. Part of me used to like that. I could come and go as I pleased without answering to anyone.

But when my memory was erased, I'd painted pictures of

what I wanted my life to look like. I did something important, and I was surrounded by people who loved me. The reality did not measure up. I set a hand on the table, holding myself up against the sinking, sucking feeling at my center.

I breathed in the smell of sugar and cake to calm myself. Touching the charm at my neck, I remembered the bakery owner downstairs had given it to me for my birthday one year, along with my favorite cupcake. Her name was Cheri, and she was always nice to me and made good coffee. We weren't close enough to be considered friends, but in my mind we were. She was the closest thing I knew to a friend but going in every week for something sweet didn't exactly constitute a real relationship. In her eyes, I was a regular. Still, the necklace meant more to me than she knew.

"I've been a bounty hunter for three years." I continued to stroke the dented and marred wood of the table. "Before that, it had been a string of shitty, odd jobs. But I'd finally found something that truly suited me."

"Hunting people?" Grim asked, finally straightening.

"Yeah," I said, musing. "What does that say about me?"

Grim walked over to stand on the other side of the table from me. Shadows still covered his face, and I was grateful I couldn't see his expression. The god of death himself must have felt so debased to step into such a small, shitty abode.

"It means whatever you want it to."

I snorted. "I live like a trash panda, hunt sketchy criminals for a living, and no one noticed I was missing."

Grim rounded the table and caught my chin in his hand, taking me by surprise. "You are not judged by what you do, or even how loved you were. What matters is that you lived in a way that was true to your soul."

The moonlight hit his eyes, turning them into liquid amber. Then I felt as though we were encased in a bubble.

There was safety and warmth in our private pocket. No matter he was the most lethal being on Earth, the need to step fully into his arms was overwhelming. I wanted to melt into Grim. Let him kiss me senseless even if he killed me when he was done.

I spent so much time keeping people at a distance since my parents died, even though I told myself I wanted it that way. But these last few days, forced to be his prisoner, we'd come to understand each other. Granted, we annoyed and infuriated each other, but there was a seed of intimacy at its center.

Grim was the only one who cared if I lived, even if it was to use me as bait. And suddenly, more than anything, I wanted him to need me.

My voice was hoarse when I spoke. "Are you telling me people who win the popularity contest don't get an automatic pass-go card?"

He stepped in closer, his thumb lightly brushing my chin now. "I'm saying I am an excellent judge of soul and *you* have lived in such close alignment with yours that you don't know how to do or be anything else."

My vision blurred, but I continued to meet his gaze. Grim dripped his head, lips nearing mine. His fingers skimmed along my jawline as they slipped into my hair at the base of my skull, causing hot tingles to race up and down my spine.

Despite not needing to breathe, I became lightheaded, practically vibrating with need. My hand flattened against the table, bracing for what I knew would come. My eyes drifted closed.

The lights flicked on, chasing away our intimacy with a harsh brightness. Grim and I jumped apart.

Timothy stood there, an eyebrow raised as he examined

the two of us. He'd come in a separate car, having to handle something first before joining us. After a moment of tense silence, he asked, "Find anything that would lead us to the master?"

"My laptop," I blurted out. I turned and went to my bed. Lifting the far edge of my mattress, I pulled out an old, refurbished computer.

Opening it up, it didn't take long to boot. I didn't remember my password, but my fingers flew with muscle memory, typing it in automatically.

The first thing to pop up was a mug shot of a man. There was a smile tugging at the corner of his mouth as if he kept a secret that he never planned to share with anyone. Thin blond hair, light eyes, and a trimmed beard. He looked average, unremarkable, yet setting eyes on him made my skin crawl.

Grim placed his hand on my lower back to alert me of his presence as he leaned in. "Landon Crane. Says he was arrested for an outstanding number of parking tickets. He missed his court date two months ago, and no one has been able to get a hold of him. They thought he was on the run."

My body went as cold as when I'd woken up in that freezer. I focused on the heat of Grim's hand as I dug my knuckles into the table on either side of my laptop. "It was supposed to be easy money. I found him on a dating site and set up a date. I'd done it a couple times at this Italian restaurant. I'd get the skips to leave with me before dinner showed up. I'd give them the idea I was hot and heavy to put out. Most of them fell for it, but not this guy," I said, shaking my head.

"Why didn't you arrest the marks the moment you found them?" Timothy asked, his tablet away for once.

"Not only was it better to have a drink and let their

defenses down, I liked the restaurant owners. They knew what I was doing and the waitstaff knew to not even put in the food orders. I didn't want their place to get trashed. I usually got the skips to follow me out through the back where I could cuff them in the alley without causing a fuss."

Grim's fingers skimmed my bare back with reassuring pressure, out of Timothy's eyeline. "What happened?"

"I tried to get to the restaurant fifteen minutes earlier than my date, but Crane was already there." I remembered my instincts being on high alert, though I couldn't pinpoint why. Crane seemed friendly and relaxed. He was a middle class, white-collar worker from some tech company. The most interesting things about him were he enjoyed gadgets from Brookstone and went to ball games when he had the time.

"When I suggested we take the party somewhere else, he said he liked things to go slow. I could tell he wouldn't budge, so we chatted a while."

Grim's hand stilled. "What about?"

I wished he would continue his light massage but didn't say anything about it. "Not much. I told him my cover story, how I was an Uber driver in between jobs. Gives men a chance to tell you what they think you should do, and you learn a lot about them real quick. He didn't. I got the sense he knew I was lying. Instead, we drank wine and talked about..." I searched my memory. "Fires and ice, maybe something about global warming. It's fuzzy."

Timothy shook his head as if he tried to find any significance in that and failed.

"What then?" Grim prodded, stroking my back again.

"Nothing." I shrugged. "I don't remember anything after that. I woke up a cold block in a corpse drawer."

Timothy and Grim exchanged a look. "This man is

either our master or connected to him," Timothy said. Then gesturing toward my laptop, he asked, "May I?"

Nodding, I backed up while he used his tablet to snapshot all pertinent information. My back pressed against Grim, his hands holding my arms. He didn't touch me like he had when we first met. A piece of meat he needed to make sure didn't make a getaway. It was more as if he were trying to steady me, reassure me he was there. I turned my head and looked up into his eyes.

His amber depths seemed to hold apprehension and regret. As if he was also aware my usefulness was almost fulfilled, and he knew our time would soon come to an end.

I told myself I was projecting. I was the one who didn't want to die. I was the one who wanted to lean up and kiss those lips again. I wondered if he'd give me one last kiss, or hey, maybe a roll in the sack before he killed me. His hands dropped away, leaving my skin cold as he took a step back.

Then I remembered he was Anubis, the Egyptian god of the dead. I still hadn't had time to absorb what all that meant. But I did suspect gods didn't offer parting bangs to vampires on the chopping block.

Timothy spoke while he worked on my laptop. "I may have some resources, or perhaps Ms. West would help me see about further looking into this man's identity."

I ripped my gaze away from Grim to look at Timothy as I said, "Leave Miranda out of it. I know she wants to help, but she's in over her head and I don't want her or her kid to get hurt."

"Agreed." Grim walked across the apartment to look out the window.

Timothy stood, tucking his tablet under his arm. "I'm on this. I'll take the car back to Sinopolis, then send the driver back to pick you up to give you some more time to...investigate." He gave us a nod, but his eyes lingered first on me, then shot Grim a look before making his exit.

"So," I said, blowing out a breath. "I guess my name isn't Vivien."

Grim didn't say a word.

I swung my arms back and forth, trying to loosen the tight knot that had formed in my chest. "I'm a Jane. A plain Jane." Then I muttered, "Serves me right."

"I think Vivien suits you," he said, turning to look at me. "You should keep it."

I bit my lower lip.

"Truly," he went on. "You died and have been reborn, for all intents and purposes. And I'm not so sure Jane could face off with Vivien." One side of his lips lifted.

"Ya think?" I asked, releasing my lower lip. "Well, Vivien has had enough of memory lane for today. So it's back to my prestigious job as worm on a hook." Then with a laugh, I said, "Maybe I should wriggle right here. See if the master or his minions show up at my pad."

The windows to our right exploded as a figure launched through them. I closed my eyes against the assault of glass. More windows smashed, and I heard numerous pairs of boots hit the ground. When I opened my eyes again, I found ten people in my apartment. No, not people. Sekhors.

"I would hate if a million dollars and a bazooka would appear in my hands," I announced loudly.

Unfortunately, my magic trick only worked with the first thing I said. Damn.

27

M y hands elongated into claws so I could rip the sekhors apart. Vivien was next to me, kicking, punching, and smashing through our assailants. Sharp incisors cut through my arms, my legs, my back and chest as they threw themselves at me. Those who sunk their teeth into my flesh had to die first. They could not be allowed to drink the blood of a god.

No matter how many vampires I decapitated or shredded, more kept coming. The smell of their blood hung heavy in the air and splattered the walls. When they first came smashing through the windows, I pushed Vivien behind me, intending to fight all of them off. But in no time, they overwhelmed me, engaged her and drew her out. Slowly but surely, she was forced to move farther away from me. They were intentionally separating us.

"Vivien," I yelled.

Her eyes met mine, just before a bag was thrown over her head. Three sekhors tied her in rope and carried her away.

I fought to follow, but there were six sekhors on me. One

bit into my leg, tasting my blood, then another on my arm. I could not allow a single one of them to drink my blood and live, which prevented me from getting to Vivien. I was losing time as distance expanded between us.

Rage screamed through me in a fiery blaze, and the thick black smoke of my power filled the room. Violence overtook me as the look on Vivien's face before she was taken burned in my mind. Then I let it out in a piercing howl as my body exploded into monstrous muscle and sinew, my skin turning as black as the sand of the Nile. My sharp fangs sunk into the head of a sekhor before I ripped it off. Blood fountained from his decapitated neck.

I'd kill them all and find Vivien if it was the last thing I did.

When I returned to Sinopolis, Timothy was there to meet me at the private entrance. I was covered in blood, naked, and bite marks abounded. Despite my appearance, he didn't stop to comment. He followed me to the elevator, tablet up.

"I tried to keep Ms. West out of it, but she insisted. With her help, and a chat with our reapers, Acissej, Llij, and Ekoorb, we were able to find out who Landon Crane actually is. The man may have been arrested for unpaid parking tickets, but he is guilty of far worse." Without waiting for me to prompt him, he barreled on. "Mr. Crane has been stalking and murdering women for the past twenty years. There have been seven in total, so far. I'm sure if we interviewed with more of our reapers we will dig up even more." He followed me into the penthouse and into my room. I pulled a black tee-shirt over my head, pulling it down, not bothering to clean up the blood on me.

Then I tugged on a pair of sweatpants. I didn't know if I'd have to change back into my god-likeness again and sweats were more forgiving.

I had judged the souls of stalkers and murderers. Often, parts of their souls were missing, or turning rancid. Hate and evil was a cancer that rotted their souls. I knew their kind all too well.

"How did he choose his victims?" I asked.

Timothy pulled up a gallery of photos. Young, blonde, blue-eyed, fair-skinned women. I remembered the gymnasts I'd fought at Wolf Town. They matched Crane's tastes. If Landon Crane was the master vampire, that still didn't explain why he wanted Vivien. She had auburn hair, emerald eyes, and was made of fire.

Timothy's lips had all but disappeared. "What do you think his plan is?"

I shook my head. "I don't know, but he has Vivien. I have to find her. I need to get her back."

"You mean, you have to find the master, so you can kill him?"

A snarl emitted from my throat as I jerked my head up to meet Timothy's eye.

Instead of responding to my aggression, he maintained a cool, calm demeanor. "Sire, the sekhor. You know none of the others would permit Vivien to live, especially not *him*."

He wasn't talking about the master. My aide was referring to the one being I answered to. Whatever *he* commanded must be obeyed by all.

"I'm not going to let anyone hurt her." The words flew out of my mouth before I could think.

I waited for Timothy to tell me it was impossible, unreasonable, and dangerous. But losing Vivien had thrown me off the rails, and I was hanging on by a single strand. If it snapped, the nearest being to me would feel my wrath before I tore this world apart to find her.

There was a crash out in the main room. Timothy and I ran out in a flash to find Ms. West stalking toward us. The whites of her eyes nearly swallowed up her dark irises. "Jamal is missing."

Timothy and I exchanged a glance. My aide voiced my thoughts. "The master tried to use Ms. West against Vivien, so we can infer that..."

Miranda pointed a finger at us. "That you are going to help me find my son or I'll bury both of you." Rage rolled off her in waves. She was a guided missile, seeking her son, and she'd destroy anything in her way. Despite being a mere mortal, I believed her when she threatened there would be hell to pay if we didn't find Jamal.

Then Miranda seemed to finally register my bloody, unkempt state. "Where's Vivien?"

I wasted no time heading for the elevator. Miranda and Timothy followed. "She's been taken."

Bianca's words returned to me. *Don't let her out of your sight.* My gut clenched.

"What are these vampires planning?" Miranda asked me, as we stepped out into the hotel. Her eyes were stamped with fear and fury.

"I don't know, but I don't plan to wait around and find out. I know someone who can help," I said as Timothy and Miranda kept pace with me across the black marble floor.

The reapers were out searching for a trail of bodies, but it was taking too long. I had to find Vivien and I refused to wait.

"That's unadvisable, sire," Timothy said, his voice tight.

"Who?" Miranda asked.

"Someone who has the ability to find the vampires," I said.

Miranda's jaw set. "Then do it."

Timothy put an arm in front of me to halt my steps. I wanted to throw him across the room for getting in my way, but I controlled myself.

That's all I'd been doing, I realized. Controlling myself. Around Vivien, stopping myself for reaching out though I wanted her. She'd sparked something inside of me and now that she was missing, the fire I'd felt had gone missing with her.

Unlike with Qwynn, I wasn't Vivien's plaything to manipulate and contort. Vivien was bold, irreverent, while also playful, intentional, and relentless in the pursuit of what she wanted. And I didn't intend on losing her and adding to my long list of regrets.

Timothy spoke to Miranda. "Give us a moment."

Recovering her child was all that mattered, but Ms. West saw the look in Timothy's eye and dutifully walked out the front doors of the hotel and paced out front.

Timothy was also a god, and though his power and talents were vastly different from mine, I could tell he needed to have his say on this matter. "If you go to Bast, she will likely kill Vivien."

"And you care if she lives?" I asked. "Admit it, man, you are worried I won't kill her when the time comes. You say I should worry about the others, but you are the one concerned."

"Viven poses a threat. That is undeniable, even if she doesn't know it. But I have transcribed enough of time and life to know that nothing is certain, especially not a person's nature." Timothy shook his head. "But you are the one who has grown attached. I'm beginning to think you don't care about the rules anymore."

"So what if I don't?" I said, my tone freezing him out.

"Consarn you, you are losing yourself and you can't see it." Timothy reverted to older curses when he was deeply stressed. Though I didn't need his words to tell me that, a line of worry had gathered around his eyes. "Regardless of what you and I believe about Vivien, there will be consequences if she lives."

"I will deal with her when the time comes." I said the words, but they came out hollow, empty of promise.

"Anubis." Timothy's voice gained a hard edge he rarely used. "Are you willing to throw the world into chaos for this sekhor?"

"This is about finding the master," I snapped. "I know my duty. Don't think I've forgotten it for a single second." I was done with this conversation. I needed to act. I needed to find Vivien and Jamal. I would worry about the details later. Or better, never. That was why I had Timothy, so he could see to those. "Now you and I know there is only one who has a way to find the sekhors." I paused expectantly.

My aide dipped his head. "You'll find her at The Kitty Claw Café."

I WASTED no time traveling up the Strip. Ms. West couldn't sit on her heels, so I sent her to check security footage of anyone who may have been following us. Though Timothy and I knew I was going to the only person who could help.

I pushed the door open to the cat café and bookstore. The smell of fresh coffee, pastries, and new books curled in the air. Tabbies, Siamese, and black cats roamed free throughout the shop. One skittered to avoid my heavy foot falls. Most of the felines had squeezed themselves in the shelves on top of the books. They watched me pass by with lidded eyes. I strode to the back of the café where large windows overlooked the hotel pool below. A woman was curled in an oversized Tiffany-blue chair with a book and a glass of red wine.

"Why Anu," the dark-haired woman said with open surprise. "What are you doing here?" She rose with fluid elegance from her cozy spot, setting aside the wine. A cat jumped from her lap with a discontented meow as she stood. One feline lay along the back of the chair while four more were sprawled nearby. I worked to keep my lip from curling. I never cared for cats.

"I need your help, Bast."

Bast went by the name Galina now, but when I called her by her old moniker, her eyes glowed bright green for a second. I had her full attention.

A line formed between Galina's eyebrows as she took in my bloody, disheveled state. Galina was tall, elegant, and lithe. Black wavy hair was cut above her shoulders. She wore designer yoga pants and a large white sweater that was miraculously free of cat hair.

Feeling the slip of time through my fingers, I had no time to ease her into things. "There are sekhors in our city. I was using one of them as bait to lure out the master vampire when he managed to grab her and take her back to his hideaway. She was my only lead. My reapers cannot track sekhors, but your servants can."

Galina's mouth hung open, gobsmacked. A finger still held her place in the hardback she'd been reading. When she recovered, she grabbed a bookmark on the table next to her and slipped it into the book and set it down. "Really,

Anu, we don't call them servants anymore. They are my envoys." The cat who'd jumped off her lap sat near my feet. It stuck a leg straight up and began to lick its privates. *Lovely.*

"I need your help, Galina," I urged.

Galina slipped an arm through mine. "Tell me everything. How did you discover the presence of the sekhors?"

"We have no time, Galina." I closed my fists, wanting to punch a hole through time and space to get to wherever Vivien was.

Giving me an even look, Galina was thoughtful for a moment. "Do the others know about this?"

"Only Timothy and Bianca. Fallon is aware I am taking care of the situation."

Her mouth tightened into a thin line. "You should have come to me sooner." She made a pss pss pss sound. All the cats straightened, looking at her. A couple gracefully leaped from their shelves and walked to her feet, giving her their full attention.

I didn't explain that I'd intended to take care of the situation quickly and quietly. That alerting the others would create a panic, and gods did not deal well with fear. The aftermath usually left a scorched trail in the earth.

Pupils thinning into slits, her eyes appeared cat-like as they glowed green. Within moments, the cats all dispersed, off to find Vivien. I could only hope they would find her and Jamal in time. Otherwise this world would suffer my wrath.

28

Someone pulled the bag off my head, leaving my hair a wild, staticky mess. I couldn't smooth it back down or away from my face as my hands were currently shackled to the chair I was in. Cold metal bit into my wrists and ankles. The smell of crushed concrete and fresh-cut metal filled my nose, making me want to sneeze.

Blinking against the bright light in my face, I couldn't see past the flood light, but I recognized the scent. We were in the tunnels under the Vegas Strip.

I fought the panic rising up in my chest.

For one day, I'd stayed down in the notorious tunnels before realizing my mistake. There was an abundance of homeless people squatting under the Strip.

When the blood lust hit me, the need to hunt had struck me as hard as when the master stoked it in me. It wasn't just the blood of transients calling to me, I wanted to stalk them in the darkness, maybe let them run a bit before I caught them and drained them. The prospect sent thrills through my entire being. A part of me had whispered, *This is your new nature. Don't fight it. Hunt, drink, kill.*

But I fought it. Fought it hard. I was ready to walk into sunlight before I let my impulses take over.

I'd somehow gotten a hold of myself enough to run to a remote end of the tunnels, far away from any and all persons. I'd been a miserable, hungry, shivering mass, waiting it out until the sun set so I could escape to a more secluded hideaway. The sewers I'd found were not nearly as comfortable as these tunnels, and they sure as hell didn't smell pleasant. But there were no people I could endanger.

But I had endangered Grim. Last I'd seen, he was fighting off the sekhors as best he could. Even with his supernatural strength, they were overwhelming him. Death and violence surrounded him in a black cloud as he fought back. But even a mass of army ants can overtake an elephant. Blood had seeped through his clothes as the vampires latched on like leeches.

Right before I was nabbed, Grim's gold eyes met mine and they flashed with fear and alarm. In that moment, I knew with certainty his concern went beyond keeping me around as a meat snack. Longing and need stretched between us like a physical tether. That is, until I was wrapped up like a sausage and carried away. Grim didn't want anything to happen to me, despite the fact he claimed he'd have to kill me once I'd served my purpose.

My throat tightened with deep longing and the need to know he was okay. I knew he was an immortal god, but the way those sekhors tore into him...they intended to take him apart. My un-beating heart clenched at the thought they could hurt or possibly kill him.

I wanted to be with him so badly, right now. I'd let him judge my outfit, look down his nose at me and I'd poke fun at his perpetual glower. He could even parade me around in an old-timey dress decked out in frills if that's what he wanted. Anything as long as I knew he was okay.

The reality that I'd caught feels for Death and that Death had caught feels for me was so wrong...and yet, so right.

He would come for me. I knew it down to the marrow of my bones.

A figure stepped in front of the lamp. "Hello again."

Gooseflesh rose up along my arms and neck. Fear flooded my mouth with a metallic taste. "You."

My eyes adjusted, taking in the features of Landon Crane. Last time I'd seen him, he'd looked average, harmless. Now, I knew what he was. A wolf in sheep's clothing. "What did you do to me?" I demanded, asking the question that had plagued me for weeks.

"I'd say the question is, what did you do to me?"

Hands held behind his back, Crane wore a striped button-up shirt tucked into jeans with a belt. The combed-back blond hair was thinning at his temples. He'd shaved off his beard, revealing a narrow chin, making him look ten years younger. That secret, unnerving smile pulled at the corner of his lips and his eyes were too fixated, as if he were swallowing information with them. He should be listening and laughing at a co-worker's stories by the water cooler at some tech company, not lurking in the tunnels under the Vegas Strip.

My face twisted with confusion. "*You* turned me into a vampire and dumped me in an alley, then sent a bunch of your sekhors to kill me." It didn't add up.

He rubbed his chin as he stepped away from the lamp. "Yes, I can see how none of this would make sense. But I never intended to kill you. I had sent my people to *retrieve* you." Annoyance thinned his lips and clipped his words. "Unfortunately, the brutes I've been turning sometimes get it in their pea-brains to go off-book. The bloodthirsty beasts are not in the habit of controlling their rage. But I didn't let them hurt you." His eyes rounded and glazed over. "I would never let them hurt you. You're special. The moment they became loose cannons, I grabbed their will and forced them to walk away."

I remembered how Bruiser's face emptied every time he boiled over, then he walked away. Same thing with Milky-eye. The master had pulled the leash on his minions, hard. Well, I killed his doggos in the end.

He smoothed my staticky hair back. "I tried to show you that you and I were meant to be together, but you didn't like the love note I left for you in the alleyway?"

I wanted to jerk my head away, my skin recoiling at his touch. But when I looked into his eyes I saw something more than a mild, inoffensive man.

I remembered this. Something tapped on my brain, waking up an old memory, the moment I realized Landon Crane wasn't who he seemed.

When I walked into the restaurant twenty minutes early, Landon was already seated and waiting. Two glasses of red wine were on the table, but it didn't seem as though he'd touched his. I didn't move to touch the wine either, since I was A) a beer girl, and B) technically on the job.

I'd done my research, looked into his background. Made sure there would be no surprises. Crane had been pulled over and arrested when the officer discovered the car's registration had expired and Crane had several unpaid parking tickets from all around town. Most people didn't realize you aren't allowed to pay parking tickets from jail. They'd released him, but he never paid the tickets, missed his court date, and seemed to all but vanish. That was four months ago.

But I'd found him online under an alias, Landon Bird (clever devil), and gotten him to agree to meet for a date. He was on multiple matchmaking sites. After a brief introduction and exchange of basic information at the restaurant— *Hi, I work as an Uber driver, love puppies, and hope to travel in Europe someday*—I'd pulled my move.

I'd leaned back in my chair and sent him a penetrating look coupled with a seductive half-smile. "Why don't we cut to the chase here, Landon. I'm here to have a good time. While we could sit here, exchange some surface information about ourselves, we both know we are really waiting for what comes at the end of the evening. I like what I see and I'm suggesting we do what two consenting adults all too often deny themselves. Dessert before dinner."

Most dudes were taken aback by my forward approach, but ultimately, I was a breath of fresh air. I took all the work out of the situation and promised a guilt-free nookie cookie most men would happily partake in.

Landon Crane only blinked at me.

I studied him back, wondering if he was slow. "Sex," I finally said. "I'm talking about sex, Landon." The waiter had started to approach but when he heard my words, he did his best to casually pivot past us.

"If we are dispensing with the pleasantries, don't you think there will be something lost to the experience?" he finally asked.

"Are you telling me you aren't interested in sex?"

"On the contrary, I am an avid thrill-seeker." Eyes flicking up to mine, something unidentifiable lurking behind them, he added, "Contrary to my appearance."

I decided to switch to a goading tactic. With a shrug, I

ran my finger around the rim of the wine glass. "True, if I had to guess I'd say your idea of a wild night might be doing your taxes."

Even after all my digging, it seemed his worst sin was that tidy stack of unpaid parking tickets that had gotten out of hand.

"A true thrill-seeker does not seek attention," he said, straightening the napkin in his lap.

What the hell did that mean?

Some men instantly fell over themselves with the need to prove their masculinity or sexuality. But not this guy, cool as a cucumber.

The reality that I might actually have to stay and order food peeved me off. But then again, maybe getting him full and lethargic would add to the ease of slapping cuffs on him once we left the restaurant. Still, I didn't relish spending a meal with this dude. He set my teeth on edge.

I shot him a flirtatious wink and gave him an obvious onceover. "What kinds of thrills do you seek?" I wanted him to take the bait, I wanted to get this over with and get away from this creepy vibe Landon Crane emitted.

"Do you ever wear lipstick?" he asked, changing the subject abruptly. His tone was too even, empty. There was a fathomless hunger about him that yawned open, threatening to swallow me whole.

Suppressing a shiver, I said, "Not unless I have to." I'd opted for a pineapple-flavored Chapstick for a little gloss, but lipsticks were high maintenance and often ended up smeared across my face. I was more a dark eyeliner kind of gal.

"Pity." His eyes slid down to my lips. "You would look famously beautiful in a shade called Fire and Ice."

My blood froze as everything inside me stilled. My

instincts crested in a wave of realization that was so insane it couldn't possibly be true. My imagination was getting away with me. I'd been told that my whole life. Too much whimsy and ridiculous notions. Still, I couldn't shake the thought that gripped my brain. "Can you excuse me for one minute?" I asked with an apologetic smile. "I downed a big gulp earlier and it's come back a-knocking." Landon nodded ever so slightly.

I couldn't feel my legs even as they carried me back to the bathroom. Alarm bells went off in my head, drowning out the sound of the restaurant. Once I'd flipped the lock, I pulled my phone out and pulled up a search.

Fire and Ice lipstick. The parking tickets. They were pieces fast arranging themselves as Landon's voice echoed in my mind. "I'm an avid thrill-seeker."

A number of women's bodies turned up over the last year. Correction, bodies missing their limbs. The news reported the cops suspected a serial killer, but nothing was confirmed. But I took skips to the police station, and I overheard the cops talking about the link between the bodies. Fire and Ice. It was a cheap, common drugstore lipstick, but it had been applied to every girl's lips, postmortem.

I searched my phone for the location of the bodies, discovering what I hoped I'd been wrong about. Crane's vehicle was ticketed relatively close to four of the six. Letting out a breath, I braced myself against the wall. That was too many to be a coincidence.

Could I leave? Pretend I never saw Landon Crane's mug shot? The payout wasn't worth the danger I suddenly felt steeped in. But my damned conscience told me I needed to get him off the streets as fast as possible. I'd talk to the cops at the station, tell them what I found and make it their problem.

After a quick pep talk in the mirror and a splash of cold water on my face, I went back out.

Once I was seated again, Crane said, "For a moment, I didn't think you were coming back."

My laugh sounded forced. "Can't get rid of me that easily."

There was an almost imperceptible change in his demeanor, as he if were listening closer now to what I was saying.

Anxiety crowded in around me until I couldn't breathe. I had no idea if I sounded or acted normal anymore, and not like I was sitting across from a serial killer. "You were saying I'd look good in Fire and Ice? Was that a color your mother wore or something?" From what I knew, serial killers mainly came from messed-up childhoods. Epically messed-up childhoods.

Darkness flickered in his eyes for a moment. "Or something."

Shit, I shouldn't have asked. But now that I had a suspicion about who he was, it was emblazoned in my mind in big neon letters, *serial killer*, complete with blinking arrow pointing at his head.

Landon toyed with the stem of his wine glass. "You're right. Why deny ourselves dessert. Sitting here with you I've become quite...hungry." Then he did something wildly terrifying. He smiled.

I doubted his neighbors would pull any of that, "I never would have suspected that guy of murder." They would one hundred percent be the witnesses saying, "There was always something off about him, but what are you going to do?" Because his smile gave me the absolute willies, like a toy clown from the seventies that was still way too pleased to meet you and your delicious spleen.

Despite his terrifying grin, I was grateful this was almost over. Out the back and a quick car ride to the cops with him in my caged back seat. I threw him a look that was both coy and smoldering.

"But first"—he lifted his glass of wine—"to thrill-seekers."

I picked mine up and our glasses clinked. Usually, I would have only pretended to take a sip but Crane downed his, making pointed eye contact to make sure I did the same. The pinot was decent as it slid down my throat. Hell, it might even help my nerves.

I proposed we exit out the back because I knew a fun spot to get the party started. He threw a twenty on the table and followed me out.

As we walked past the kitchen, I began to feel flushed and lightheaded. My stomach started to churn fire. But it wasn't until the heavy steel door shut behind us, that I realized he'd drugged me.

I wanted to turn around and bang on the door for someone to open it back up. But the thick door automatically locked when shut—usually a bonus, so my skips couldn't run back inside. The kitchen staff was used to ignoring any ruckus in the back alleyway when I was around.

On shaky legs, like a newborn colt, I took two steps, stumbled, took another, then fell into Crane's arms. His words echoed around me as I was swallowed by darkness. "You thrill me."

29

"You drugged me, you son of a bitch. Drank my blood, then tossed me in an alleyway," I yelled at the psychopath standing above me. This was why I didn't like drinking red wine at the Wolf Town Club, and why I refused to accept that Ken-doll's drink. While I didn't consciously remember, my instincts had and they'd been warning me.

Crane continued to pet my hair back even as I jerked to get away. "An unfortunate calculation on my part. But at the restaurant, I knew you were special. Normally I wouldn't even give someone with your features a second glance; I prefer those of a lighter, colder complexion. But you were different from the rest, smarter. I saw it in your eyes when you figured out who I was and what I'd done. I'm not sure how you did it, but I knew the instant you did." He chuckled low. "And how you knew about my mother..." He trailed off, in wonder.

He stepped back, his hand falling from my hair. I desperately wanted to jump under a hot shower until I could scour away his touch. If I had been blonde and blue-eyed, would my limbs be scattered about the state by now? Like all those women he'd tortured and cut into pieces? Undead didn't seem like the worst of the two fates, but it was still out for debate.

He went on. "Do you know how often I am surprised? Rarely. That's why I not only drugged you, I added blood of the Original to your glass when you left for the bathroom. But all the same I wanted you to be the one by my side, helping me plunge the world into fire and make it new. I've been looking for an equal for so long, and I knew I'd finally found the one. I'd say perhaps I've become too much of a romantic when I suggest that you would be my queen in a new land."

Crane said the last bit with the bashfulness of a schoolboy, the sick fuck.

"Hey, psycho, if you wanted me to be your queen, why did you dump me in an alleyway?"

Then with an uncomfortable tug at his collar, he said, "You had a different reaction to the blood than I. When I drank the blood of the Original I changed, while conscious, in a relatively short time. You appeared to actually die."

"So you decided, might as well fit a meal in?" I asked, turning my head to the side to present my scarred neck though it was veiled by my leather ties.

He shrugged, not seeming all that embarrassed. "If you'll remember, we didn't have dinner. I was starving by the time we made our exit. Waste not, want not." Then he grinned. "Though I believe that my feeding on you has psychically bound us. It is why you have been able to hear my dulcet whispers in your mind."

"You made me carve your message into my own hand with a steak knife," I said, fully pissed now. I'd once worried the master vampire had started out like me and twisted into a hateful, monstrous bastard. But this sicko started out perverse and violent, and there was no possibility of my ending up like him.

Kneeling by me, he laid a hand on mine. I wished I could snatch it away, but I was shackled up good.

"Another note of reassurance to let you know I was coming for you. Ever since I learned of your rebirth, I've been desperate to get to you."

"If you were so desperate, how come you didn't come get me yourself?" I asked.

A woman's voice answered for him. "Because he was trying to hide what he'd done."

Qwynn stepped into the light of the cell.

"I knew your skanky ass was caught up in this!" I exclaimed, my shackles rattling.

Her arms were crossed over what appeared to be a number of black straps criss-crossing over her torso and breasts up to a collar that wrapped around her neck. If I didn't know any better, I might think she was biting off my BDSM flavor from the Wolf Town Club.

Half her long, black hair was pulled up into a pony while her eye makeup was dark and seductive. Qwynn's cat-like features were caught between annoyance and amusement. "I have to say, being chained up like a dog suits you."

Then dropping her arms and turning to Crane, her annoyance flared. "You little snake. You tried to hide making a master from me. You will kill her at once, and never think to step out of line again or I'll rip your head off."

Crane was unmoved. He regarded her with cool boredom, as if she were nothing more than a silly, useless girl. I wondered if he was aware she was a goddess. The goddess of manipulative skanks, but to each their own.

"You need me," Crane said in an even tone. "And you

need me happy. If you kill me, all of the sekhors die, and you'll have to start all over again. Except this time, you won't have the element of surprise on the others. Can you really afford to kill me?" He walked over to my side and gripped the back of my neck with cold, clammy fingers. "What does it cost you to let me have a queen so that we can both serve you?"

Qwynn looked close to grinding her teeth, but I guessed she would never do anything so outwardly unattractive. Her eyelids lowered in a scathing look of disdain that would have frozen the blood in any man's veins. "You made another master. Had you simply turned her, we would not be having this conversation."

"I can control her," he replied as if trying to appeal to his mother to let him have a puppy. *I swear I'll pick up after her, walk her, and feed her every day.*

"Fat chance of that." I snorted.

Neither bothered to look at me. "Prove it and you can keep her," Qwynn said.

"Gosh, do you really think you're old enough for such a big responsibility?" I taunted.

Releasing my neck, Crane crossed over to Qwynn, a grin on his face that made my insides turn cold. "I have just the method to demonstrate." He clapped his hands, and one of the sekhors came forward, a bundle slung over his shoulder. He set the small human form on the ground, a bag covering their head, with hands and feet tied. Crane sauntered over to the newcomer, a smile on his face, then pulled the bag off as if performing a magic trick.

My stomach turned to ice as panic exploded inside me. The kid had a gag shoved in his mouth, tear-stained cheeks, and wide eyes full of fear. It was Jamal.

30

Galina's envoys traced the sekhors quickly, but not quick enough to my liking. I wasted no time making my way down to the tunnels below the Strip. I'd texted Timothy and Miranda, telling them to meet me down there. Galina lent me one of her envoys to lead me to the sekhors, while she waited at the mouth of the tunnel for Timothy and Miranda. I didn't know what we were walking into, but I planned to take point.

It was widely known that homeless people nested in these tunnels, and I passed by several cots, piles of clothes, and water-stained paperbacks. But my instincts told me these squatters had cleared out. More accurately, I sensed the death lingering in these tunnels. A perfect hiding spot for the master and his sekhors.

Careful not to make any noise as sound echoed down here, I followed the fluffy white Persian into the darkness.

The cat stopped to lick its paws and I realized Galina's envoy would go no farther. My eyes glowed, casting light into the tunnel. Eventually, it opened up into a large space. A pile of drained bodies was left discarded in a corner.

"She's not yours, you know." A man's voice echoed through the chamber.

Looking around, but seeing no one, I said, "I don't know what you mean."

"I've seen how you look at her. How you protect her." The master. It had to be. His tone was cool and aloof, but underneath I could sense the hungry obsession tinging his words.

The voice seemed to move around me from above—the acoustics causing the sound to bounce. I tried to discern where it was coming from.

"I've been using Vivien to find you," I said, trying to keep him engaged in conversation so I could pinpoint his location.

"No," he hissed. "You came for *her*. I understand. I couldn't resist her either. I'm not sure even she understands, but you do. Jane is special. Her spirit is immutable, and her intelligence is unique. I have taken many a woman, pulled them all apart, and have seen nothing like *her* before."

Crane said it with all the disconnection of a professional surgeon or scientist. He disgusted me.

He went on. "But the moment I saw Jane, looked in her eyes, I knew she'd been through fire already. And now she doesn't fear the burn, the changes that will come because she knows who she is. Do you know how many people actually know themselves?"

My senses stretched outward, as I tried to track where his voice was coming from, but it bounced nebulously in the cavernous space. I tried not to let his words penetrate but I couldn't help agree. Vivien could survive more than even she knew.

"I have shown so many women who they are, put their beating hearts in front of their eyes and they could not handle the truth. But I've seen Jane does not even fear anything. Isn't that the kind of woman you want at your side?"

"Why are you doing this?" I asked. "How did you know to take the blood of the Original?"

"I told him," a feminine voice answered. Qwynn stepped out of one of the tunnels, along with three sekhors behind her.

"Qwynn, have you gone mad?"

She shrugged and walked toward me. "Aren't you tired, Anu? Aren't you tired of having to care for all those souls? Don't you want a break?"

She was trying to get me off track. "Where is Vivien? Where is the child?"

Qwynn cupped my face in her hands. "I did this for you." The usual glint of mischief was missing from her eye. She was serious.

"This shall not be borne," I said.

"Aren't you tired of judging souls? For all eternity, judgment is your burden."

"My responsibilities are important and necessary."

"Not if there aren't any souls to judge." Her eyebrows rose.

"So that's it. If sekhors return to the world, trapping the soul to the body, you think I'll, what...have more time for you?"

"Aren't you tired of living in secret? We are gods, we should rule this world. Yet we are told we must keep our heads down and obey law." For a moment, the façade slipped as she stepped forward, her hands framing my face as she searched my eyes with naked need. "For us. For love, Anu. I am trying to free you. We belong together in a world where we make our own rules and live eternally as we see fit. Join me, and we can use the sekhors to upend this so-called order and take this world."

"At least you can finally admit it," I said, covering her hands with mine. "That you care about nothing except power." I stepped away, moving her hands off me. "You don't want me to spend all my time judging souls, Qwynn? I believe that is the only thing you ever cared about. How much power I wield and trying to bend that power to your will." Letting power flood my voice, it layered and echoed off the tunnel walls. "But it ends now, Qadesh."

Ice entered Qwynn's eyes as she pursed her lips and stepped back. I'd destroyed any and all illusions I would be her ally and lover again. "I should have known you would be like this. You could never think outside of the box. Excuse me," she corrected herself with a snide smile, "the sarcophagus."

I didn't respond with words. I released my power, dark tendrils of death surrounding me. I slammed it into Qwynn, sending her flying across the tunnel until she hit the wall with a boom. The tunnels shook with the impact. She fell to her knees in a crumble of concrete. When she looked up with malice shining in her narrowed eyes, there was still a smug smile curving her lips. "You think we haven't been busy preparing, Anu? Crane," she said louder, "be a dear and send in our friends."

Sekhors emerged from the tunnels on all sides, violent, vacant-eyed soldiers, fangs dripping with saliva. I'd fought my way out of the overwhelming number of sekhors at Vivien's former abode, but there were ten times that amount down here below the city, maybe more. My muscles coiled.

"So sorry, my love," Qwynn said, getting to her feet, step-ping back into the throng of vampires. "They are really all quite hungry and have been told the blood of a god is a delicious ambrosia they can't miss." She disappeared into the darkness of the tunnel as the sekhors erupted in a cry, rushing at me with crazed blood-lust.

I was at a great disadvantage as they came at me from all sides. Not waiting this time, I changed into my god-likeness, bones cracking and muscles lengthening and swelling as I shifted into a massive black jackal. With a roar that reverberated through my being and shook the room, I smashed my fist into a group of sekhors rushing me, and they exploded backward in a wave, downing the sekhors behind them. I threw another punch, raking out my claws and severing the heads of several more.

The bite marks had healed from earlier, but my flesh broke again as they all sought to sink their teeth into me and drain me.

In moments, I was buried in vampires. I thought of Vivien, somewhere in these tunnels, so close. She needed me. I could feel it as if she were sending messages on the air.

Power built in me until I exploded, vampires flying off me and back into their own horde.

"I thought you might need a hand, but looks like you've got this covered," Fallon said, entering from the same tunnel I came by.

I grabbed the nearest sekhor and twisted her head right off and threw it into another coming at me. "Are you going to just stand there?" I asked my brother blandly.

With a shrug, Fallon jumped into the fray, eyes alight with violence in moments. He worked his way through the throng until we were fighting back to back.

Qwynn and Crane were getting away, and they might be taking Vivien with them. If Crane escaped he could make even more sekhors.

That's when Timothy, Miranda, and Galina showed up. They wasted no time jumping into the fight.

"Where is Jamal?" Miranda yelled to me. A vampire flew at her on the left, but she reared around and shot the sekhor between the eyes.

"I will find him," I said, using the opportunity to break off to follow in the direction Qwynn had disappeared. I needed to find her and Crane and stop them. The rest would hold off the sekhors. I trusted Timothy and Galina to protect Miss West, though I'd no doubt she'd hold her own.

With super speed, I raced through the tunnels. I stopped on a dime when I caught sight of a barred cell on my left, in an alcove. It was a recent construction.

A human figure was inside. It was sitting, hunched over. I recognized the warm glow of a sekhor, but unlike Vivien's this was muted, dull. Whoever it was, they were talking. "Oh god, oh god, oh god."

"Vivien?" I said, my voice echoing down toward the figure. The figure twisted and I saw Vivien's eyes. They were bigger than usual and blood red.

The second she saw me, she got to her feet and stumbled to the bars with a sob. She hung on them as if helpless. I grabbed the locked door and ripped it off the hinges, throwing it behind me. Everything inside me shouted with joy as Vivien fell into my arms. She was okay.

She clutched my arms as her words tumbled out. "Tell me this is a dream. Tell me you're not really here. This is a nightmare and you're not here." Vivien seemed out of her mind, gripped by fear and anxiety.

"What did he do to you?" I asked, every part of me coming to attention.

A sob bubbled out of her throat as she shut her eyes tight. "You are here, aren't you?" I smoothed her wild, messy hair away from her face, but I couldn't soothe away her tortured feelings which radiated out of her as if from a gaping wound. Then her eyes snapped open. "You can fix this. You are the only one who can fix this."

Then she was tugging on me, urging me over to where she'd been kneeling on the ground. I saw the source of her pain. I grimaced.

Jamal lay on the ground, his neck a mangled, bloodied mess. She'd fed from him. His warm brown skin had turned ashen. Even in the darkness, I could see his soul was barely clinging to his body. She'd all but drained him.

"I tried to stop." Vivien pulled at her hair and shut her eyes again. "I tried everything I could to stop, but the master was in my head. Crane is so much stronger since he made an army of sekhors. His power is growing. He forced me to feed, then took my strength."

The fact she had left anything of Jamal showed great control on her part, but the child was still not long for this world. Then turning to me, she grasped at my shirt. "You have to save him."

"I can't do that," I said quietly.

She grasped at my shirt, bunching the fabric in her hands. "I didn't trap his soul in his body. I didn't make him drink my blood. He won't be a vampire. You can save him." She choked on a sob. "You have to. Jamal doesn't deserve this. He shouldn't have been here."

I'd faced the pleas from millions upon millions of souls. Death was part of the cycle of life. Yet Vivien's entreaties tore at me. "I can't...I never meant to...I tried to stop. But you can save him."

I gripped her arms with a bruising force. Her tortured babbling cut off abruptly as she focused on me. I spoke slowly, deliberately. "Death is necessary, and it is natural."

A new fire lit in her eyes as she pointed at Jamal's prone body. "This is not necessary. This is our fight, not his. And if you have the power to save him, you would do it. You were the one to say that you valued human life. That Qwynn betrayed you when she used mortals. Don't let him be collateral damage in this battle. Don't let her win. Don't let that bastard, Crane, get away with this." Her words broke at the end. "Take my soul. Anything."

"You know you don't have a soul to bargain with." As soon as I said it, I knew that wasn't entirely true. No force in this universe was without a cost. And while I could not take Vivien's soul to save Jamal's, there was another price she could pay to preserve the balance. There was something I could take from her that would permit me to save the boy while keeping the scales of fate even.

But if there was one thing I learned about Vivien, she would never agree to the price.

"There will be a cost." The words came out before I knew what I was saying.

Her head bobbed emphatically. "Anything. Just do it. Do it now." Eyes continuing to flicker to Jamal, she knew he had mere moments left.

"Vivien, you must know the price—"

"Now, Anubis." She appealed to me using my real name, and power surged in me. Her use of my true moniker left me heady as energy pulsated through me anew. There was power in a name.

"You need to drink my blood."

Vivien's blood-red eyes widened. "I can't," she whispered. She thought she would hurt me. She thought it would make her a monster. She didn't know the truth but there was no time to explain.

"Then the boy dies," I said, my voice stony.

Knowing we were out of time, she swallowed and stepped closer to me. She brought her mouth close to where my neck and shoulder met. Her lips hovered there a moment, her breath warming my exposed flesh, causing prickles of sensation to shoot throughout my body.

"We don't have any time for you to make up your mind. If you want to destroy the master and save the boy, you will drink my blood and you will do it now," I commanded, my voice infused with power. I was teetering on the edge, about to take a header. But I couldn't stop now.

Emotions pounded through me in a confusing tandem as I urged her on. I wanted this. Everything about this was wrong, but I couldn't and wouldn't stop now.

Then Vivien's fangs sliced through my neck.

31

As soon as his blood hit my tongue, I moaned in pleasure. While I'd already been warmed by Jamal's blood, my temperature continued to rise.

Grim didn't taste like human. No, this was unlike anything I'd ever experienced. Flavors unfolded on my tongue that I could no sooner name than I could describe colors my eye had never seen before. I clutched Grim's solid back and arms and latched on like a leech. I could hear myself continuing to moan and mewl as I sucked away.

"Enough."

I barely registered his gruff whisper.

My knees shook, my entire being trembled. Oh god, I needed more. I needed it all. Somewhere at the back of my mind, I felt a snap as if some connection had been broken. I rubbed my body against Grim. My nipples had pebbled, and the feel of his hard body only stoked the fire blazing inside of me. I wanted to burn up.

"Vivien, enough," he said a little louder.

Where human blood was life, Grim's blood encompassed all of the cosmos. As I drank, it was like spinning through the universe while realizing at the same time, I was also the universe. Everything was made of the same fabric. I was made of the same burning particles that composed stars. Time and space expanded and stretched endlessly before me, and I understood everything. Then everything fell away, leaving only Grim. He was the entire point of my being, and I could never detach from him again or I would die. I needed all of him in every way. I would drink his blood until I turned to ash.

"I said enough." His voice boomed through the tunnel, breaking through my sensual psychedelic trip.

A cold hand gripped my will with an iron fist. My back straightened with a snap and I backed away from Grim.

Though I instantly wanted to cry, having parted with his neck, I knew something worse had just transpired.

"What did you do to me?" I breathed.

His shoulders rose and dropped with exaggerated movements. Regret lay heavy on Grim's brow. Blood trickled down from the puncture wounds where I'd been drinking. The urge to lick up his neck and latch back onto him nearly sent me to my knees. But I forced myself to look in his eyes, which had turned entirely black. "What did you do to me?" I repeated myself.

But I already knew. Ice dripped in my stomach. I felt the bond form between us. He'd taken my will. He'd commanded me to stop, and I'd obeyed.

Grim didn't answer. Instead, he walked over to Jamal. I saw one of his reapers pawing at the ground next to Jamal. "Nyliak," Grim murmured, and the dog backed up, bowing his head.

Suddenly, I could see Jamal's soul. It was beautiful. Pure white and golden light of pure energy. It hovered over his body and was connected to it by a mere tendril. Grim reached out and grabbed hold of it. Jamal, or the bright wispy light that was his soul, struggled in his grasp. Grim closed his eyes in concentration. Slowly but surely, he strengthened the tether between Jamal's soul and his drained body.

"He'll be alright," Grim said when he was done, not looking at me. "We still need to get him medical attention."

"Jamal." Miranda's voice echoed through the tunnel.

"Over here," I called out, my voice scratchy. I stumbled to get away from Grim, needing to get far away from him. He didn't follow.

Miranda's voice continued to lead me down the tunnels. But I was lost to the aftereffects of Grim's blood.

I was tied to Grim. I needed him, craved him, and it physically hurt to run away from him. I couldn't think about the look on his face, as if he'd done something so deeply regrettable that I was now an object of pity. Tears pricked at the backs of my eyes.

With thoughts and emotions swirling around me like a tornado, I rather felt like a cow swept away into the death winds of something more massive than I could understand. And I certainly didn't expect Landon Crane when he stepped out in front of me.

The master psycho gripped my face in one hand, nails digging into my cheeks and forcing my lips to pucker. He backed me up several steps. Crane's once perfectly combed-back hair was now tousled, and his button-down shirt was a rumpled mess. Violence and frustration vibrated off his compact form.

"You will go and kill them, and then you will come back to me like an obedient little bitch." He gave my face another shake before releasing me. I rubbed my face and curled my lip at him.

"Kill them." Crane pointed down the tunnel where my sensitive vampire hearing could pick up Miranda's quick, light footsteps.

I still didn't move.

Crane's nostrils flared as he concentrated on me. Crane said with more force, "I command you to kill them."

Then I realized the cause of his anger. I narrowed my eyes. "Looks like whatever psychic tie we shared has been cut, Landy boy."

"No." He stomped his foot with all the fury and petulance of a child about to throw a tantrum.

I threw my knee up into his balls. Crane doubled over with a cry of pain. It was cut short when I threw a jab into his face, breaking his nose with a spectacular explosion of blood.

"I know it's not Fire and Ice, but the shade suits you," I said, referring to the blood slicked across his mouth, now dripping onto his shirt.

"But I think you could use a second coat." I threw a second punch into his mouth. He wailed like a furious child.

"Do you know what it's like to be controlled? Do you know what it's like to be maimed and murdered? No. You think you can play god."

He tried to intercept my next kick, but I was stronger now. He stumbled back under the force of my fury. I took the opportunity to take another step and pivot to throw a roundhouse kick that connected with the side of his head. I heard the crack of his neck, but Crane still didn't go down. He was powerful with his army of sekhors feeding his strength, but I'd swallowed blood from an actual god. That, and I was as livid as a cat trapped in a dunk tank.

"My life is not for you to control or toy with. Those girls were not your playthings, and this world is not your playground." I continued my furious onslaught, making each point with a smashing punch or a swift, vicious kick.

"But while we are here, I might as well perform an experiment on *you*."

A couple of old two-by-fours lay in an abandoned pile and I used my toe to flick one up into my hands. Before Crane could take another step, I jabbed the makeshift wooden stake through his heart.

Crane's already waxy skin paled. His mouth formed an "o" as blood dripped out the corners.

His skin cracked, making it appear as though there was a map of red glowing rivers all over his body, up his neck, across his face. Then with one last grunt he exploded into ash.

"You deserved worse," I whispered. When I turned, I found Grim standing off a ways, watching me. A shadow cut across his eyes, but I could see the hard set of his jaw.

The master vampire was dead. I'd completed my purpose. Grim had made it all too clear the moment I'd outlived my usefulness that he would end me. I waited, expecting him to close the distance and put an end to my existence. Especially now that I'd drunk his blood.

He didn't move. As the minutes stretched out between us, I realized he wasn't going to kill me. Was he waiting to do it later? Or did this have to do with my drinking his blood? I didn't know, but I'd take advantage of my borrowed time. Jamal needed help, now.

Turning my back on him, I ran toward Miranda's voice. I finally met up with her and we grasped each other's arms, relieved to see each other.

"Jamal?" she asked, her voice tight with worry.

Blood smeared along her neck, face, and arms. I was

about to answer when I was struck by a realization. "Is that vampire blood on you?" I asked.

"Some of it theirs, some of it mine," she said, pushing some of her hair back, smearing more blood into it. She still wore a sling on one arm, and the scent of gunpowder surrounded her in a thick haze that made me want to sneeze. She'd come to the rescue packing some serious heat. Miranda West was a patent badass.

Then I realize something. Every time I was near a human, I was drawn to their blood, no matter how much I'd already drunk. It called to me like a siren. This close to Miranda, covered in her own blood, it should make me want to lick her like a popsicle on a hot day, but I felt...nothing. No draw, no hunger, no nothing.

Grim had done something to me. Something I couldn't explain, but I knew to the marrow of my bones I didn't want it.

"Later, you will have to explain to me about Grim and his superhero friends, but tell me," her voice more insistent, "do you know if Jamal is alright?"

"He needs help but he's going to be alright," I said, then pulled her toward where her son was.

We would get help. Jamal would live. But I might be killed once Miranda found out I was the one who bit him.

32

Jamal was recovering in the hospital, and Grim hadn't deigned to kill me. In fact, he hadn't spoken to me since we left the tunnels. He went straight to shower and get changed while Timothy, who looked the most unkempt I'd ever seen him, having laid waste to all of the sekhors with Miranda, Fallon, and some woman, presumably another goddess, named Galina, stared off after Grim.

"You'll need to get showered and changed," he said to me.

"Why?"

His lips tightened as if he were reluctant to tell me what was coming.

"Come on, Timmy," I goaded. "Tell me what's going on."

While Timothy usually let things slip for either my benefit or his need to share, this time he was locked down tighter than a prison after a breakout.

"There will be a change of clothes laid out for you when you are done cleansing yourself. You will be meeting with..." He trailed off, as his face scrunched into an expression that I didn't comprehend until after he'd left. As the elevator doors closed behind Timothy, he added, "Don't forget to wash behind your ears."

Fear. It had been fear that cut his explanation short. Timothy was afraid of whoever I was supposed to meet with. When I asked myself what a god was afraid of, the best answer I could come up with was a gigantic evil Stay Puft Marshmallow Man.

After I showered, I found a white, flowing gown laid out on the bed. I balked at donning the beautiful feminine confection and the delicate golden sandals that went with it. Instead, I walked to the closet where I knew I could dig up something with a bit more sass. My confidence was on shaky ground, so slipping into something more my style would bolster me for whatever the hell was about to happen.

Was Grim going to make a show of killing me? Would he sacrifice me in the white gown to some volcano? Would he tear it from me and take me on some altar? Okay, that last one caused heat to spread across my cheeks and between my thighs. But I still didn't want to be anywhere near him after tasting his blood.

When I opened the closet, I found it had been cleared out, leaving only a large sign and my combat boots at the bottom.

Dear Vivien,

Do not even think about it. Put on the gown.

Thank you kindly,

Jeeves

Touché, Timmy. I put on the dress, unable to help enjoying the soft texture of it slipping against my skin. I felt like a goddess in it, which was both empowering and gave me a bad case of imposter syndrome. I walked back out to the living room, but it was empty. Needing something to do with my hands, I French-braided my hair.

When Grim emerged from his room, he was only wearing a set of black slacks. His feet were bare, and his hard, sculpted torso was displayed for my viewing pleasure. *Holy blood bags.* I fought the drool that threatened to leak out the side of my mouth.

Dammit brain, did Jenkins pull that lever? The boys running my brain were totally getting a pay cut. But Grim's body was a masterpiece from his wide, muscular shoulders to his tapered, washboard abs. He'd also showered, and his wet hair fell over his forehead though he tried to push it back, and his caramel skin glistened with moisture. And lord help a vampire, but the cut of his hips was positively sinful. It was the perfect trail for a finger, or maybe a tongue to trail along.

But layered into all this desire my body felt, urging me to attack and mount Grim in one go, was a different need. It left me weak and woozy. Before, I never detected what flowed through his veins, but now the liquid gold underneath his skin beckoned to me. I wanted to sink my fangs into him again and lose myself.

My hands shook until I closed them into fists. I was jonesing. Bad. Human blood had been one thing, but I could never allow myself to drink from Grim again.

The features of the god in front of me were made of stone, giving nothing away. I felt shy under his gaze, my stomach a squirming mess. So, I lifted my chin and stared back. Grim didn't react, he didn't even give me a onceover, which I found slightly offensive. After all, I looked like a damn angel over here. I would have made some crack or called him on it if there hadn't been something in the air

since we'd returned from the tunnels. It hung as heavy as
sopping wet clothes on a line.

His eyes did touch my neck, then my feet. I'd wrapped
the piece of leather around my neck again and skipped the
sandals for the heeled combat boots.

I did my best to wrangle in my lust, desire, and hunger
as distrust parted the air between us like the red sea.
Drinking his blood had changed things between us on a
basic, undeniable level. I wouldn't allow my physical need
for him to dictate my action.

"What am I now?" I asked.

When Grim finally met my gaze again, he said, "You
paid the price for the boy's soul."

"You said you couldn't reap my soul."

"I didn't reap it. I bound it."

"What does that mean?"

He didn't answer, only continued to regard me with his
black stare, as if he were looking at a dead woman. But I was
undead.

Despite Jenkins and the rest of the crew running the
cogs of common sense in my brain, I walked forward until I
was standing in front of him. I could do this. Be near him
and control my every screaming urge.

My voice was low, dangerous. "Tell me. I won't ask
again."

"We made a blood bond and now you belong to me."

"Belong to you?" Then I remembered. Grim spoke of the
ancient times where sekhors had been slaves to the gods.
"You made me your slave?"

I might have drunk his blood, but it was Grim who had
siphoned power from me. He took and took from me until
he possessed almost all of me.

Then I remembered how he ordered me off him, and I

jumped back. I hadn't moved of my own free will; it had been Grim's command that controlled me. It was the same as the push Landon Crane had done to my mind when he stoked the thirst in me and set me on Jamal.

"But your fate has not been entirely decided." He motioned me to enter the elevator when it opened without looking at me. "There is an authority even I cannot defy."

Remembering Timothy's fear, I followed Grim in.

I remembered how he once slammed his hands on either side of my head in here. How his fury had morphed into lust as he pressed against me. Even as he chastised me, I'd been turned on, wanting to get even more under his skin, like how he'd gotten under mine.

Now the space between us was leaden and cold. He reached past me to press the black button and the elevator smoothly descended. When the doors opened again, he took my arm. I wasn't sure if it was to keep me from running, or because I was liable to fall over.

The realization I was Grim's prisoner left me the rubble of a fallen tower. I didn't know what to think or do, so I let him lead me through his antechamber. The torches blazed, casting ominous shadows through the room.

Maybe whatever monster was in the side room was going to reckon with me. I didn't care. I would either remain a prisoner or cease to exist. Either way, my life was not my own anymore. Instead, he led me around his throne to the wall behind it. I hadn't noticed before but an ancient mural of a giant set of scales decorated the wall.

Grim set his hand on the wall and closed his eyes. Light glowed around his hand until the walls parted in a burst of light. We stepped through. When the glare subsided, I found myself standing with Grim on a black-sand beach. Tall reeds rustled as black birds cawed, streaking across a clear blue sky. When I looked behind me, I found any trace of the antechamber had disappeared.

I threw my hands over my head, expecting to sizzle into ash. Panic closed my throat off. Grim pulled my arms away. "You are safe here. That is a different star," he said, pointing to the sun.

"So we aren't on Earth anymore? We are on a different planet?"

He shook his head. "Not a different planet. This is where worthy souls go after they have been deemed worthy of the afterlife."

"Wait, this is heaven?" Shock made my eyes wide as saucers.

"In a way. Yes, it has been referred to as that," Grim said.

Huh. I didn't see any bakeries or cafés. How great could heaven be if you couldn't get any cookies?

"Ahoy," a man called out. A grizzled old man, with broomstick limbs, and a bright white beard waved us over to his shiny black boat which reminded me of a gondola. He leaned against a staff he'd stuck in the water to keep it from floating off.

Without a word, Grim swept me off my feet and walked through the marsh before depositing me in the boat.

"I could have walked myself," I grumbled, crossing my arms. Grim jumped in next to me.

"And ruined your combat boots?"

"So this is her, huh?" the white-haired man huffed as he pushed the boat off from the shore. He had the brightest blue eyes I'd ever seen, but a scowl that could have shamed a nun. "She's what all the fuss is about? She shouldn't be here. When he finds out you've brought her here, there is going to be hell to pay."

"Hush, Hraf-haf," Grim said.

"Don't tell him to hush." I stuck my hands on my hips. "You can't boss everyone around. If the captain wants to judge me to my face, I can take it just fine."

The old man's eyebrows shot up. Then a grin spread across his face and I found his teeth were even whiter than his hair. "Oh, I like this one." Then turning to Grim, he said, "Did you hear that? I'm not just a regular ferryman, I'm a captain."

I patted his shoulder as he sent the boat gliding forward, cutting through the crystalline water. "Absolutely. Isn't every man with a boat a captain?" Hraf-haf, the ferryman, went on to talk all about his boat and how he built it himself and there was no other like it. Even though I didn't understand half of what he talked about, I nodded as if I did. He helped distract me from the jitters that made me sick to my stomach. Grim was silent, but instead of looking forward to where the ferryman was taking us, he'd turned to watch me.

Once we reached another shoreline, I found myself looking up at a massive palace. It reminded me of the temples of Egypt except while those were old, crumbling structures, this gleamed as if brand new. The structure was painted in colorful blues, greens, and whites.

I saluted Hraf-haf and said that was the smoothest boat ride I'd ever taken. He chuckled, then captured my hand, landing a kiss on the back of it. "It sure was lovely to meet you, miss. Shame he'll likely kill you."

A chill shot down my spine. Who? Who was going to kill me? This seemed like such a nice place. Surely no one was ever murdered here.

Before I could respond, Grim lifted me once again into his arms and carried me the short distance to land.

The ferryman leaned against his staff and waved.

We walked through the temple until we came to a set of

massive doors. Grim stopped, looking up at them with trepidation. He didn't want to go in.

Then in one motion, he pulled me to him as his lips pressed against mine. The kiss was scorching. Fire zinged through me. My insides turned into a shivering, hopeless, helpless mass. I wanted to lose myself in Grim and forget everything but the roughness of his unshaven jaw. I wanted his perfect, sexy hands on me everywhere. I was on the verge of exploding into a fiery inferno if I didn't rip his clothes off and taste every last inch of his decadent, caramel skin. Then I'd drink his blood and fall backward into space as his lifeforce pumped through me again.

Despite the cacophony of needy, wanty desires, I managed to stay perfectly still under his skilled mouth. When he stepped back, breaking off the kiss, my chest tightened. I deserved a gold star sticker— screw that, I deserved a medal, a tiara, crown jewels for resisting that kiss. Yet somehow I managed.

"What was that for?" I said, proud my voice didn't sound nearly as shaky as I thought it would.

"For luck," Grim said. His eyes were the color of melted dark chocolate.

I'd gripped my fists so tight, my fingernails cut through my palms. The pain helped me not get swept up in his mystic power.

"I don't need luck," I managed to say in a scathing tone. He did not need to know he'd turned me into pudding and left a slick need between my thighs.

One of his eyebrows rose almost imperceptibly. "Who said I was talking about you?" Grim stepped forward and gave the door a sharp, rhythmic rap.

I was confused, turned on, and terrified. What did he mean it wasn't for me?

What could the god of death possibly need luck for? He was invulnerable. Right?

Grim rolled back his shoulders. He was nervous. I'd never known Grim to be nervous. Pissed off, sure. Annoyed, often, and by me. But nervous? Well, if he was nervous that meant I should be filling my panties with bricks.

The doors swung open, slowly, and without the help of anyone. Grim walked forward with measured steps and I did everything I could not to trip over my feet. Suddenly I wished I hadn't worn the boots. They echoed loudly across the stone floor.

It was part palace, part oasis. Ornate golden columns framed old Egyptian pictures and hieroglyphics that adorned the walls with shades of browns, turquoise, and burnt oranges. We walked across a sandstone floor toward what appeared to be a raised dais under a gazebo. It reminded me of the throne I'd seen in Grim's antechamber, but this was a hundred times grander.

There was no ceiling here, allowing the noonday sun to warm my skin. The throne platform was surrounded by sparkling waters that acted as a miniature moat filled with tall grasses and elegant stork-like birds.

Behind the throne, a wall shifted back and forth between another ornate mural and an open oasis that instilled peace simply by looking at it.

But you know what didn't instill peace?

The dude sitting on the throne. He had icy blue skin, and enlarged, blueberry-colored eyes that lacked irises. A tall white hat that curled slightly at the top, matching his white pajama-like outfit. At first, I thought a glare was coming off his white clothes, but I soon realized the man was simply too hard to look directly at. He glowed and effervesced with a raw, awe-inspiring power that penetrated my bones. There was an alienness to him that sent prickles of alarm along the nape of my neck and down my spine.

He did not acknowledge our approach.

Admittedly, I wasn't big into mythology, but I knew some of the basics from school. And there was no doubt who this big mamba jamba was. If the being beside me was Anubis, then the god across from us was Osiris.

When he blinked, I nearly peed myself and fell to the floor. I didn't remember when Grim took me by the arm, but he was the only thing holding me up as my legs turned to liquid.

Those blue eyes trained on me, and everything in me stilled. It felt as though lasers were traversing from my head to my toes, scanning me for something.

When the god spoke it was like listening to a hundred different, individual voices at once. "You killed the master sekhor."

"She did," Grim confirmed, but stopped when Osiris raised a hand.

"Let her speak for herself."

I suppressed a shiver of fear. Walking on eggshells was not my strong suit. Talking on eggshells, even less so.

"I did, you're, uh, Highness." With Grim it had been a taunt, but with Osiris, I meant it. In his presence, I was painfully aware of the meaningless worm I was. No, I was lower than that, the dirt a worm burrowed through.

Osiris tilted his head ever so slightly. Again, I was struck by his alienness. "And yet you are a master sekhor yourself."

I nodded, not trusting myself to say anything. Grim had brought me before Osiris for judgement, I realized. Captain Hraf-haf had it right. I didn't have to worry about being Grim's slave, Osiris was going to stomp me out of existence.

Osiris's attention shifted to Grim and relief swept

through me as if I'd been released from some tractor beam holding me in place.

"And you bound her to you." Again, the words were said with a removed curiosity.

"I did. She wanted me to save a boy, and agreed to the price," Grim said.

"A forbidden price."

"She did not know, and she has been a useful ally—"

A boom cracked through the room, though there was no actual sound. Grim stopped speaking.

Holy crap. Do not soil this pretty dress, do not soil this pretty dress.

"Indeed, she has assisted in uncovering the conspiracy," Osiris said, eyes falling back on me. Again, pressure closed in on me from all sides. While I tried to seem as nonthreatening as possible, I was sure that my eyes were bugging out of my head.

Grim spoke again. "Qadesh was behind the conspiracy, but she got away—"

Another soundless crack boomed through the room.

Something shimmered into view on the stairs leading up to where Osiris sat. Like a mirage coming into focus, soon I saw Qwynn hovering in midair, completely naked. She didn't seem aware of our presence as she clutched at her ears, eyes brimming with absolute terror. Though I couldn't hear her, it looked as though she was screaming.

Osiris spoke again. "Qadesh has been apprehended and her punishment is being seen to."

The way he said it made me think she wasn't even really there, that maybe it was only some kind of hologram of her, wherever she was.

I didn't like the slut-bag one iota, but my hands itched to pull her out of whatever cone of hell she seemed wrapped up in. Seeing her in abject pain grated in a way I hadn't expected. I believed in justice, but I didn't believe in torture.

Qwynn shimmered out of view again and we fell into silence. Only chirping frogs and the occasional flap of wings filled the space.

Osiris spoke again, his voice less layered this time, but still unearthly. "Qwynn was a pawn, as the master sekhor was. There is a conspiracy in our midst, and I do not know who is behind it."

From what Grim told me, Qwynn wasn't driven or even smart enough to pull such a big stunt, and apparently papa Osiris agreed.

"I need to know who is attempting to upset the balance." Osiris blinked. How could a blink be terrifying? I vowed if I lived through this to practice in the mirror until I managed the same amount of intimidation.

"Do you believe yourself to be the target?" Grim asked.

"I do. And I believe it to be one of our own. You have proven yourself to be faithful. I wish for you to discover the source of this conspiracy and put a stop to it and bring me the perpetrator."

Grim bowed his head. "As it pleases you."

Osiris tilted his head in Grim's direction. "As for the sekhor. She has proven useful, as you say. But her existence is forbidden, as is the blood bond you formed with her. What do you have to say for yourself, Anubis?"

I chanced a look when Grim didn't respond. There was a hard set of his jaw, and his eyes blazed with maybe loyalty? Pride? Duty? I wasn't sure, but after a moment Osiris gave a slight nod. "I see."

I didn't see. Grim didn't answer out loud, so how did Osiris "see"?

The thought the god could read minds suddenly

shocked me with fear. In case he wanted to eavesdrop on my thoughts, I forced myself to fill my mind with useless junk.

Cat memes, mud, that dick pic I got from one of my skips.

Damn.

A cola jingle, the route I used to take to my favorite coffee shop, explicit, crude amateur porn.

Double damn.

"You will keep the sekhor under your watch. She will assist you in uncovering this conspiracy. She will do what she does best."

Wait, what?

The doors opened behind us once again.

"Wait, that's it? I get to live?"

Grim's hand squeezed my arm so hard I thought my muscle might pop out of my flesh.

Osiris's eyes landed on me again, making me regret speaking out loud. "Anubis knows the rules. You have a rare, fleeting advantage. Don't make me regret granting it."

I resisted the urge to salute as Anubis dragged me out of the throne room in haste, probably afraid I would say something else.

We made our way back to Hraf-haf. He grinned. "Glad to see you've lived to see another day, miss."

33

I waited until we were back in the antechamber to ask my questions.

"What did he mean, I will do what I do best?"

Grim didn't answer right away.

"Now. You are telling me everything now. I'm not waiting any longer, so you can kaput with the cryptic bullshit."

"Hunt. You hunt people, and you hunt sekhors. You even suspected Qwynn where I was blind to her abilities yet again. Osiris wants you to help me discover the conspiracy against him because hunting is what you do best. One of the gods seeks chaos and upheaval. That is no small transgression."

I crossed my arms, still trying to keep up. "And how are we supposed to do that? Go door-to-door around the world and ask each god if they did it? How many are there? Plus, I don't travel well. I get sick on airplanes."

Grim failed to cover his smile.

"What? What's so funny?"

"You ramble when you are nervous."

"You straighten your suits when you're nervous," I shot back.

His expression emptied. "We do not have to travel the world to see the rest of the gods."

"And why is that?" I tapped my foot.

Grim sat on the arm of his throne, one foot on the seat, positioning himself in an impossibly alluring pose. "Because they are all here. In Vegas."

My foot stilled.

He entwined his fingers. "All of the gods reside on the Strip. As I own Sinopolis, they have staked their claim on other such hotels. They are all here."

All the gods were in one place. In Vegas. Was that where the saying *what happens in Vegas, stays in Vegas* originated? Because otherwise a god might smite your ass.

"What are the rules?" I asked, referring again to our talk with daddy Osiris.

He spoke more slowly. "I think you already know that human blood will no longer sustain you."

I nodded, not trusting myself to speak.

"That is because you are now bonded to me. You require my blood, and my blood alone, to stay alive."

Did the floor drop out from under me? I checked. Nope. Must have been my heart falling out of my chest. "Literally, no one else's blood? Not even another gods?"

Grim shook his head, his expression as serious as only Death himself could manage.

"You not only control what I eat, you can control my will. Like how they used to do in the old days," I said, hearing the snarl in my voice. "I had enough of that with Crane."

He was on his feet in the blink of an eye. "I won't abuse the power, Vivien."

"It's enough that you have it in the first place." He didn't understand. I had worked so hard to get out of anyone's control, and to end up like this...I wondered if this wouldn't be worse than death for me.

"There is only one rule I will bind you to," he said, now towering over me.

My breath caught in my throat. I didn't want to be bound. I didn't want to be stuck with having to feed on Grim. I wanted to go back to my shoddy apartment and figure out a way to turn my little meaningless life into something I actually wanted. Maybe learn how to actually be a baker and open up a shop, find a nice little butcher shop I could get delivery blood from.

"You can tell no one that gods walk amongst them."

An invisible vice squeezed around my throat so hard that my hands reached up as if to pry the invisible force from me. It passed after a few seconds, and I knew that Grim used his power to magically bind me.

Which meant at the first opportunity I was going to go find a loudspeaker and see if I could get the words out.

"Is that it?" I glowered at Grim, hating the power he had over me. "Can I go now?"

"You'll have to stay close by since you need my blood."

Irritation flared in me. "Do you have to be so—"

"What?" he asked, his eyebrow rising.

"Do you have to act so damn cold and calculating like this is some business transaction?"

"It was a transaction. I gave the boy more time on this Earth and you will serve the blood bond."

"Tell me the truth, did you pick the price because you knew it would make me hate you?"

He ran a frustrated hand through his dark, unruly hair. "What makes you think I intentionally want you to hate me?"

"Because you were scared of what was growing between us. You felt something for me and you had to stop it, and you couldn't bring yourself to kill me." Tears filled my eyes and I hated myself for it.

Grim grabbed me by the shoulders, hauling me to him, kissing me again. It was fierce, hot, and possessive. My soul soared at the contact and then took a nosedive off the cliff he'd pushed me over. I could never love someone who controlled me. I pushed him off me. A sound slap rang through the air. My hand stung from where I'd connected with his perfect cheekbone.

Grim's eyes went flat.

"Never again. You never get to do that again."

An absolutely predatory smile curved his lips. "Only if you beg for it."

I turned and walked away so he couldn't see the tears fall. I hated him and yet I could never escape him now.

34

"Why did you do it?"

I didn't react, though Timothy took me by surprise, sneaking up from behind. He was now in order once again.

"Why did I let her drink my blood? Because I couldn't take her soul for Jamal's. It was the only option."

"Mmm." Timothy watched Vivien's retreating form next to me. He didn't believe me.

The truth was far more terrifying. I needed Vivien. I couldn't end her, so I'd chained her to me for all eternity. And she'd hate me for just as long.

Or for at least as long as Osiris deemed her useful. But unearthing a conspiracy amongst the gods could take years, centuries, millennia perhaps. Or everything could explode with the fall of a mighty hammer in a matter of hours. Either way, Vivien would live for a little longer.

"Did you tell her you broke every rule in the book to save her?"

"It doesn't matter. She despises me. I've imprisoned her."

"And you now have a weakness I've never known you to indulge in."

I turned to him. "You are not to tell her. Just as you are not to tell her what would happen if she were to drink too much of my blood."

Timothy sniffed. "I would never."

Vivien did make me weak, in more ways than one. She made me forget duty and responsibility. Though I wanted to believe I had done things from a place of cool calculation, my emotions had gotten the best of me. After I'd thought they'd long hardened.

Now the trick was to stay close to Vivien without actually being close to her. I sighed and sat in my throne. There were many judgements I must proceed with, and I could use the distraction.

Though I knew there would be nothing that could erase those glinting green eyes, full of passion, the feel of her lips under mine, or the sting of the slap against my face.

There was no rest for the wicked, and certainly never for Death.

EPILOGUE

"So this is your new place?" Miranda asked as I poured her a glass of red wine. I even poured one for myself. I didn't want to let that dickwad Landon Crane spoil anything for me. I'd force myself to love wine to spite the horrible thing he'd done to me. Seemed fair.

I'd confessed to Miranda what I'd done to Jamal, expecting her to shoot me. Instead, she grabbed my hand and said she knew it wasn't my fault. After all, I had saved him. He was released from the hospital and having lots of long talks with his mom about what they once thought to be true about this world. She'd said to him, "Life has the endless ability to surprise us. In this case, dark, scary creatures that we never thought could exist. But that also means there are endless possibilities for the expression of love, hope, and good in the world." I informed her that I was an orphan and demanded she adopt me right away.

When I asked if Jamal was terrified of me, she explained he thought I was a superhero. He knew I was manipulated by the bad guys. I absolutely did not tear up when she told me that.

So I told Miranda about the blood bond, that I could only drink blood from Grim now and had quit humans for good. Didn't even need a patch. She knew he was different, she just didn't know how. Miranda was only aware she had been around a lot of supernatural beings lately. Thank god she was the coolest, toughest chick I knew and didn't melt into an incoherent puddle of fear. I wanted to be her when I grew up.

Miranda's hand wrapped around the giant balloon glass, as I passed it to her and said, "There was no way I was going to live in that penthouse with his majesty."

Though he rarely spent any time up there, which was why it was a great makeshift prison for me in the first place, it was still his. It smelled of him, his taste was everywhere and inescapable. I may be on a short leash, but I intended to take every inch.

"So I demanded my own digs. It's still in the same hotel, but don't you love it?" I asked Miranda. We were standing in one of Sinopolis's greatest suites, complete with two bedrooms, a kitchen, and an infinity pool that butted up to the glass and overlooked the sparkling lights of the Strip. Of course, heavy duty blackout curtains were installed to keep me from ending up a pile of ash.

"I mean," she said, eyeing the piles of clothes everywhere, "it's impressive you trashed it so hard in what, six hours?"

"I got a hold of his majesty's credit card and have done a lot of online shopping." I examined the mini mountains I'd made. "And I'm still trying to figure out my new look. Jane had a certain kind of style, but now I'm Vivien. And Vivien totally has a look. I just haven't figured it out yet."

Miranda eyed my mess with the barely restrained

censure only a mother could manage. "And a maid will be by to pick up all of this?"

"Exactly." I nodded, clinking my glass against hers. Jamal was sleeping over at a friend's house, leaving us a blissful girl's night. And now that I had memories, I could count the number of these occasions on one hand.

She shrugged and sighed, seeming to give up the itch to lecture me to pick up after myself, and sipped from her glass. "So are you going to tell me what Grim is yet? Or Timothy or those other two ya-hoos who fought off those vamps with me?"

I took a longer slug from the glass. Still wished it was a beer. True to Grim's word, I was bound to not reveal the identity of the gods. Oh, believe me, I tried. Immediately, many times, with Miranda in fact, but I barely got a puff of air out every time I tried. My throat would squeeze the words down before they could really get up at all.

"You know I can't," I said. "Why do you ask?"

Miranda pinched the stem of the wine glass and rolled it between her fingers. "Grim offered me a position with his security team, here at Sinopolis."

I froze. "Are you going to take it?"

"It's chief of security. The job comes with housing, five times the pay I was receiving at Castlegate, and the benefits are out of this world. He even promised that the owner of Castlegate wouldn't put up a fight, as he would personally see to compensating for my transfer."

The idea I could flounce down and bother Miranda any time I wanted made my heart soar. I was planning on doing that anyway, seeing as the hotels connected by a windowless corridor, but it would be so much more satisfying to do it on Grim's dime.

"But I don't know what kind of man Grim is."

He's not a man at all.

I shrugged. "From what I can tell, he treats his staff very well and as far as I know he doesn't do any shady shit, if that's what you're asking."

"Then I can tell him I'll take the job in the morning."

I squeed and raced around the bar to squeeze Miranda in a near bone-breaking hug. Then we lounged on the couch and chatted about how Jamal was doing, picked over the clothes, some of which I forced her to take with her because she had a banging body and actual, defined arm muscles. Sooner than I liked, Miranda headed home, full of cocktails, in a cab. Somehow, out of all of this I'd come out with a friend. That was more than I'd had in my previous life. And it sure as hell wasn't nothing.

My phone buzzed. It was a text.

You're late for dinner.

I sucked in a breath though I didn't need it. It was going to be like this now. I'd have to go to *him* for blood every single night.

Heading to my new pile of shoes, I picked up a new pair of combat boots with steel spikes sticking out of them.

My anger and fear were still fresh as a damn daisy. In essence, Grim owned me. He swore he wouldn't abuse the power, but I knew control was everything to him. Sooner or later, he'd slip and yank my leash so hard I'd choke on it.

Dropping the boots, I changed my mind, a spot of brilliance hitting me. I grabbed the ruby bikini I'd worn when I was playing bait. Was that really only a week ago?

I threw on some heels and tied a sheer black "cover-up" around my waist. I'd give the explanation that, of course, I'd want to go for a swim after my meal.

Grim could congratulate himself on holding the power

in our relationship, but I intended to make him regret every second of it.

Every second.

Want a bonus epilogue where Vivien goes and meets Grim for that 'drink?'

Visit www.hollyroberds.com and download it now!

KISSED BY DEATH

Here's a preview from the next exciting installment in the series

"What happened here?" The British voice was edged with both shock *and* appall.

"What?" I cast a glance around me. The hotel suite I lived in looked as it had for the last five days. I stood and crossed the room to meet Timothy, tiptoeing over stacks of plates, takeout boxes, and piles of dirty clothes. Most of the food had been scraped off the platters, but after a while, I decided I didn't need to hoover everything down. Dried cake pieces, half-eaten burgers, and cold French fries decorated the platters.

"Mother of pearl, Vivien, this place is positively disgusting." Timothy must have been really shocked to use that kind of language. He appeared to be in his late twenties, but Timothy was several millennia old. And he only reverted to old-fashioned curses when he was particularly aghast.

Not that it was too hard. He was the most fastidious and

tidy person I'd met. Next to him in his perfect suit, not a gelled hair out of place, tablet in hand, I resembled a hobo. My rocking lounge wear consisted of lime-green sweatpants, two sweatshirts pulled over each other, and fuzzy socks. Well, one sock.

Where did that other bugger get to?

I took a closer look at my surroundings. "Yeah, I guess I should take a time out from watching reality television and pick up a bit."

The Asian man looked about with open astonishment. "Why haven't you let in the maid service to handle this?"

"What? And invite *his* spies in? No, thank you." To show I didn't need help, I grabbed a stack of takeout boxes that had only started to smell, and delicately perched them on the already full trash bin.

Okay, maybe I needed a little help.

Timothy began muttering to himself. "No, maid service won't do. We'll simply have to burn everything in here to get it properly cleansed."

I stuck a hand on my hip, officially offended by his offense. "It's not that bad."

He must have left the door open because Miranda walked in. "Whoa, that's pungent." My friend covered her nose, joining Timothy in his horror as she observed my pad. Her fro of tight curls bounced as she reared back. A portion of her hair was braided back over one ear, giving her a seriously badass look. She wore her security uniform, having just got off her shift.

"What?" I threw my arms out. "It's not that bad."

Miranda gave me the onceover, her expression becoming more pained from behind the hand still covering her nose. "Did you throw a party and not invite me? It looks like you invited a ton of people over and ordered from every junk food place available."

"Not all of them, but most of them," I corrected. Then with a grin, I said, "Miranda, while you've been busy with your new job as chief of security of the hotel, I have been living the dream."

Timothy and Miranda exchanged a wary look.

"I can eat whatever, and however much I want, and never get fat." I threw up my hands in triumph and did a booty dance.

For some reason, neither of them joined in with my victory dance.

Miranda spoke first. "Um, Viv, isn't that because you drink blood now, since you're a vampire and all?"

I stopped mid-booty shake.

Timothy cleared his throat. "That's why I'm here. You need to drink blood." His tone was careful, as if worried he would spook me. Too late. I was spooked.

Suddenly, I was a torrential cleaning machine. I pulled out a new trash bag and started throwing takeout boxes and entire cups and plates into it as well. "I don't need it. I don't need *him*."

Ever since I woke up a vampire without any memory of who I was a month ago, I'd needed to feed on blood every day to survive. But when I made a deal with the devil—or I guess more accurately, with Death himself, to save Miranda's nine-year-old son from dying—my needs changed.

I had fed from the God of Death, and now only his blood would sustain me. And because a blood bond had been created between us, Grim could control my will whenever he damn well wanted to. Just like the master vampire slash psycho serial killer had done. But if Grim thought he could snap his fingers and I'd come running, he'd better guess again.

"You haven't seen him in five days," Timothy pointed out.

"Did Grim send you here?"

"No."

"You're lying."

Timothy let out an exasperated sigh. "Well, you've ignored his calls and texts when he's done everything from cordially invite you to dinner, to threaten to pull you by the hair to get you to see him."

Timothy was a god like Grim, but he considered himself Grim's aide. I really didn't understand the dynamic, but I often felt Timothy was the Alfred to Grim's Batman. Though Timothy was young, and Grim wasn't a vigilante. Just a beast.

I resisted the urge to stick my tongue out at him. "And now he's sent someone to butter me up because he's too afraid to come see me. He knows if he showed up at my door, I'd kick his ass." For good measure, I threw some pretty intimidating karate chops into the air.

But that wasn't entirely true. Even on my best day with all my vampire strength and speed, Grim was a god and could rip my head clean off with little to no effort. I'd seen him do it to a number of vampires, or sekhors, as he called them. The first time he used the word, I thought he was calling me a sucky whore, but sekhor is the original, ancient term for vampire.

And I was the last one in existence. I couldn't let myself think about that one too long. Apparently, vampires, or sekhors, were around aplenty in ancient Egypt when everyone was worshipping Grim as Anubis, but then the sekhors went crazy with boredom and bloodlust and tried to take over the world. It was decided by the gods that the sekhors were too dangerous to be allowed to live. Turned out humans couldn't handle immortality without going batshit crazy.

Maybe that's where the myth about vampires turning into bats came from? So far I hadn't figured out how to sprout veiny wings, but I could make annoying high-pitch squeaking sounds.

Long story short, Grim wasted all of them, and until he met up with my fangs a couple weeks ago, he hadn't seen a vampire in five million years. Dude was not happy about it.

But we destroyed the master vampire and his little army, and I was given special dispensation to continue with my undead life as long as I help find out who managed to create a master vampire after all that time.

So help unearth a conspiracy plot amongst the gods or have my head ripped off. Sure, I can play Scooby Doo to save my neck. I was, after all, a bounty hunter in my last life. Piece of cake. Mmmm, cake.

"Do you want to take this one?" Timothy asked Miranda in a sidebar, as I furiously jammed the trash bag to its limits with junk. I pulled out another and left the kitchen to tackle the living room.

"Yeah, I didn't realize how bad things had gotten," Miranda said. "Give me a minute with her."

"No problem, I'll get someone to take care of...this." He cast a last look around the room with fearful dread before stepping out, his phone already to his ear.

Miranda finally dropped her hand and came as close as she could without knocking over my impressive skyscraper of pizza boxes. "Vivien, sweetie, you need to eat."

"If you were paying attention, you'd notice that's all I've

been doing." I crammed a throw pillow that I'd spilled spaghetti on into the trash bag.

"You know what I mean. You can't live off human food anymore, and Timothy said you haven't been to the penthouse in five days. I know you're in pain."

I stopped to glare. "I am not." Yes, every movement made my very atoms feel like they were being scraped against a chilled cheese grater, but she didn't need to know that.

Miranda took advantage of my pause to grab the garbage bag away from me. "You are wearing at least two sweaters, and I'm betting you have at least one pair of leggings on under those sweatpants." She gave a pointed look at the piles of blankets that nearly swallowed the couch.

Ha! Showed how much she knew. It was actually a pair of pajama pants between the leggings and sweatpants.

I'd heard about vampires being as cold as corpses, but nowhere in the lore did anyone capture the fact that if I didn't feed on blood, I'd become as cold as a witch's tit in a frozen hell after a blizzard. Miranda didn't even know about the multitude of heating pads hidden amongst the blankets, and I didn't enlighten her. Now that I was out of my cocoon, it hurt to move. It hurt to stand still. Everything in me pounded with thirst and need, making me weak as a kitten and feel as though my head were shoved full of cotton. At least being hungry now didn't make me want to lunge at Miranda and rip her throat out anymore. Ever since Grim's blood hit my lips, my desire for human blood disappeared in a magic puff of smoke. He was the only thing I craved.

Nope. I don't need him. I don't crave him. Not in any way whatsoever.

"Not to mention," Miranda went on, hands on her hips, "you look like death."

I crossed my arms. "I *am* dead. Or undead. And I don't need him."

"So you're going to die from a case of stubbornness?"

"I'm testing a theory. If I eat enough human food, maybe I'll magically turn back into a human, just like in a fairy tale."

Miranda's brow arched. "We read very different fairy tales." Then she licked her lips and dropped her arms, as if preparing herself. "What are you really afraid of, Vivien?"

"You think I'm afraid?" I barked out a laugh. "I'm not afraid of anything." I'd survived on the streets as a vampire for several weeks on my own without killing anyone, destroyed the master vampire, and literally laughed in Death's face. I was a straight-up badass. No, I was Taylor Swift—Fearless.

Miranda straightened and said in a firm tone, "Great, then you'll have no problem going to him tonight and getting what you need. Now get in the shower," she said, pointing in the direction of the bathroom. "Pull your big-girl panties on and go see him."

"But—"

Miranda's face darkened, and she pulled the scariest weapon out of her arsenal. Her mom voice. "No buts, missy, you do what I tell you right now or I'll show you what they taught me in Special Forces." Only slightly less scary, Miranda was ex-Army, but the Special Forces bit was new to me. I trudged off to the shower, throwing only one mournful, resentful look over my shoulder to let her know I wasn't happy.

By the time I emerged from the shower, barely warmed despite having the water set to scalding temperatures, Timothy had made fast work of my rooms. Not one but four cleaners rushed about the place, throwing away garbage, cleaning surfaces, and vacuuming. Miranda sat perched at the kitchen counter, drinking a cup of tea.

A satisfied smile spread along Miranda's mocha-colored face. "There now, don't you feel better?"

I had to admit I felt better after a thorough cleaning. My hair had transformed from a dark, scary rat's nest to thick, smooth auburn waves. Strangely enough, I felt more fragile now that I was cleaned up, as if my loofah scrubbed away both the grime and the lie I told myself that I'd never need to face my dependency on someone else's blood again. I'd put on some thick black eyeliner. It was the closest thing to war paint I had, and I felt it help cover up my vulnerability.

I wore a crop top, leather pants, and pulled on a bulky, cheetah-print, faux fur coat. The combo made it look like a style choice, rather than that I really needed the damn coat because my teeth were chattering.

"Do you think I pull this off?" I said.

"It's Vegas," Miranda said. "You could wear a green spandex suit and walk on stilts down the Strip, and no one would think you looked out of place."

"You're right," I said, pulling the coat closer around me. "People will probably think it's pimpin'."

And in Las Vegas, one could totally get away with wearing a pimpin' coat.

"Wait, do people say pimpin' anymore?" I said.

"No one has said pimpin' in thirty years," Miranda pointed out.

"Oh god, what will it be like when I'm thousands of years old, dropping outdated slang like a fuddy duddy? Like Timothy?" I shuddered.

Timothy rolled his eyes before clicking off his tablet. Pretty sure the guy would expire if he wasn't directing, scheduling, or controlling something on his little iPad. Then he practically pushed me out the door, locking the deadbolt behind me.

I turned to Miranda, who'd been ejected along with me. "Did I say something?"

"Constantly." Despite her dry accusation there was no real judgment. Beneath the heart of a tough-as-nails mom and ex-Special Forces soldier was a sarcastic hellion after my own unbeating heart. Ever since she stumbled upon me and a far scarier vampire in an alleyway, she owed me her life. Or I guess she'd also saved mine, but we had a mutual save-each-other's-butt thing going.

I'd never really had a friend before. I finally got the appeal everyone was talking about. Someone who cared about you, made you laugh, and was willing to get in hijinks. Though I doubted others were as likely to get tangled up in a supernatural war. Then again, Miranda was clued into vampires but had no idea that Grim was the god of the Dead. She knew something was off about him, but had no idea gods walked amongst us. And I was forbidden from telling her. As in, I literally couldn't; Grim used the blood bond between us to bind my will so that I could never tell Miranda. So naturally I tried a hundred times to tell her or write it down but every time I hit a wall that prevented me from revealing that fact to Miranda.

Probably for the best. Miranda had enough to come to terms with after finding out vampires were real and my almost killing her son when the master vampire took my will and forced me to feed on him. I still wasn't sure how Miranda could stand to be around me, even though Jamal was as right as rain now, if not suffering a minor small case of anemia. She said it wasn't me, so it didn't count. Part of me still thought she was hanging around to kill me, but so far she'd kept her claws in.

Miranda and I took the elevator down to the lobby of Sinopolis. The pyramid hotel was the epitome of exclusive wealth and a hub to the high rollers. When the doors opened, tropical flowers, fresh soil, and water filled my senses. In the center of all the onyx tile and gold accents was an honest-to-god oasis.

When Miranda kept pace with me as I approached the private elevator to Grim's penthouse, I raised an eyebrow. "Acting as escort?"

She gave me a terrifying smile. "If I need to twist your arm to get you on the elevator, I will."

I stuck my tongue out. "I'm a scary, strong vampire. I'd like to see you try."

Miranda stuck an arm out, pushing me. I flailed and stumbled, barely saving myself from splatting on the tile floor.

"Whoa, not cool," I complained, rubbing my arm. I think she may have bruised me.

"Yeah, super scary and strong. Now get your butt on that elevator," she said, pointing at the call button. I pressed it, but not without considerable grumbling. The buttons were programmed to recognize my fingerprints now, or lack thereof.

They opened with a bing. Dread pooled in my stomach. I stepped inside and turned around, pressing the gold button that led to the top of the pyramid-shaped hotel. Where *he* was waiting.

Miranda gave me the thumbs-up and I did the same as the doors closed. Though the second they shut, I wanted to pry them back open. But the elevator had already started its descent. I backed up to a corner of the elevator and closed my eyes, trying to psyche myself up.

"You are strong, independent, and don't need anyone.

You are just here for a quick bite." I couldn't even laugh at my own joke. "You will not be affected by his presence. You will have a dignified meal, slam, bam, thank you man for the blood, and be on your way." I silently added, and *do not, under any circumstances, let him know that he turns you into putty.*

Get Kissed by Death now to find out what happens next!

WANT A FREE BOOK?

Join Holly's Newsletter Holly's Hot Spot at www.
hollyroberds.com and get the Five Orders Prequel Novella,
The Knight Watcher, for FREE!

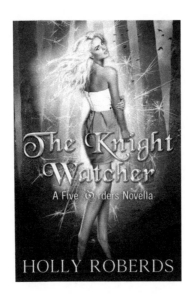

Plus you'll get exclusive sneak peaks, giveaways, fun lil' nuggets, and notifications when new books come out. Woot!

A LETTER FROM THE AUTHOR

Dear Reader,

Thank you for reading!

I loved writing this story and have so much more in store for Grim and Vivien as they discover the cancerous root amidst the gods and learn the limits of trust and love.

Loved this book? Consider leaving a review as it helps other readers discover my books.

Want to make sure you never miss a release or any bonus content I have coming down the pipeline?

Make sure to join Holly's Hotspot, my newsletter, and I'll send you a FREE ebook right away!

You can also find me on my website www.hollyroberds.com and I hang out on social media.

Instagram: http://instagram.com/authorhollyroberds

Facebook: www.facebook.com/hollyroberdsauthorpage/

And closest to my black heart is my reader fan group, Holly's Hellions. Become a Hellion. Raise Hell. www.facebook.com/groups/hollyshellions/

Cheers!

Holly Roberds

ABOUT THE AUTHOR

Holly started out writing Buffy the Vampire Slayer and Terminator romantic fanfiction before spinning off into her own fantastic worlds with apocalyptic stakes.

Recently relocated to New Hampshire from Colorado, Holly is exploring the possibilities of become a witch (as one must consider when living in New England) and is hard at work implementing the word "wicked" into her vernacular.

She lives with her husband whose handsome looks are only out done by his charming and wicked supportive personality.

Two surly house rabbits supervise this writer, to make sure she doesn't spend all of her time watching Buffy reruns.

For more sample chapters, news, and more, visit www.
hollyroberds.com